The Onedin Line: The Iron Ships

Cyril Abraham

TANDEM
14 Gloucester Road, London SW7

First published in Great Britain
by Allan Wingate (Publishers) Ltd, 1974

Published by Universal-Tandem Publishing Co. Ltd, 1974

The cover design includes a photograph of Philip Bond as Albert Frazer and Michael Billington as Daniel Fogarty in the BBC-TV production of 'The Onedin Line'. The series was devised by Cyril Abraham and produced by Peter Graham Scott. BBC Copyright photograph by Nicholas Acraman.
The photograph of Jessica Benton as Elizabeth Frazer is by Wim Heyblom.

To

Bill and Mary

Printed in Great Britain by The Anchor Press Ltd
and bound by Wm Brendon & Son Ltd
both of Tiptree, Essex

TANDEM

The Onedin Line: The Iron Ships

The sun had a pale, anxious look and the air was still and sultry. 'Set storm canvas,' said James. 'We're in for a blow.'

The emigrants were driven below, the hatches secured. Every possible ingress through which the sea might force a way was firmly stopped and caulked. The royals and topgallants were fished and sent down; the standing rigging was checked and tautened. The *Pampero* crouched in the sea, pricking her ears as the sails filled; her head rose high as though scenting danger. She snarled at the sea foaming about her bows, then she lay still and quiet again, waiting.

Anne came to stand beside James on the quarterdeck. 'Will it be bad?' she asked.

'Very bad,' he answered simply. 'And you must go below, Anne, and stay there. No matter what you divine to be happening on deck, you stay below. Is that clear?'

'I understand,' she said. Her hand sought his and their fingers locked together. They stood side by side, not speaking, content in each other's strength.

The Onedin Line story by Cyril Abraham

Book I The Shipmaster

Published in hardback by Allan Wingate (Publishers) Ltd at £2·25 and in paperback by Tandem Books at 35p

Chapter One

The *Pampero* slid through the dawn sea mist like a grey wraith while Anne, warmly wrapped in a heavy woollen cloak, strained her eyes for her first glimpse of America.

They had left Lisbon in brilliant winter sunshine thirty-eight days ago, a great white bird spreading its wings, and taken the clipper passage south and west. A broad road of wind and sea curving across the Atlantic to sweep the *Pampero* out into a boundless waste of sky and water. At the bottom of the curve the wind shifted to blow steadily from south and east. The yards were braced round, the ship heeled, and the bow sliced into deep green water as they headed north and west toward the Caribbean and north again to the cold skies and slate-grey seas of the American seaboard.

Anne thought the *Pampero* quite the loveliest ship she had ever seen.

Painted white, with a figurehead of an immodestly dressed maiden with long flowing tresses and warning conch shell held to her lips, trail-boards and stern richly carved and touched with gold, the *Pampero* was two hundred feet long and thirty-five feet broad with long raking clipper bows as sharp as a knife. Masts of yellow pine towered a hundred and twenty feet above the decks to carry a press of thirty-six sails. A vast cloud of snow-white canvas that drove the ship sweetly through the water and carpeted the sea with a long creamy wake.

Beneath the poop the dining saloon was elegance itself, of rich Spanish mahogany with columns relieved with gold and a ceiling of white and gold. Their own private stateroom was a dream of sybaritic luxury. Panelled in white satin-wood, with a Turkey carpet upon the floor, chairs and settee upholstered in blue velvet, curtains of Roman cloth banded with plush and a dining table of polished walnut inlaid with mother-of-pearl, it was, Anne considered, a room of unsurpassed splendour, while the appointments of their bedroom were worthy of an Ottoman. Entering, she remembered, had been like opening the door to Aladdin's cave, for the *Pampero*'s previous owner, that poor drowned madman, Captain Thomas, had nailed and boarded up the threshold and daubed scriptural texts above the lintel exhorting the beholder to flee the wrath to come and beware the snares of Jezebel.

The ceiling was of Japanese leather-paper and the walls of brocaded silk. Their bed a magnificent brass four-poster with a green counterpane whose tassels reached down to the floor of polished parquet glowing like honey. There was even a hanging wardrobe of ebony and gold with a large plate-glass mirror, a somewhat masculine piece of furniture which frowned disapproval from beneath heavy brows of ogee moulding at the feminine frippery of her personal dressing table with its ruffled valance and frilled muslin bunched around the petite toilet mirror framed in lovers' knots and plump cupids.

After the cramped quarters of the *Charlotte Rhodes*, with its single narrow bunks and low head-cracking beams, life aboard the *Pampero* seemed to Anne to be one eternal round of gracious living.

There was only one problem. Time hung heavily on her hands. Whereas James and Mr Baines never seemed to have an idle moment, she felt like a wealthy recluse with too many servants to do her bidding. There was Jão, their steward, a rubbery-faced, bulbous-eyed, little Portuguese who kept their quarters spick-and-span and bright as a new pin, and fetched and carried and anticipated every wish until she could have screamed from sheer boredom.

She had once taken it upon herself to have a thorough

spring-clean and was happily turning out the bedroom when Jão had entered, taken one horrified look, burst into tears and scurried off to James to appeal for justice. What unpardonable sin had he committed, he had demanded of the heavens, that he should be so belittled before his fellows? Had he not worked his fingers to the bone? Served the gracious lady well? If his work was not satisfactory he was prepared to be hung by his thumbs and have the flesh torn from his body.

Baines had translated.

'Perhaps we should take him at his word,' he had growled. 'Give him a touch of a rope's end. He'll squeal a different tune then, I'll warrant.'

James had shaken his head. 'Tell him,' he had said gravely, 'that it is Mrs Onedin's habit and custom to periodically inspect the manner in which her servants carry out their duties. Should she ever have occasion to complain, assure him that he will be the first to know.'

Baines had poured out a torrent of spluttering Portuguese and Jão's head had bobbed with such rapidity that it had seemed in imminent danger of shaking loose from its moorings. Then he had bowed deeply and strutted below with the air of one who had won a famous victory.

Anne had half-smiled. 'Poor man,' she'd said. 'All those non-existent servants. He must imagine us to be members of the quality.'

'Aboard ship, we are,' James had told her flatly. 'And the explanation I gave is the only one he could be expected to comprehend. In the event it should serve to keep him up to scratch.'

He had turned away, obviously dismissing the subject from his mind, but she had felt the implied rebuke keenly and later had questioned Mr Baines.

She was fulfilling her promise to teach him the three 'R's and their daily lesson had become a ritual. Baines was a slow but dogged learner and had progressed from

'The cat sat on the mat' to the stage where he could painfully suck the venom from the serpentine prose of the *Liverpool Shipping Gazette*, a tattered copy now three months out of date. Baines had much preferred the simplicities of the multiplication tables until he found himself faced by the impossible hurdle of eleven times eleven. His mouth had opened and closed like a great clumsy Groper fish swimming out of its depth and he had sighed with relief when Anne changed the subject.

'You see, ma'am,' he had explained, 'he probably had to dip into his pocket in order to acquire the job in the first place.'

She had stared blankly. 'The man had to buy his way into his situation?'

'A backhander. The crimping master would dock part of his wages. A pound a month is usual, made out in the form of an allotment note. It's a common enough practice, ma'am, but you can see how the man would be afraid of losing his position.'

She had had no idea that such practices were prevalent and had expressed her opinion sharply and forcibly. Why, the unfortunate wretch was paying out more than a third of his wages to some vile rapacious parasite simply in order to secure menial employment. Such exploitation of the simple-minded was not to be borne and on their return to Lisbon she would see to it that the rogue was put behind bars.

Baines had looked uncomfortable. 'The thing is, ma'am, Cap'n's steward is a much sought-after position. Pickings and perks, y'see?'

She didn't.

'Pickings from the galley—him and the cook eat cabin fare, share and share alike. Then of course he's not required to turn out and turn to and up aloft in all weathers, saving only the safety of the ship. And he has first choice Cap'n's cast-offs, takes care of the slop chest on behalf of the Captain, then he'll expect a fat tip at the end of the voyage. Never fear, ma'am, he'll make up his wages long before he pays off.'

She had been quite unaware that such venal practices obtained aboard ship and had taken her plaint to James.

He had shrugged it off. Like most shipmasters he loathed and despised the crimps but looked upon them as a necessary evil. They controlled the waterfronts of every major seaport and demanded that all men shipped must pass through their boarding houses at a fat profit to themselves. They supplied the crews, taking a month's wages in advance as their fee.

'Blood money,' was James's description.

Anne's indignation had given way to perplexity. Surely the authorities could not permit such pernicious practices to go unpunished?

James had smiled sourly and enlightened her. The crimping masters not only controlled the waterfronts by means of gangs of bully-boys, but also owned—he ticked off on his fingers—boarding-houses, dance-halls, brothels and taverns. It was a town within a town where the crimps were a law unto themselves, where anyone not of the fraternity, whether policeman or parson, would soon find himself shanghaied aboard an outward-bound Yankee blood-boat. 'And Baltimore,' James added, 'is a crimp's paradise. Wait and see.'

So she stood on the poop deck, and the winter sun rose to turn the mist into a golden haze through which the leadsmen's monotonous chanting had the eerie sound of disembodied spirits forever condemned to call and call from a nether world of curling vapour.

'By the ma-ark—seven. By the de-eep—eight. By the de-eep . . . By the de-eep . . .'

James came to stand beside her. He hrrmphed drily and pointed.

Over to starboard the mist swirled and shifted and then vanished as though an unseen hand had whisked aside a fine silk curtain. For a moment the air seemed as clear as crystal and ships' masts stood as thick as an enchanted forest of trees, stark and bare, stripped of leaves and hung with the webs of phantasmagorical spiders.

'Baltimore,' said James.

She could see the wharves and the scurrying figures. A stumbling horse pulling a heavily laden dray. Long low timbered sheds bearded with ice and bewigged with snow and three dark figures hunched against a shed. There was something odd about them. They seemed to be wearing conical hats and from this distance looked like gnomes. Anne picked up the ship's telescope and focused carefully.

The three figures leaped into view. She could see every detail and felt that if she could stretch out a hand she could touch them. They were blackamoors and each wore a thin tattered shirt and cotton trousers. The conical-seeming hats were simply the corners of sacks worn as capes. They were squatting on their haunches in an icy slush of churned snow and their heads hung down in the attitude of resigned misery common to unfortunates the world over.

Even as she looked—feeling as though she were an intruder upon private suffering—a tall man in a beaver coat and astrakhan hat stepped into her field of view. He was drawing evenly upon a cigar clenched between his teeth. He paused a moment then, throwing away the cigar, casually kicked the trio to their feet.

She saw, with almost total disbelief, that their hands were manacled and their necks yoked together by means of a long rope.

Baines was about to go forrard. She clutched his arm.

'Mr Baines. Surely Maryland is not a slave state?'

Baines followed her gaze, took the telescope and squinted through it.

'No, ma'am, it ain't,' he said. 'But I reckon them niggers to be catched runaways. They often heads for a seaport hoping to slip aboard an outward-bounder—

stowaway or sign as crew—either way they don't stand a chance. There's always a handsome reward for their capture. Now that tall bully in the fur coat is likely a slave-catcher.' Baines hawked and spat over the side. 'Bounty hunters, you might say. At around a hundred dollars a head slave-catching can be a mighty profitable business. For them that has a bent for the work.' He hawked and spat his disgust again.

'It's scandalous,' said Anne.

'Yes'm,' said Baines. 'Excuse me, ma'am,' and hurried away to attend to the ceremony of dropping the anchor.

Anne again peered through the glass. The group had reached the corner of one of the buildings. They paused for a moment, evidently uncertain as to which direction to take. One of the negroes, a big heavily-muscled man with a couple of days' growth of beard, seemed to look full into her eyes. Despair and a sick longing showed in the droop of his shoulders and the hang of his head. No doubt his gaze was concentrated upon the illusory freedom of the river flowing quietly toward the sea, but in the restricted and magnified view of the telescope his anguish seemed to reach out to her and her alone.

The tall man shoved them forward again and then the ship swung across river and the jib sail obscured her vision.

The anchor leaped from the cathead to the welcoming embrace of the sea and the cable roared through the hawse pipe as the jib rattled down to give Anne a wide panoramic view of Baltimore.

A straggle of wooden buildings reached back from the docks to the spired churches and squares and parks of Monument City.

It was America. The Promised Land. The Land of the Free and Home of the Brave. The *Pampero* had arrived.

Chapter Two

Robert's shop was crowded to the door with a mass of sour-smelling humanity. Scottish and Irish would-be emigrants with silver and gold sewn into the linings of their coats. They shuffled and lowed and murmured like cattle, rolling hopeful eyes at the casks of flour and barrels of biscuits open for their inspection. Smoked hams and flitches of bacon hung from the beams and mounds of dried peas and lentils flanked fat round cheeses. Sarah's hands flew like windmill sails as she wielded the butter spatters, slapping and moulding the soft yellow substance into rounds and cubes and squares.

There was no doubt about it, Robert considered; coming to terms with Mr Miles, the lodging-house keeper, was the best day's work he had ever done. In return for a fifteen per cent commission Mr Miles arranged for his runners to shepherd his lodgers to Robert's shop where they would be provisioned for the voyage.

'Next,' said Robert. He worked in shirt sleeves, sweat trickling down his face. His feet hurt and his legs ached but solace would come later when the shop was closed and they counted the takings. Silver brought its own balm.

The man was tall and had a craggy look of raw-hewn rock. He wore the remnants of a Highland kilt and plaid and a broad worn leather belt held an ancient basket-hilted claymore. He followed the direction of Robert's gaze and touched the hilt.

'It was my father's,' he said in the soft lilting accent of the Western Isles. 'And his father's before him.'

'Ah,' said Robert, preparing to get down to business.

'I am Dugald McCraig of Dunvegan and myself, wife and bairns are wishful of voyaging to Canada.'

The woman was gaunt and thin. The children clung to her skirts and peered fearfully at a hostile world through large starveling eyes.

'Fine prospects,' said Robert briskly. 'Fine prospects.'

'The gentleman recommended we should come here for our necessities.'

'Best provisions at competitive prices backed by a lifetime of experience. No finer recommendation,' parrotted Robert. 'You will require . . .'

Dugald interrupted. 'I understand,' he said, 'that the ship is obliged to provide a sufficiency of victuals for the duration of the voyage?'

'Ah,' said Robert. He picked up a board to which was pasted a printed list bearing the coat of arms of Her Majesty's Government. He read rapidly: 'Each adult passenger is entitled by law to be issued each week with the following rations, to wit: 21 quarts, water. 2 and a half pounds, biscuit. 1 pound, wheaten flour. 2 pounds, rice. 5 pounds, oatmeal. Potatoes when available as substitute for aforesaid rice and oatmeal. Children to share with parents. You'll not grow fat on that, Mr McCraig.'

'We'll survive,' said Dugald.

'Long voyage,' countered Robert. 'Shipboard fare is not of the best and a known cause of scurvy and ship fever. Once at sea you'll require to supplement your diet with extras—and extras come very high priced aboard ship.'

'I had in mind,' said Dugald, 'a pound or two of bacon, a dozen pickled eggs and perhaps a small cheese.'

Robert glanced across toward Mr Miles's runner, Gruber, standing guard at the doorway. The man had the scarred brutal face of the one-time prize-fighter, a chest muscled like the hoops of a barrel, arms like giant lobster claws. His function was to shepherd his flock to Robert's shop, to ensure that none welshed nor ran away, or were grabbed by rival runners. He bared broken yellow teeth in a grin of acknowledgement and nodded his head.

Robert was satisfied. Emigrants, in his considered opinion, were a shiftless lot who, were it not for the agency and good offices of men such as Mr Miles and himself, would never succeed in placing one foot before another, much less make the perilous journey across the wild Atlantic.

'Mr Miles issued you with a list,' said Robert. It was a statement rather than a question. He and Mr Miles had long come to a mutually satisfactory arrangement by which each emigrant was supplied with an identical catalogue of provisions. It served the dual purpose of saving unseemly bickering between partners and of reducing the often absurd requirements of the emigrants to simple and manageable proportions.

'He did,' responded Dugald, producing a much-folded piece of paper from the recesses of his plaid. 'I have removed several items. I conseeder tea and coffee luxuries we can well do without, nor do I see the need for a loaf of baked bread which must be eaten before the ship sails or be as stale as a stone.'

Robert had heard it all before. He spiked the list on a file, plunged beneath the counter and hauled up two wicker baskets.

'Company rules,' he said, looking toward the bruiser in case of trouble. 'Each emigrant is to take aboard, at his own expense, the following additional provisions: 7 pounds of bacon. 12 pounds of hard cheese. 14 pounds of dried peas. Ditto lentils. 4 pounds of onions. 3 pounds of lard. Ditto butter. 2 pounds of tea. Ditto coffee. 6 pounds of dried Hamburg meat. 2 dozen pickled eggs. 7 pounds of salt. 4 ounces of pepper. 1 cottage loaf. 1 bottle linseed oil. 1 box of fever pills. All contained within one best quality wicker basket. Total value three sovereigns. You'll live to thank me for it, Mr McCraig.'

'Six pound!'

McCraig's voice of protest rose above the gibble-gabble of chatter behind him.

'It's an ootrage!' he hooted.

'Company regulations,' said Robert nervously. 'Very strict.' Out of the corner of his eye he saw the burly figure of the runner shouldering his way through the crowd.

Then Dugald seized Robert by the beard and banged his head on the counter.

'Ye're a liar and a cheat,' howled Dugald.

Sarah screeched and flailed at the Highlander with the butter spatters. The man's gaunt wife, wailing a high-pitched heathen gibberish, clawed at Sarah.

Robert's head rang, tears came to his eyes and his nose felt like a squashed tomato. Then mercifully McCraig released his grasp and Robert saw through blurred vision that the villain had been brought to his knees while the bruiser pounded his face with bone-crunching blows from fists as hard as ironwood.

Sarah was screaming. 'The ruffian! The savage! Drag him out of here, the murderous hooligan! Out, out, out!' she shrieked. 'All of you. Out, out, out!'

The remainder waved their bits of paper and protested eagerness to purchase while the unconscious Dugald was dragged to the door and pitched into the gutter. His wife, keening and wailing, followed, her children howling with terror.

Blood ran from Robert's nose in a steady stream to splash upon the counter in scarlet pools. He put an unsteady hand to the bump on his forehead, thereby daubing his face with the red mask of the devil's imprint. He felt sick and the bile rose to his throat. They were barbarous wretches. Unwashed, evil-smelling, brute-natured riff-raff. It seemed to be in their very natures to be disorderly and uncivilised. Blood-thirsty ghouls totally undeserving of humane consideration.

'Throw them out,' he said nasally. 'Ebery last one. Lock and bar the door.'

They backed away before Sarah's furious advance, out into the street where Dugald McCraig lay groaning while his woman dabbed ineffectually at his shattered face with the hem of her shawl. The wind blew wet and cold off the river and tattered remnants of clouds streamed like pennants across a darkening sky.

They grouped on the pavement, shuffling and bewildered, waiting helplessly to be told what to do next.

Sarah addressed herself to Mr Miles's runner.

'Keep them here. We shall re-open within the hour.'

She stormed back into the shop, slamming the door behind her and shooting the bolts. A bewhiskered face, begrimed with dirt, swam against the whorled glass. The lips curled back in a gap-toothed ingratiating smile and a grotesque hand pushed a copy of the list against the pane.

Sarah yanked down the roller blind and turned to face Robert.

'Oh, the monsters,' she said. 'The conscienceless, unprincipled monsters.'

Robert, his head held back, was trying to staunch the flow of blood steadily pouring from his nose as though from a tap.

'I dink he's broke by dose,' he said.

'You must go and lie down, dearest,' said Sarah. 'I shall prepare a vinegar compress.'

Walking with the high-stepping gait of a blindfolded man searching for invisible obstacles, Robert allowed her to guide him through to the parlour behind the shop.

He lay on the sofa with his head hanging down over one arm while Sarah hurried away to fetch vinegar and water, wishing with all his heart for the day when they could serve a better class of customer.

It was James's fault, he thought. All James's fault. His troubles emanated from the day the *Charlotte Rhodes* arrived captained by a stranger with a foreign-sounding name and a limited command of the English language. The man bore a letter the contents of which Robert now knew by heart.

It introduced Captain Miguel Esperanzo and instructed Robert to pay the crew, arrange to put the wine in bond, write to a dozen or so wine merchants advising them of the safe arrival of their wares. He was also to dispose of a part cargo of 450 gallons of turpentine at a profit of not less than twenty per cent. He was then to re-victual the ship and pack her off to sea again, fully laden, with the minimum of delay. Remember, James had admonished, idle ships eat money. Robert had remembered, knowing full well whose pocket would suffer. He had huffed and puffed, thumped the table and stormed angrily about the house, waving the letter and roaring refusal at the top of his voice until the baby had wakened and added his piercing squawl as makeweight to Robert's thunder.

'Victual the ship! Pay the crew! Harbour dues! Docking fees! The man must think money grows on trees. Did I, or did I not, dissolve the partnership?' he had demanded of Sarah. 'I will not be responsible. Not one penny piece!'

Sarah had considered carefully. 'If a ship can make a profit for James there is no reason why it should not make a profit for us.'

Robert had grunted peevishly. 'I know nothing of buying and selling cargoes. What rates would I charge? And how do I set about the business? Knock on people's doors asking for the favour of their custom?' He had snorted derision. But he had been worried. There was no gainsaying it, he had been worried.

'First things first,' the practical Sarah had responded. 'Sell the turpentine and use the money to finance the ship. As there is no partnership we should be entitled to all profits.'

'James will have something to say on that score.'

'No doubt, but even James's voice will not carry from America.'

Robert doubted it, but before he could argue a customer had entered the shop. He was an Irisher newly arrived from Dublin and spoke with an accent as thick as turnip broth. He'd bought a farthing candle, a ha'porth of lamp oil and a twist of tobacco and given Robert his great idea.

'Emigrants,' he'd announced after the man had gone. 'There's a trouble-free cargo. They walk aboard at Dublin and ashore at Liverpool. We can afford to cut rates—just enough for the *Charlotte Rhodes* to earn her keep.' He had rubbed his hands exultantly. 'Emigrants. That's the trade, for even that scrofulous rabble must eat.'

They had sat far into the night perfecting the details of Robert's wonderful scheme.

Like all great ideas it had the merit of simplicity.

Irish emigrants, congregating at Cork or Dublin, were packed aboard ship like so many salted herrings in a cask. Arriving at Liverpool they were unceremoniously bundled ashore where, sick, cowed and bewildered, they were left to the mercy of touts and man-catchers—lodging-house keepers' runners—who vied and fought with one another over their prizes, often separating husbands from wives and wives from children before dragging them off to low boarding-houses where the unfortunate wretches were cheated, lied to, fleeced and robbed.

Robert's notion was to organise a hopelessly disorganised business. In a small way, of course, but out of little acorns giant oak trees grow.

Mr Miles was a gross blubber-lipped hunchback with eyebrows as thick as ship's fenders and a mind like a counting frame. He had been quick to grasp the essentials: The *Charlotte Rhodes* would deliver emigrants by the shipload direct to Mr Miles's lodging-house by the simple expedient of including in their fare a ticket entitling them to one night's board and lodging. The rest was up to Mr Miles who no doubt would extract value for money in his subsequent charges.

There was money to be made in the emigrant trade and many a lodging-house keeper, starting from humble beginnings, had waxed and grown fat. There was no good reason, in Robert's view, why an honest chandler should not also turn an honest penny.

Apart from today's contretemps he had reason to be well satisfied. As provision merchant he had a contract to supply Mr Miles's rapidly expanding hostel with cheap provisions such as bacon bones, rancid butter and lard spurned by cash customers, and salt and potatoes, which commodities the Irish never seemed to tire of eating. Then he had a little arrangement with Mr Simpson, the butcher, to dispose of offal and the more unsavoury cuts of meat which would provide nourishing stews. Nor was Mr Jenkins, the stableman, forgotten. He supplied twice weekly a horse and dray to carry the emigrants' boxes and bundles under the protection of Mr Miles's runners. Naturally, as was only to be expected, Mr Simpson and Mr Jenkins showed their appreciation of a superior intellect by a weekly consideration of ten per cent discount.

It was true, thought Robert, staunching the flow of blood from his nose, that unthinking and evil-minded persons had been known to protest that a charge of three pounds for a guinea's worth of goods including wicker basket was extortionate. But such malicious rumourmongers obviously did not take into account the fact that emigrants as a class, and the Irish in particular, were notoriously feckless and improvident and the prey of every shark and villain with a ready tongue and a mountain of rubbish to dispose of. More often than not the miserable wretches were sold suits that disintegrated at the first shower of rain, boots that fell apart after a day's usage, and useless and unnecessary items such as pocket mirrors, flintlock rifles, powder flasks, glass beads for sale to the Indian tribes and counterfeit American dollars in exchange for good English gold. In Robert's considered opinion he and Mr Miles dealt fairly. Business was business and a man must strike a profit where he could.

Sarah held the cold vinegar compress to the bruise welling up on his forehead. Robert sat up, leaned forward and gingerly touched his nose. It seemed to have swollen to pumpkin size and throbbed in concert with the duck's-egg lump above. But not broken, he thought thankfully. He sniffed and snorted experimentally.

'Be careful, dear,' said Sarah, soothingly. 'Try not to mark the carpet.'

Robert obediently pulled back his head while Sarah carefully wiped his face and beard with a flannel.

'They are savages,' she said. 'Savages. They should be left to fend for themselves.'

'Business before sentiment,' said Robert, heroically.

Sarah dried his face.

'You are as brave as a lion, dear heart, but I am determined you shall not be called upon to face that pack of ravening wolves alone again. This time Mr Gruber shall be posted by the counter ready to fell with one blow any miscreant who dares so much as raise his voice. As for that Scotch rogue—words fail me.'

Robert considered. 'Send him to the back of the queue,' he decided. After all, business was business, and a rogue's money rang as true as that of any honest man.

Sarah nodded approvingly. 'He shall have the poorest quality hampers. With no reduction in price,' she added in qualification, and went to fetch a glass of Robert's favourite medicinal whisky.

They dined that night with Albert and Elizabeth.

While Robert modestly exhibited the scars of battle and Sarah breathlessly recounted the stirring tale of his titanic struggle against insurmountable odds, Elizabeth sat brooding over her own predicament.

Now seven months pregnant, she was daily racked with a torment of doubts and fears. Her sleep was disturbed by nightmares in which the child was born a mirrored likeness of Daniel Fogarty; where Albert, with outraged pointed arm, banished her to a wilderness of empty streets with doors closing and shutters slamming at her passing.

Dear Albert. She could cry real wet salt tears. She didn't deserve him. If only he wouldn't be so kind, so tender, so attentive to her every need. Sometimes, at her wits' end, she would fly into a tantrum and snap vexatiously at the poor man, or rail at the servants. But Albert would remain calm and considerate and the servants would smirk and nod knowingly. It was the child, of course, that was receiving all this consideration, not her. She was simply a receptacle condemned to drag this wearisome burden around until one day. . . . Then she had fresh nightmares with the memory of Sarah's screams and screeches ringing in her ears. Elizabeth thought she had never been so unhappy in her life. It wasn't fair. It simply wasn't fair. All her life she had longed for a splendid house, with servants and a carriage and pair, and a tender-hearted self-effacing husband. All the comforts that money could buy. She'd been granted her wish and was cossetted and cared for as never before, but for all that she felt as though she were imprisoned between walls of cotton wool with demons of fear clawing and chattering outside.

Even her favourite reading matter offered no solace. Without exception every single one of the soiled heroines suffered at the hands of outraged respectability. In *Virtue Triumphant* Gloria Mandrake died rescuing her child from a blazing fire. 'She took her Secret to the Grave' read the caption, and an imaginative artist had portrayed a terrified Gloria, hair ablaze, falling back into a raging inferno. Nor did *Iris Pinworthy's Secret* help. Miss Pinworthy came to her end standing on a sandbank, her baby held at the full stretch of her arms, while the waters closed over her head and the despairing hands of the rescuers reached out from a lifeboat. Others came to less spectacular ends, hanging themselves from beams or swallowing copious draughts of poison. Elizabeth had no intention of following their example which was principally why she had invited Robert and Sarah to dinner. With luck she might be able to stop up one source of gossip.

She came out of her reverie to hear Albert saying: 'You should fit the *Charlotte Rhodes* with an auxiliary engine. Such a machine would more than pay its way in the saving of time alone.'

'They are only emigrants,' said Robert. 'Time does not matter.'

'I doubt,' said Albert drily, 'that even a parcel of poor emigrants relishes the prospect of drowning. An auxiliary would serve to keep the ship off a lee shore.'

'Hmph,' grunted Robert, bored with the whole business. 'You should take it up with James. It's his ship, not mine.'

Albert caught Elizabeth's eye and came to his feet.

'I think, in view of my dear wife's condition, we shall reverse tradition and the gentlemen shall leave the ladies. We shall take cigars and port in the billiards room, Robert.'

He planted a chaste kiss upon Elizabeth's forehead, closed one eye in a slow conspiratorial wink and guided Robert from the room.

'A hundred up, Robert,' he said cheerfully. 'And the loser's forfeit shall be to crack a bottle of wine.'

He really was, Elizabeth considered, the most delightful husband imaginable. Civil, mannerly and the very soul of tact. But there was steel beneath the urbanity which brought prickles of fear to her heart. If ever he should learn of her deception! And one deceit seemed to pile upon another until she seemed to be living upon a mountain of lies and half-truths. Even her coming conversation with Sarah had had to be carefully stage-managed. 'Dearest,' she had said. 'I want to talk to Sarah alone. About her confinement.' She had babbled on and Albert had smiled and reassured her that she could have anything her heart desired. 'You shall converse with the Queen herself, if you think it necessary. Indeed she should be quite an authority, having had more children than the old woman who lived in a shoe.' He had been bantering but his eyes had shown concern and he had warned her against listening to old wives' tales. 'Doctor Loveless will give you all the advice you need,' he had added.

Doctor Loveless. The name suited him. A more loveless creature she could not imagine. He called daily—a tall cadaver of a man with mutton-chop whiskers, all-seeing eyes, and the stern face of the dyed-in-the-wool moralist. She dreaded his arrival and knew with absolute certainty that he believed not one word of her pretty confusion about dates. He would take her pulse in total silence, prod her with a bony finger, ask if she felt comfortable, leave a bottle of evil-tasting medicine recommended as an enrichment for the blood, advise her to compose herself and pray regularly, and warn her that children were born in travail but that a beneficient providence would bring merciful oblivion *in extremis*. Then he would formally take his leave to greet Albert haunting the corridor beyond the closed door. But though she strained her ears with all her might she could never wrest sense from the gobble-gobble-mutter-mutter of their conversation. There was always a heart-stopping moment when the door reopened and Albert entered until she could tell from the mingled concern and delight on his dear face that the sour-visaged old crocodile had kept her counsel for yet another day.

Elizabeth laced her coffee with brandy and trundled the decanter across to Sarah.

'Spirituous liquors will curdle your milk,' said Sarah disapprovingly, helping herself liberally from the same Devil's pipkin.

'I don't care,' said Elizabeth miserably, and poured out her doubts and woes in a torrent of tear-splashing self-abnegation.

Sarah listened in vinegar-faced silence then, hoisting her nose above tightly pursed lips, expelled a breath of exasperation and pronounced firmly:

'The child is Albert's. Of that there can be no shadow of doubt. You must banish such wicked thoughts from your mind instantly or you will give birth to a monster.'

'But,' wailed Elizabeth, 'you know the child is Daniel's. Mrs McCready told Robert and Robert told you. It's a family secret.'

'It won't be much longer if you carry on like that,' snapped Sarah. 'I really don't know where you get such notions. Presumably from that wretched Mrs McCready who, Robert has assured me, was the worse for drink at the time. It is our considered opinion that that dreadful creature simply took advantage of a young girl's innocence to fill her head with fanciful rubbish.'

Elizabeth beat her fists upon the table.

'But you knew, you knew, you knew,' she sobbed. 'You even planned to pack me off into the country to stay with your family until it was born!'

'It is well known,' said Sarah acidly, 'that women of unstable character who find themselves with child are frequently afflicted with wild imaginings. We simply offered, out of the kindness of our hearts, to send you for a quiet sojourn in the country because you were obviously suffering from a morbid distemper of the heart.'

'Because of Daniel,' said Elizabeth like a child learning its lesson. She dabbed her eyes and tried to look contrite. It was obvious which way the wind was blowing. Sarah and Robert were preparing to bury their heads in the sands of ignorance in the hope of avoiding the murky taint of scandal. Without doubt they were now preparing to perjure themselves into perdition rather than admit foreknowledge of her condition.

So be it. There would be no tittle-tattle from that direction.

'When I was with child,' Sarah was saying, 'I concentrated my mind exclusively upon dear Robert's features. As a result our little Samuel is the perfect image of his Papa. Everyone comments upon it.'

Anything less like Robert than that pudgy, button-eyed creature Elizabeth could not imagine. It reminded her of nothing other than a suet dumpling wrapped in pudding cloths.

'You must put aside all impure thoughts,' continued Sarah, 'and wholly concentrate your attention upon your confinement.'

'Yes, Sarah,' said Elizabeth, meekly. Really, things were working out much better than she had expected. Better, certainly, than that unhappy creature in *The Shame of Clara Cartwright*. She had had the mortification of being denounced from the pulpit.

Chapter Three

The notice, one of a job lot run off overnight by a journeyman printer, read:

The Celebrated First Class
Clipper Ship
PAMPERO
Newly Arrived DIRECT From
LISBON PORTUGAL
Has For AUCTION
Her Cargo Of
850 tons Best BAY SALT
And
150 tons First Rate CORKWOOD

The Above PRIME CARGOES To Be
SOLD By AUCTION
On Behalf Of The Owners
By CAPTAIN JAMES ONEDIN
Aboard The Above Named VESSEL
At TWO O'CLOCK 15th January, 1861
Pier 17
Baltimore

It was but one of a rash of posters plastered over the walls and pillars of the Baltimore waterfront and partly overlapping one offering a reward of one hundred and fifty dollars for the apprehension and return of Josiah Kane, a runaway slave, age 28, ears nicked and bearing marks of the lash. Beside it another poster was headed 'STATES RIGHTS!' followed by a couple of dozen lines of closely reasoned text, the quality of the argument, however, being difficult to follow because someone had daubed across with a brushful of tar 'Liberty and Union, Now and For Ever!'

A third placard left the political arena for straight-from-the-shoulder commerce. '2 Dollars a Day and MORE for Strong and Lusty Men!!!', it bawled in letters of fire. 'Tracklayers and Platelayers Required. Come One, Come ALL! 2 Silver Dollars Each and EVERY Day! Apply J. J. M'Guire. Chesapeake R.R. Co.' Beside it a giant locomotive belching fire and brimstone mowed down hordes of helpless women and children, its writhing smoke bearing the dire warning: 'Locomotive Railroads Spread DEATH and Destruction! Mothers Look Out For Your CHILDREN! Down With Railroads!'

Anne, trudging back to the ship in the teeth of a wind that tore gaps in steadily falling snow, paused for a moment to brush away the clinging white crystals beneath the hood of her cloak. She idly re-read the now familiar notices and then surreptitiously tore Josiah Kane's description in half. The paper, wet and sticky, came away easily and she watched the strip twist and turn in the wind to disappear into swirling white oblivion. Her conscience eased a little by what she knew to be a pointless gesture, she shifted the weight of parcels against her hip and bowed her head once again into the wind. A distant church clock clanged a muffled hour and ships' bells took up the refrain. It was three o'clock and she wondered if the auction had been a success. The posters had given fair warning, at least ten days' notice. Of course there was the inclemency of the weather to take into account but Baltimore merchants, James had assured her, were not likely to place comfort before business.

She walked on in a white world of muffled sound until the *Pampero*'s jib boom rose high above the pier. The snow-covered masts and spars gave the ship the insubstantial air of something seen in a dream. Half-blinded, she found the gangway with difficulty and made her way across the dark chopping chasm between wharf and ship-side. A child's snowman stepped forward and reached up a helping hand. The figure shook itself like a dog and a shower of snow fell to the deck. Jão's liquid eyes held a reproachful look as he took her parcels and, clucking disapproval, shooed her to their quarters.

She entered the saloon to find an angry James pacing forwards and backwards, turn and turn about, while a more philosophical Baines munched at a diminishing pile of sandwiches specially prepared for the would-be buyers. Anne stared around the empty saloon.

'Where are they?' she asked.

'They're not coming,' snarled James. 'Baltimore blood-suckers!' He clasped his hands behind his back, drew a mass of air through his nostrils and blew it out again in a whistle of impotent exasperation.

She could only parrot her incomprehension.

'Not coming? Ever?'

'Never. We've been boycotted. The dealers have formed a price ring. You sell through them, at their price or to no one at all. They're even trying to push a bill through Congress making ship auctions illegal. They call it the liberty of the individual to make a profit from both ends. Grasping middlemen!'

She had never seen him so angry before.

'We cannot deal direct?'

Baines took another sandwich, wolfed it in one mouthful, and shook his head.

'The salt merchants have the monopoly.'

She thought for a moment.

'To whom do they sell?'

'Butchers. Fishmongers. Meat packers. Picklers. Cooks. Everyone uses salt but they pay the dealers' price or do without.' James snorted again. 'I've eight hundred and fifty tons to dispose of so I can hardly trundle a barrow around the streets selling it off in job lots. We'd be here until doomsday.' He perambulated around the saloon again. 'There's no choice—I must sell at a loss. It is Senhor Braganza's vines which are of prime importance. But no doubt,' he added sarcastically, 'there will be a dealer in vines as well. This country is going to the dogs!'

Baines grunted through a mouthful of sandwich.

'The backwoods is infested with vines. They're there for the picking. All that is required is labour.'

James brightened a little.

'That shouldn't be too difficult to come by.'

Baines took the last sandwich and shook his head.

'There's not an able-bodied man to be found. The taverns is half empty and even the crimping masters is feeling the pinch.' He gulped the bread and salted ham, washed it down a cavernous throat with half a tumbler of James's best whisky, belched, begged Anne's pardon, and added: 'They're all off building railroads at two dollars a day.' He smacked his lips and reached for the bottle again. 'No wonder they call it the Irishman's paradise. Two dollars a day!'

James blinked.

'Irishmen?'

'Shiploads of 'em,' said Baines. 'They're out there now, digging their way across country like dogs digging for bones. Leastways they will as soon as this wind shifts and the snow stops.'

'Irishmen?' repeated James.

'Thousands of 'em,' said Baines.

'I've heard it said,' said James, thoughtfully, 'that an

Irishman lives off potatoes and a handful of salt.'

Baines nodded his head. 'The Irish is demons for salt. I once shipped a crowd of emigrants. They ate salt like a Turk eats sherbet.'

Anne had seen that look on James's face before.

'James,' she protested. 'Even an Irishman cannot eat his way through half a ton of salt!'

'Given time, he can,' said James. 'Given time. Mr Baines!' he snapped sharply. 'The contents of that botttle will be deducted from your wages.'

'In that case,' said Baines, tucking the bottle beneath his arm, 'I'd best make the most of it.' He bid a cheerful good afternoon and tramped contentedly off to his cabin.

'Hrrrmph,' said James. He rubbed his hands together. 'That leaves but one problem. To sell the corkwood and pick up a cargo for home. Top off with grain, I think.' He sniffed and harrumphed again. 'I do think you should lose no time in removing those wet garments, my dear, or you may find yourself with an attack of rheumatics in your—ah—hrrrmph—extremities.'

Anne smiled. James was his old self again. He was, she thought, really a most remarkable man. Most remarkable.

J. J. M'Guire picked up a fresh slab of 'Lover's Friend' chewing tobacco. A mixture of rum, molasses and tobacco, 'Lover's Friend' was, in J. J. M'Guire's often reiterated opinion, the best damn chew in the entire United States. But today he found little pleasure in his favourite vice. Taking a two-inch bite he wedged the cud into the side of his cheek, lumbered to his feet and opened the door of the railhead hut. He looked up at the leaden skies and the softly falling snow and cursed slowly and fluently, without heat or passion. The long-drawn-out maledictions of a man tried beyond endurance. He looked far over to his right to a straggle of timber shacks and scattered tents, dark figures moving against the snow, the curling smoke of camp fires. Pots and pans clattered.

Voices surged and broke in waves of sound. There was a shout of laughter punctuated by the staccato discord of a quarrel. The sweet smell of wood smoke drifted across to draw a thin blue haze across the shifting white curtain of snow.

Snow lay everywhere, burying the rails beneath a crumpled white sheet, the forest line alone standing etched in black. M'Guire ejected a stream of tobacco juice in a long practised arc. It hit the snow with a faint hiss, left a dark brown stain running along the sides of a minute chasm. Then the chasm collapsed and the snow engulfed and mortared over the fissure until the white face of the surface was once again hatefully smooth and bland.

M'Guire raised his bored eyes and saw a figure that seemed to rise from the earth itself. Then a horse neighed and floundered from a bellydeep snowdrift. The rider was hunched forward, bouncing like a sack of potatoes, one hand firmly clutching a stovepipe top hat clamped to his head. He was obviously heading directly for the railhead hut.

M'Guire spat again, returned inside and kicked shut the door. A coffee pot simmered on the round-bellied stove. He added an extra handful of coffee grounds and a mugful of water, then settled back in his chair to await the arrival of the stranger.

The coffee was burbling and bubbling and giving off its uniquely rich aromatic odour by the time he heard the clink of harness and the blowing of a horse.

The door opened to M'Guire's barked 'Yeah?' and the visitor stepped into the small hot room. The man removed his top hat, politely shook the snow outside and kicked his boots against the step. He was a tall man, M'Guire noticed, of lean face, long nose and pale blue eyes as hard as pebbles. He wore a seaman's fearnaught coat and worsted trousers stuffed into leather lace-up boots.

The apparition warmed its hands at the stove.

'You'll be Mr M'Guire, I take it?' The long face

brooded over the stove but the eyes turned towards M'Guire. It occurred to M'Guire that they were not the sort of eyes that would take prevarication easily.

'I am,' he said. 'How the devil did ye find your way to this wilderness?'

'By map and compass,' said James. 'I took a bearing from time to time,' he added as though that were explanation enough.

M'Guire looked again at the face. It was the face of an outdoor man. Brown, weatherstained, pared and eroded by wind and sun.

'You a company surveyor?' he asked. 'Because if you are we need you like a dog needs fleas.'

'No,' said James. 'I'm master of the *Pampero*. Berthed in Baltimore. My name is Onedin.' He stretched out a hand. M'Guire hoisted himself to his feet, took the hand in a paw the size of a ham, shook it briefly and poured coffee into two tin cups. He rooted in a cupboard and produced a jug of hard whisky. Slopping a generous helping into each cup he grinned at James.

'As you're not a company man you'll not object to a taste of Irishman's Delight—to keep out the cold?'

James raised his cup in a toast.

'Medicinal purposes,' he said.

The scalding liquid scorched a path down his throat and lit a bonfire in the pit of his stomach. The fumes seemed to make his head swell to balloon-like proportions, but the numbness was leaving his body and the cold stiffness his face. No horseman at the best of times, he felt saddle-sore and weary and harboured a conviction that every bone in his body had been shattered. He looked again at M'Guire. He was by far the biggest man he had ever seen. Even the gigantic Baines would be reduced to pygmy size beside this gargantuan behemoth. The man bore the stamp of Ireland in every lineament of his features and spoke with the accent of St Patrick himself.

'And what can I do for you, mister?' M'Guire asked,

settling himself once again in the only chair.

James perched on the edge of a makeshift desk and took stock of his surroundings before replying. The hut was about twelve feet square and contained, in addition to the stove, an unmade truckle bed, the solitary wooden chair occupied by M'Guire, the desk cluttered with a paraphernalia of rolled plans, contour sheets and data sheets. Time schedules and a progress chart were pinned to the walls.

'How many men do you employ?' James tried to make the question sound casual.

M'Guire sucked his teeth, spat out a coffee ground and waved a dejected arm.

'I got near to three thousand out there eating up good railroad money waiting for this Goddamighty snow to stop.'

'They're great salt-eaters, I'm told,' said James.

'Salt is it, at four dollars a ton take it or leave it from them prating thimble-rigging merchants? Why?' he demanded with sudden suspicion. 'You got salt?'

James nodded. 'A shipload. Eight hundred and fifty tons.'

M'Guire stared at the madman.

'Now what in the name of all the devils in hell would I be wanting with eight hundred and fifty tons of salt?'

'Turn a profit.'

'I'm no salt merchant, mister, I'm in the railroad business.'

'A dollar a ton,' said James.

M'Guire's suspicions hardened.

'I'm not buying.' He held up a finger as thick as a post. 'The factors will pay two dollars fifty. You know it and I know it. So why ride through a snowstorm to put money in my pocket? What's the game, mister?'

'I have something you want, you have something I want.'

'And what might that be?'

'Labour,' said James. 'Three thousand men up to their ears in snow and waiting for the day of judgement. Lend me a thousand men to pick vines. One day's work . . .'

M'Guire cut him short with a snort of derision.

'Vines? Now I know you're crazy. The only vines out here are those of the wild grape. Shrivelled little things as bitter as gall. We burn 'em by the cartload.'

'I want one hundred thousand, and I want them now.' He smiled his thin smile at M'Guire. 'While the snow is falling. One thousand men—one day's work—each man to dig up one hundred vines. It won't cost you a red cent and in return you make a clear profit of twelve hundred dollars.'

M'Guire hoisted his booted feet to the top of the stove and remained for long seconds sombrely viewing the toe caps. He looked up suddenly.

'You serious?'

'I'm serious,' said James.

The giant came to his feet, held out a hand.

'You got a deal,' he said.

After three days the snow ceased falling, the skies cleared and a pale sun leaned across the harbour. The temperature fell to sub-zero and ice crackled underfoot and overnight turned the *Pampero*'s mooring lines into bars of iron Small ice-floes began to drift down the Patapsco, meeting and coalescing into larger masses. All ironwork seared and burned to the touch and the furled sails hardened into a state of petrified rigidity.

But work went apace. M'Guire had been as good as his word and the vines, roots wrapped in straw, had been delivered and were now safely stowed in the 'tween decks and the holds filled with grain. The crew, possibly because of the ferocious cold, had worked with a will until all that remained was to batten down the hatches and clear for Lisbon on the morrow.

James yawned, stretched his arms, and sat back in his

chair with the contented air of a man well-satisfied with the order of events.

Anne, seated by the fire, was engaged in reading the latest edition of the *Baltimore Sun*, the ponderous prose of which held a gloomy foreboding enriched with the unmistakable whiff of gunpowder. The editorial succeeded in being both ominous in tone and convoluted in argument. Citizens were sternly admonished to keep cool heads and at the same time warned to be prepared to take up arms in defence of the Constitution. Little mention was made of the issue of slavery, the article concentrating its invective against the hotheads of South Carolina who had apparently seized the coastal batteries at Fort Moultrie and, no less than a fortnight since, opened fire upon a United States merchant vessel bound from New York.

There was a further reference to a place called Fort Sumter, apparently occupied by regular troops. The name meant nothing to her. She gave up the attempt to struggle through the labyrinth of American politics, neatly folded the newspaper and leaned back in her chair. Strangers hung from the bars of the grate and a crust of coal fell into the maw of the fire sending up tongues of orange flame. The oil lamps bathed the room in a warm soft light and added their warmth to that of the fire. At such a time, she thought lazily, a ship's cabin was really the most comfortable place imaginable. It was like being cocooned in luxury with the rigours of the world outside kept at bay.

James coughed: 'I reckon on clearing 38 cents a bushel on grain alone. Set the vines against the cost of the salt, add a hundred and five dollars a ton for corkwood—less three and a half per cent for those damned middlemen—deduct expenses of the voyage—and I calculate a profit of fifteen thousand dollars. Half to Senhor Braganza and half to me—plus a half share in the *Pampero*. Not bad for a beginning, Anne. Not bad.'

'I sometimes think,' smiled Anne, 'I married a magician.' She apologetically stifled a yawn.

James stood up, closed his ledgers and rubbed his hands together. 'Hrrrmph. Time for bed,' he announced briskly. 'I intend to sail at four in the morning. I want to be clear of the Chesapeake before this damned weather closes in.'

There was a tap-tap at the door then Baines stood swaying in the threshold. His face was rubicund and the unmistakable fumes of rum hung about him like a rich ambrosial incense.

'Beg pardon, sir—ma'am,' he enunciated thickly. He removed his hat as an afterthought and shuffled his feet.

He seemed, thought Anne, to be exhibiting a most unusual degree of embarrassment, one that could hardly be accounted for by a man of Mr Baines's known fondness for the devil's lamp oil. There must be something else, and a closer look at Mr Baines's unhappy features showed only too clearly that he was schooling himself to impart bad news.

He sucked in a breath. 'Ship battened down fore and aft,' he began.

James nodded impatiently.

'Drawing twenty feet forrard and twenty-two feet aft, sir.'

'Good,' said James. The ship was trimmed exactly to his liking. 'We sail at four. Are the hands aboard?'

Baines unhappily shook his head as though the entire responsibility was his and his alone.

'They've skedaddled,' he said. 'Off to build a railroad for your friend M'Guire.'

'What . . . ?' James for once seemed to have lost the use of his tongue. There was total disbelief in his voice.

Baines's shoulders slumped. 'Jumped ship every man jack of 'em—'cepting three—one sick in the stomach, one homesick, and your steward. That devil M'Guire 'ticed 'em away with promises of whores and high wages, begging your pardon, ma'am.'

James choked back his anger. It was no new thing. Crews jumped ship or were grabbed by crimps. It meant signing a new crew and a short delay. But no real harm done. At least he would have the satisfaction of saving their wages.

'We must have another crew without delay,' he said. 'Tomorrow we'll try the crimping houses.'

Baines shook his head. 'The last able-bodied man has been shipped aboard a Yankee whaler.' He managed a grin of delight. 'They even shanghaied two of the crimping masters to keep 'em company.'

James stared. 'No one. No one at all?'

'Not a man to be had for love nor money. They're all off building railroads. It's become a mania in this country has railroad building.' Baines sounded as though the very order of nature had been overturned.

The colour seemed to drain from James's face and for the first time Anne saw fear in his eyes. He sat down slowly.

'Then we're done for,' he said. 'And Braganza with us.'

Anne could not comprehend. 'Surely we could send for a crew? From New York? Philadelphia, perhaps? There must be hundreds of seamen eager and willing to take ship?'

James shook his head, defeated. 'It would be too late. By the time they arrived we would be ice-bound. Stranded. Frozen in for the winter. And if Braganza loses his vines, I lose the *Pampero*.'

Chapter Four

BAINES'S GARGOYLE features were twisted into a grimace of anguish as he struggled to chart a course through the rocks and shoals of his daily lesson.

Anne had set him the task of reading aloud from a page

of the *Baltimore Courier*, a newspaper with a more simplistic syntax than the elliptic prose of the *Sun*. Even so he was making heavy weather of the piece and she only half-listened to his mouthings, her mind on other problems.

James was worried beyond measure and marched up and down the room and in and out like a bee in a bottle. Every few minutes he would scurry up on deck to glare in frustration at the growing barrier of ice forming across the river then, unable to bear the sight longer, would hurry below again to resume his aimless pacing.

He and Baines had been ashore haunting the waterfront and scouring the taverns, but to no avail; there simply was not an able-bodied man to be had. Nor were they alone. At least four other ships were in a like plight with masters equally desperate for crews.

' "A mob of roofyans",' read Baines slowly, "marched upon the Culver Street bar-racks in which are housed forty-two recaptured runaway slaves awaiting transportation to the re-bell-us" . . . ?' He blinked hopefully at Anne.

' "Rebellious State of South Carolina",' Anne corrected absently.

' "Ree-bellyus State of South Carolina",' continued Baines. He set his jaw stubbornly and ground his way through the next paragraph.

' "The Mayor sent for a detachment of militia who successfully prevented the more violent excesses of the outraged citizens . . ." '

James snorted. 'So a mob suddenly becomes outraged citizenry!'

' ". . . and by prompt action forestalled the intent of the leaders, among whom are believed to be many well-known Abolitionists, of releasing the unhappy negroes . . ." '

'It is disgraceful!' raged Anne. 'Is this a free country, or isn't it?'

'Mobs are mobs the world over,' said James sourly. 'Able-bodied idlers with time on their hands and villainy in their hearts. There are times when I could wish back the days of the press gangs. Good ships lying idle while a parcel of lazy dunder-pated idiots parade the streets beating drums and mouthing empty slogans!' He banged his hands together and quickened his perambulating gait.

'I was not speaking of the justifiably incensed townpeople,' said Anne, tartly. 'But rather of those poor unfortunates held in durance with naught to look forward to but the branding iron and the lash when all they sought was freedom.'

'They have no more right to freedom than a herd of cattle,' snapped James.

Anne was horrified. 'James! You do not believe that?'

'They are property,' said James flatly. 'And it is not a question of belief. It is a question of law.'

'An evil law.'

'No doubt, madam, but it is not in our power to change it. You really must stop trying to alter the world to your liking, Anne.'

'Yes, James,' said Anne, meekly. She knew from experience that when he addressed her as 'madam' he was in no mood to brook argument. And really, she thought sadly, what could she do? What could anyone do where the entire juridical process of the United States had failed?

'It's a pity,' interjected Baines wistfully, 'we can't buy 'em. They make first-rate hands does the blacks. I shipped with a checkerboard crew once—port watch white, starboard watch black. Black as tar they was. But first rate hands. Give me a crew o' tar-babies and I'll give you the smartest ship afloat.'

'It can't be done,' said James. 'In a free State it is a criminal offence to buy or sell slaves.'

Baines yawned and stretched his arms. 'I shouldn't

worry, ma'am, they'll be freed soon enough if I know anything about mobs. I doubt the soldiers, being northeners, has their heart in it. I wouldn't change shoes with one of them slave-catchers for a mountain of gold. Within twenty-four hours they'll be hanging from lampposts, mark my words.'

Anne shivered. 'A terrible prospect even though they are wicked cruel men.'

James stopped his pacing. 'Yes,' he said, thoughtfully. 'I daresay they would require little persuasion to leave, and by the same token the authorities will be glad to see the back of them.' He picked up hat and cloak. 'I'm off ashore,' he announced. His face twisted into a lopsided grin. 'To tout for passengers.' He deposited a chaste kiss upon her forehead and was gone. They could hear him whistling cheerfully as he tramped along the deck above. Anne stared at Baines. 'Passengers? But we have no crew!'

Baines shrugged: 'Mr Onedin knows what he's about, ma'am.'

James swung away from the docks and walked briskly past the grain warehouses, the tobacco sheds and, with the lowing murmur of cattle in his ears, skirted the stockyards to turn into Market Street with its rows of tumbledown wooden-framed buildings. Then the town opened before him into neat squares and well-kept parks with plane trees stark and bare in the winter half-light. He paused to take his bearings, then asked the way of a passer-by, a pesky little man with a goatee beard and the cantankerous eyes of the born nosey-parker.

'Whaddya want with slavers?' he demanded. 'You for free labour, or slave?'

'I believe every man to be worth his salt,' replied James ambiguously.

'Long Abe'll settle their hash, give they uppity secessionists their come-uppance.' He hopped from one leg to another like a demented grasshopper and poked forward an accusing head: 'You one of they long-nosed Britishers, ann't ya?'

James gravely acknowledged the charge.

'Paul Pry. All Britishers is Paul Pries.' Having established supremacy the grasshopper unbent sufficiently to announce that the slave-catchers were settled in the Chalmer's Hotel on Union Street. 'Quaking in their boots and awaiting the wrath of the Lord. We is going to burn 'em out and run 'em out of town on a rail. Lessen we decide to hang 'em fust,' he added in the tone of one who has given a knotty problem considerable reflection. 'Guthrie's the feller you're set on seeing. Whaddya want with Guthrie? You going to spit in his eye?'

'Something like that,' said James, thanked the fool and headed across town for Union Street.

A crowd had gathered outside Chalmer's Hotel, a high-fronted three-storeyed building of clapboard, shuttered windows and shingled roof. The crowd was little more than a leaderless mob; aimless spectators not yet motivated to violence. There would be about thirty or forty people, he calculated. They shuffled and stamped their feet and a few with breath to spare were defiantly whistling 'John Brown's Body' while one long ragged youth monotonously tapped a drum. The portals were guarded by two soldiers muffled in greatcoats and carrying fixed bayonets. They seemed bored by the whole proceedings and the crowd reacted to their presence with the greatest good-humour as though they were part of a side-show put on for their special delectation before the main event. Pushing his way to the front, James realised that in a sense that was exactly what the two guards did represent—a sop to authority and amusement for the mob. Somebody of sardonic humour had posted two negro privates to protect a pair of slave-catchers from lynch law.

James straightened his shoulders, tried to give himself a military bearing, and stepped briskly across to the hotel entrance. One of the guards lazily extended his bayoneted carbine to bar the way.

'I am Captain Onedin,' snapped James. 'Is your commanding officer inside?'

The two guards sprang to attention.

'Yassuh,' said the first in the accents of Georgia. 'He surely are. Cap'n Bear, Cap'n, sir.'

'Thank you, soldier,' said James and walked quickly through to the hotel foyer followed by an ironic cheer from the crowd.

The foyer consisted of little more than a threadbare carpet, moth-eaten velvet curtains, a few sick-looking aspidistras, a formidable array of spittoons and a bogey stove belching sulphurous fumes. To his left was a desk with a hotel register presided over by a whey-faced clerk ready to run at the cast of the first stone.

James strode to the desk and noticed the fear in the man's eyes. There would be no awkward questions from that quarter, he decided.

'Captain Bear?' he demanded peremptorily.

'Dining room, sir.' The clerk's shoulders sagged as though bearing the burden of the world. He waved a white fin of a hand towards a curtained arch.

'And Mr Guthrie?'

'Both gentlemen are in the dining room, sir,' said the clerk, hoping James was not a man of violence.

James grunted acknowledgement and marched in the direction indicated.

The dining room was bare of guests except for a choleric man in regimentals dining alone and two hard-looking men shifty of eye and nervous of gesture conversing in low voices at a corner table. They were apparently at the end of their meal and helping themselves liberally from the brandy bottle. One was tall and lean with a short pointed beard and a long black cigar clenched between his teeth. His companion was a broad-shouldered man of about thirty with a bald patch like a monk's tonsure. It was the only monkish thing about him. He was cursed with a ferocious squint and a complexion the colour of roast beef.

The army officer sat a table or two distant where he could keep his charges under surveillance and yet not be contaminated by their presence.

James addressed himself to the bearded man without regard for conversational niceties and in a voice loud enough to be overheard by their reluctant guardian.

'Captain Onedin of the British ship *Pampero*. I'm bound for Charleston and I can ship you and your forty niggers if you've a mind for it and the price is right.'

The pair stared blankly at him for a moment and James heard a chair creak as the militia captain prepared to lumber to his feet. The tall man recovered first.

'You come at an opportune moment, sir.' He extended a hand. 'My name is Guthrie. Pray allow me to introduce my colleague, Mr Hannibal Harman.'

Harman squinted balefully at the intruder. 'I'd heard that ships was tied up for want of crews.' His voice had a harsh grating quality with a strong Virginian intonation.

'I sail at daylight,' James told him flatly, and turned his attention to Guthrie, evidently the decision-maker of the two. 'Do you accept my offer, or no?'

Guthrie extended a long thin hand and appeared to be inspecting his nails.

'And your terms, sir?'

'Twenty dollars a head.'

'In cash, I imagine?'

'In gold,' said James.

Guthrie smiled. 'Not unreasonable under the circumstances.' He spread his hands apologetically. 'Unfortunately I am not in the habit of carrying large sums of ready money about my person. I must ask you to be satisfied with a draft, Captain Onedin.' He smiled again. 'Payable in Charleston.'

'In which case,' said James pleasantly, 'we shall make it a round thousand. Five hundred payable now. Five hundred on delivery.'

Guthrie's shoulders lifted in a delicate shrug. He patted his pockets and again smiled an insincere expression of apology: 'I think you misunderstand me, sir?'

'There are only two ways out of Baltimore,' James told him brusquely. 'By sea. Or by rail. And I am not aware that the railroads have yet taken to accepting promissory notes.'

Guthrie laughed. 'You are a man after my own heart, sir, you are indeed. Hannibal will pay you the moment we set foot aboard ship.'

'Nobody is setting foot aboard no ship! Them nigras stay put until I get express orders to shift 'em. You got my word on it, gentlemen!'

The speaker was the irate army captain who now stood huffing and snorting at James's shoulder. His portly figure was crammed into an ill-fitting uniform of faded blue trousers and scarlet jacket frogged with gold. He must have been all of fifty years of age and displayed an enormous white cavalry moustache, the ends of which dipped below a bullfrog throat leading to a bullfrog chin. His brandywine face was lined with the distended veins of apoplexy and his breath reeked of an unpleasant mixture of brandy and garlic.

Guthrie seemed not in the least discommoded at the intervention. He smiled affably and reached toward the brandy bottle.

'Ah—Captain Bear, our involuntary protector. You will take refreshment, sir?'

Captain Bear's jowls took on a mottled hue and shook like turkey wattles.

'No, sir, I will not! Your very presence contaminates the air I breathe. I consider you a pair of vile seditious runagates and it is my unhappy duty to be responsible for your safety. I did not ask for the commission, nor do I relish the task, but if you have any thought for preserving your greasy necks from the rope you will obey my instructions to the letter and remain in this hotel until I give permission to move. Do I make myself clear?'

'Abundantly,' said Guthrie, lighting a fresh cigar. 'However, this gentleman...'

'I imagine, Captain,' James interrupted, 'that your first charge is the protection of persons and property?'

'Another slave-dealer?' The old man turned his head and spat his contempt to the air.

'The mob is growing in size and it is my understanding that it is their intention to burn down this hotel, hoist these two gentlemen on high, and then release your prisoners. Rioting mobs, Captain, have a way of getting out of hand. I doubt your detachment of militia is strong enough to restrain them. They'll burn this town about your ears and Washington will hold you responsible. It's a habit governments have—seeking scapegoats for their own folly.' James deliberately kept his voice cold and calm. He shrugged. 'It is no affair of mine, I am simply offering a way out of a dilemma.'

'There is no dilemma,' snapped the captain. 'I know my duty, sir.'

'The Fugitive Slave Law defines your duty,' pronounced Guthrie. ' "Federal and state officials are to aid in the capture of escaped slaves and render all assistance to constables, owners or their representatives".'

The crowd outside began a sing-song chant:

'What, bend the knee to Southern rule?
  What, cringe and crawl to Southern clay?
And be the base, the simple tool
  Of hell-begotten slavery?'

They cheered and a stone shattered an upstairs window.

'Time is short, Captain,' said James.

'You and your kind are a blot on the face of the earth,'

snarled the stout man. But he was worried and James could see his mind slowly examining alternatives.

'I abide by the law,' James said. 'To the letter, and I advise you, sir, to do the same.'

Captain Bear gave a bull-like shake of his head, but it was no more than the obstinacy of a man pushed into a corner. He made a further half-hearted attempt to save face.

'It is not possible. There is another rabble—two thousand strong, I'm told—congregated at the barracks. Any attempt to move those blacks will be resisted.'

'And the barracks, no doubt, are guarded by the main body of militia?'

Bear nodded unhappily.

'Then we must create a diversion,' said James. 'Excitement attracts riff-raff as moths to a candle. Arrange for your two sentries to fire a shot or two over the heads of the mob. The others will come a-running. In the turmoil transfer the blacks to a couple of army wagons and escort 'em to the ship. We might also spread a rumour that they are to be taken to the railroad station. During the hubbub these two gentlemen can slip out by the back door.' The hastily formulated plan stood a fair measure of success in James's view if only this puffed-up militia captain could be relied upon to carry out his part of the operation.

He underrated Captain Bear who, although perhaps lacking in qualities of imagination and a stickler for duty, was trained to act first and leave the thinking to his superiors.

Bear quickly scribbled a series of orders, roused out the frightened clerk and sent him flying off to the barracks as fast as his heels would carry him.

'And you, sir,' he barked at James, 'will do me the kindness of joining that parcel of chanting jackanapes outside and trying your hand at fomenting a little dissension in their ranks.' He fished out an enormous silver turnip of a watch. 'I give you ten minutes.' He snorted and blew at the ends of his moustache before turning a malevolent gaze upon the two slavers. 'As for you vermin, you are to make yourselves scarce the moment the first shot is fired. And once on the high seas I hope those damn' blacks rise and cut your throats!' After which malediction the gallant captain took himself to his table, poured a generous tot of brandy and placed his watch upon the table top. 'Ten minutes,' he warned James. 'Ten minutes.'

As James stepped into the street the crowd were singing, to the tune of the Marseillaise:

'Arise! Arise ye brave!
  And let your war-cry be,
Free speech, free press, free soil, free men,
  Union and liberty!'

A hot potato man and a hot chestnut seller vied for custom and the core of the gathering had now been augmented by a dozen or so ruffians armed with cudgels, axes, and even a musket or two.

One of the rowdies, a burly dull-witted ox carrying a butcher's cleaver and exuding the unmistakable smell of the slaughterhouse, barred James's way.

'And who might you be, mister?'

'A friend of freedom,' said James, knowing that nothing pleased a crowd so much as a popular watchword.

'A friend o' freedom!' bawled the butcher, brandishing his cleaver and raising both arms high. 'What news do you have, friend?'

Those nearest wheeled and jostled closer, eager for any rumour or snippet of gossip.

James raised his voice: 'News of a plot,' he began and was interrupted by a familiar pesky voice:

'He ann't no friend o' freedom,' yelped the grasshopper, squirming his way to the front. 'I know him!

He's a Southern spy. A nosey-parkerin' Britisher in secessionist pay. Stopped me in the street and ast me to direct him to Guthrie. Not an hour since!' he screeched, as though the lapse of time clinched the proof beyond the doubts of all reasonable men.

James's distaste for violence was only equalled by an almost overwhelming desire to lock his hands about the skinny man's neck and squeeze the life out of him.

The butcher growled deep in his throat, hoisted the cleaver menacingly and shoved James in the chest with such force that he stumbled back into the grasping arms of those behind.

'The man's a fool,' James rasped. 'Of course I asked directions. I'm a stranger in your town.'

'Whad I tell yer?' hooted the grasshopper triumphantly. 'He's a spy. Ast for Guthrie plain as plain!'

'You're a liar,' snapped James. 'I was looking for Captain Bear for whom I had important information. I had never heard of Guthrie until you mentioned his name.' That, he thought, was at least part true, and with the mob now pressing suffocatingly close it was no time for niceties of argument. It required little to turn a milling crowd of the curious into a ravening many-limbed beast ready to render and tear in a cumulative frenzy of madness. Already the ripples of rumour had reached the outermost fringes of the crowd. 'A spy!' 'A spy.' 'They've caught a spy.' 'A Southerner.' 'A slaver.' 'A slave-owner come for the blacks.' 'A spy!' 'They've caught a spy!' The whispers rapidly became a tumult, a clamour, then a roar of rage. The crowd surged forward, squeezing and pressing upon the centre of attention. The situation was becoming desperate. James thought quickly and addressed himself to the butcher.

'I have important information. Hoist me upon your shoulders. Quickly now!'

The man stared in dull suspicion.

'Hurry!' snapped James. 'There is no time to lose. I

must address our friends.' He laid emphasis upon 'our friends' and was rewarded by the butcher and a couple of his fellows clearing a space about them. The grasshopper started to raise his voice in protest.

'And keep that chattering dolt quiet,' James demanded. 'I cannot make myself heard above his babble.'

The butcher backhanded the little man then thrust his cleaver beneath James's nose.

'You tell the truth, mister. You tell it true, or by the Book I'll split you in half.'

His two companions lowered their heads and heaved James high upon their shoulders. He gazed around at the bobbing sea of faces. They froze, then lifted toward him, a circle of pale white blobs indistinct in the falling darkness. Here and there a newly-blazing torch threw off sparks and dark resinous smoke. The turkey-gobble died to a murmur, then to an expectant silence.

James raised his voice to quarterdeck pitch, the resonant cadences of a man accustomed to making his commands heard above the shout of wind and shriek of rigging:

'My friends. Captain Bear of the militia—a true Northerner—will avouch my credentials and confirm to you, good people, that I am come in haste to warn of treachery and black-hearted villainy. A Southern plot to seize our unhappy black brethren and transport them secretly by way of the railroad . . .'

There was a murmur of anger from the bulk of the crowd but one or two sceptics called derisively:

'We know that.'

'We stopped 'em yesterday, we'll stop 'em again today!'

'Tell us sump'n new, mister.'

'Pratin' preacher!' snarled a voice from the edge of the crowd and a hot potato flew through the air. It missed its target and brought a howl of enraged anguish from a bystander.

James held up his arms:

'Furthermore, friends, a detachment of troops are on their way to clear this street and aid those damned slavers escape our justice!'

The mob roared their anger, but James noticed with satisfaction that groups milled, like wheels within wheels, and those on the fringes looked apprehensively over their shoulders.

'There is yet time to confound their knavery.' Balancing precariously upon his bony perch he fished in his pocket to draw out two silver dollars. His eyes sought out two hungry-looking ragamuffins, street jackals whose kind invariably followed in the wake of disorder. He jingled the coins, tossed them tantalisingly in the air.

'Two fleet-footed fellows to carry a message to our supporters cooling their heels outside the barracks. Tell them to send reinforcements here immediately. Half here, and half to lay in ambush at the railroad station.'

The street arabs grabbed the coins arching through the air and whooping like Indians raced away in the direction of the barracks.

'Does that meet with your approval?' he demanded of the crowd, who promptly cheered and stamped and whistled at this intimation of action.

'And I will contribute a cask of rum to keep out the cold.' The grasshopper seemed the more dangerous adversary so he spilled a handful of coins about the fellow's ears and was rewarded by renewed cheers from the mob.

It was, James considered, an opportune moment to make himself scarce. He slid from his supporters' shoulders in time to hear a stentorian military voice bawling:

'To your homes, instanter! Instanter, I say—or I open fire. Soldiers—load and aim!'

Captain Bear could not have timed his appearance better. With scarlet coat and scarlet face he stood illumined in a shaft of yellow light like a pantomime demon. And like a pantomime demon the crowd did not at first take the apparition seriously, until the menacing carbines and the click of rifle bolts sent those nearest stumbling back upon their fellows.

James, edging away toward the rim of the mob, shouted: 'Rush them! They will not dare fire upon us! Liberty and Union!' he added for good measure and then joined the general stampede as the first volley crashed out above their heads.

He arrived back at the ship somewhat short of breath but in high good humour.

'Stand by to take on lodgers,' he told Mr Baines with unaccustomed levity. 'A crew of blackbirds and two gentlemen. Pick out a dozen good hands and knock 'em into shape; we'll train the rest when we have plenty of sea room with nothing to bump into. Broach a cask of salt beef and tell that steward he's been promoted cook. I want a kettle of broth, plenty of boiled potatoes, salt horse and pickle—they'll need a lining on their stomachs if we are to make sailors of them. Open the slop chest and put your dozen into warm clothing, I don't want them tumbling from the yards half-frozen—those niggers are worth twenty dollars a head, delivered.'

Anne stared at him stonily. Baines gave a huge grin of delight and clapped his massive paws together. 'I'll make sailors of 'em, I'll turn 'em into the sweetest-smelling, liveliest crew you could wish to sail with! By the time we clear Chesapeake every one of them tar-babies will be fit to spit into the wind with the best!'

'Sail drill, Mr Baines,' said James. 'Plenty of sail drill.'

'Aye, aye,' said Baines and departed cheerfully to roust out Jão and stir up the galley fires.

Anne waited until they were alone and then turned reproachful eyes upon James.

'It is surely not your intention to deliver those poor unfortunates into bondage?'

'They are cargo, and I am in the business of delivering

cargo according to the shippers' instructions.'

'They are not senseless packages to be bundled hither and thither. They are people,' she said fiercely. 'Human beings degraded to the level of animals by the iniquitous practice of slavery. If you accept freedom for yourself you are obliged to extend that same freedom to others!'

'In American waters,' said James, 'I am obliged to accept American law, and American law has it that slaves are property and property is protected under their Constitution. And,' he added warningly, 'I must remind you that there are stiff penalties for those who aid escaping slaves.'

'Such a law turns everyone into slave-catchers. It is a bad law, an evil law and as such it is a Christian duty to defy it. There are higher laws than those made by man.'

'It is not my Christian duty—nor yours, Anne; and I ask you to remember that my first duty is to deliver a hundred thousand vines to Senhor Braganza.'

'For profit, no doubt,' said Anne, bitterly.

'No,' said James. 'Because I gave my word.'

'I am pleased, dear husband,' she responded acidly, 'to apprehend that you retain at least a shred of conscience.'

He smiled and leaned forward to tweak her cheek.

'You are conscience enough for any man, little Anne.'

She compressed her lips and her face set into lines of sour obstinacy. James sighed. There was no doubt about it, the marital state was one of mixed blessings. Anne was a splendid helpmeet, a most remarkable woman, but there were occasions when a mettlesome spirit could prove a wearisome burden to others.

He was saved further reflection by the clatter of feet down the companionway as Baines ushered in Mr Guthrie.

James effected introductions, adding: 'I must forewarn you, sir, my wife holds strong views on the subject of slavery.'

Guthrie bowed to Anne. 'So do I, ma'am. May I hope for the pleasure of an interesting dissertation later?' He raised his head and became aware that the woman's eyes had widened into a stare of total recognition. Guthrie racked his memory.

'I am afraid you have the advantage of me, Mrs Onedin?'

'And shall continue to do so, sir!' snapped Anne and swept from the room head held stiffly in the air.

'I think she spied you through the telescope, sir,' said Baines and outlined the circumstances.

'Ah,' murmured Guthrie. 'I see. An unfortunate beginning.'

James brought him back to the business in hand. 'Where,' he asked, 'is your companion? Your paymaster?'

Gutherie spread his hands and his voice held a characteristic note of insincere regret.

'Unfortunately Mr Harman was somewhat tardy in effecting his escape. There was nothing I could do. The mob were on him like a pack of wolves. But he sold his life dearly, Captain Onedin. Yes, I may truthfully say, he sold his life dearly.'

The man was not only a theatrical mountebank, thought James, but an unmitigated liar to boot.

'I owe my life and liberty to the success of your scheme,' continued Guthrie. 'By God, sir, but that rabble scattered like chaff.' He gave vent to a neighing high-pitched laugh. 'A handful of 'em ran up the street as though the devil were at their shirt tails, only to meet a horde of their fellows hurrying from the barracks. What a business, sir! What a business!'

'And your blacks?'

'They should be here within the hour.'

'Our agreement,' James reminded him, 'was five hundred dollars on account.'

'You have a sharp head for business, sir, you do indeed.

Unfortunately . . .' And he gave that half-apologetic shrug of the shoulders.

James finished the sentence for him: 'Mr Harman carried the money belt?'

'Exactly, sir. I regret the tragedy with all my heart and must own that I am once more in your debt.'

'H'm,' said James.

'It seems we must trust one another, eh?'

'A rather one-sided obligation,' James commented sourly.

'Come, sir you have but to deliver my blacks in accordance with our agreement and you shall be paid on the moment. You have my hand and my word on it.' Guthrie extended a hand with an air of frank cameraderie.

James ignored the hand.

'We'll have it in writing,' he said.

He sat at his desk and scribbled industriously for a few minutes pausing only to ask: 'How many?'

'Forty-two.'

He passed the sheet of paper to Guthrie. 'Your Bill of Lading. Sign here.'

Guthrie eyed the document with the suspicion of a man habitually wary of the written word. 'A Bill of what?' he said.

'Lading,' said James. 'A receipt and document of title describing the merchandise to be shipped, number of pieces, and stating that payment of one thousand dollars is due at our destination.'

Guthrie's features creased into a grin as he read the neat clear calligraphy: ' "Forty-two parcels described as negro slaves the property of the charterparty Standford Guthrie . . ." Forty-two parcels! I relish that, sir. I do indeed. But what, may I ask, is a charterparty?'

'You are,' said James. 'A charterparty is one who hires a vessel in whole or in part for the conveyance of goods —in your case, forty-two blacks.'

'I see.' Guthrie's eyes had a thoughtful look. 'I take it there is some purpose in this particularisation, Captain?'

'There is, Mr Guthrie, there is. Slaves are property under United States law. Property is cargo. How else would you describe them?'

Guthrie whinnied again: 'By the Testament, sir, but you are a stickler for legalities, that you are. But permit me to assure you that your word would be good enough for me.'

James turned his cold gaze upon Guthrie. 'But not yours for me,' he said flatly. 'Two copies. One for you. One for me.'

'As you wish,' said Guthrie and appended his signature.

'Thank you,' said James pocketing one copy and giving the other to Guthrie. He smiled blandly. 'I am afraid we are a little short-handed so I shall require the service of some of your blacks before we can set sail.'

Guthrie stared at him. 'You have no crew?'

They both heard the tramp of marching feet, the jingle of harness, the creak of wagon wheels.

'I have now,' said James.

Chapter Five

THE SLAVES trudged aboard, dark faces against the darker night, hands and feet manacled and linked with chain. They moved with the slow lurching shuffle of total despair. Thirty-six men and six women yoked together in coffles of six.

Anne, unable to bear the sight longer, fled to the sanctuary of their stateroom hoping to banish the memory of those tormented ebony-black faces, some bearing the puckered brandmark R categorising the runaway burned deep into forehead or cheek. Others had ear lobes slit like cattle. All bore on shoulders, arm or leg a distinguishing brand of ownership. Without exception they wore tattered garments of thin cotton and shivered uncontrollably in the biting cold.

Even at this insulating distance she could identify the slip-slap of bare feet and the accompanying chink-chank of swaying chain. She put her hands over her ears and whimpered in an agony of shared misery made the worse by the knowledge of James's callous self-interest. She tried to excuse him, to understand the overriding imperative, the spur of necessity, his obligation to Senhor Braganza, the absolute urgency of setting sail at whatever the cost. But she could not exclude from her mind the thought that James's actions, as always, were motivated by profit. How could he possibly justify supping from that pool of degradation? Nothing, nothing could justify the use of slave labour! No matter how great the need. To succumb to such temptation put him on a level with Southern planters and men as evil as Guthrie. She wept softly for a long time until the ship fell silent and there was only the steady monotonous creak of the mooring lines and the whisper of the off-shore breeze to keep her company.

The blacks had been shepherded forward to the crew's quarters in the fo'c'sle. As the *Pampero* normally shipped thirty hands it had been a simple matter to separate the women and shut them in the sailmaker's shop. It would mean a modicum of overcrowding for the remainder but no real hardship. They had been supplied with food and bedding, their irons removed—in the face of strong protests from Guthrie—and had been padlocked in for the night with one of the remaining Portuguese standing guard outside.

All in all James considered it a satisfactory end to a satisfactory day's business.

He walked along the deck with Baines discussing the problems involved in setting sail with a raw crew.

'Once we're under way,' said Baines, 'I'll take those two Portuguese aloft and we'll rig her Yankee fashion with leech and buntlines as spilling lines.'

James nodded agreement. It was sound practice and meant, in effect, that at the first sign of a blow the sails could be rapidly snugged up to the yards by the simple expedient of hauling on ropes leading down to deck, instead of the hands being required to scramble aloft to take in sail in the teeth of a gale.

'We'll go out under spanker, jib and main tops'l,' said James. 'Until they get the hang of it.'

Baines gloated, rubbing his hands in an unconscious aping of one of James's habitual gestures: 'I'll lick 'em into shape. I've always wanted a crew o' tar-babies.'

'Gentle 'em, Mr Baines. Gentle 'em. They'll have had a bellyful of hazing on those damned plantations.'

Baines grunted and spat over the side. 'There's only one way to get a farmer aloft. He's got to be druv.'

'You're the mate,' said James. 'I shan't interfere.' He knew the problem only too well. No man in his right senses would trust himself to scramble out along a swaying yard, sixty feet or more above the deck, with the strong possibility of being knocked from his perch by a buffeting sail. His fear had to be overcome by the greater fear of disobeying an order.

They walked to the shipside and together gloomily surveyed the encroaching ice and the black chasm of water in mid-stream.

Daily a steam tug puffed and panted, stern paddle threshing the water, iron-shod bows crushing and grinding, in the laborious task of keeping the channel open. It was a losing battle with chunks of thickening ice slowing the tug's progress, heaving and bobbing in the broad wake only to reform and solidify into a creaking white field behind. One more day, James considered, and the channel would be closed until spring.

The ice squeaked and groaned, raising a fine white vapour to shimmer and glitter beneath a bone-white moon.

'I've ordered the tug,' he pronounced. 'She'll tow us as far as the Chesapeake. That should give you time to clear the tops'ls.'

Baines grunted acknowledgement.

They walked aft and in the tiny chartroom James unlocked the brass-bound chest containing the ship's armoury. He handed a long-barrelled pistol and a supply of ammunition to Baines.

'We go armed,' he told him. 'At all times.'

James had a distaste for firearms, being of the opinion that a man with a gun when faced with danger had a strong temptation to pull the trigger, a solution which served to exacerbate rather than resolve a situation. Authority, in his view, was enforced by the exercise of will and not by minatory drum-beating. But an unruly crew of half-starved packet-rats were different in kind and character from a shipload of runaways with all to gain and nothing to lose. One of the terrors of slave ships and convict ships had always been of a sudden bloody uprising of the victims against their oppressors.

'Just a precaution,' he said. 'I doubt they'll give trouble before we clear the Chesapeake.'

'And thereafter,' said Baines grimly, 'they'll be too damn' tired to turn their minds to anything but sleep.'

'Treat 'em as crew, Mr Baines. As crew, not slaves. Food to fill their bellies and routine to occupy their minds. Split 'em into two watches. There'll be a natural leader somewhere among 'em. He'll be your bos'n.'

He bid Baines goodnight and then stretched out on the chartroom settee fully clothed. He closed his eyes for a moment and awoke to find the oil lamp burning low and Jão persistently shaking him by the shoulder and the aroma of hot coffee invading his nostrils.

'Time, Senhor Capitão,' Jão announced, immediately adding, 'I no more cook, I wish for steward. I go now, wake lady.'

James sat up and discovered he had a splitting headache. 'You will cook,' he snarled, 'until I say otherwise. As for the lady—leave her to sleep. Breakfast for all hands at . . .' He stared blear-eyed at the chronometer. 'Eight bells. Eight o'clock,' he spelt out carefully. 'You compreender?' and wished, not for the first time, that he had a little of Baines's uncanny fluency in foreign tongues.

Jão rolled his eyes and departed, hissing displeasure.

James became aware of the sounds of movement, the slither of a rope dragged along the deck, someone racked with a fit of coughing, the steady chopping of ice axes, hoarse voices rasping and calling, someone stumbling and cursing on the deck above. The ship was coming alive, shivering and stretching as though from a long sleep.

He drank the coffee quickly, splashed water on his face, thrust his stockinged feet into seaboots, pulled a woollen cap over his ears and a heavy cloak about his shoulders. He paused to check the barometer, steady at 1,043 millibars thereby forecasting a continuation of clear skies, hard frost and light winds. Then he made his way on to deck.

The cold was ferocious and the breath seemed to freeze in his lungs. The deck thermometer had fallen from eighteen to twenty-two below and the air had that strange clarity indicative of being free of all moisture. The moon hung low over the horizon, a round Cyclopean eye whose bright unwinking stare peered at a world turned to amethyst and silver.

On the wharf a group of longshoremen stamped numbed feet while waiting the order to cast off the mooring lines. On deck bemused black men were being pushed and shoved into place by a fluently cursing Baines. Others stood helplessly on the fo'c'sle head while one of the Portuguese seamen waved furious arms and hissed like a kettle. Up aloft four darkies and the remaining Portuguese were strung out along the topsail yard chopping away at the gaskets holding the furled sail in position. The tarred hemp parted under the axe blows to stick out like so many dead fingers. Even as James watched the canvas stretched and sagged to throw thin sheets and slivers of ice to clatter upon the deck below.

Baines, steaming like a horse, raised a face red from exertions. ''Vast,' he bawled. ''Vast!'

Eyes rolled fearfully in downturned black faces. Santos, the Portuguese, hung easily, one foot in the rope stirrup, an arm crooked over the taper of the yard. He looked questioningly at Baines.

'Basta!' translated Baines. 'Basta!' and motioned them to return to deck.

Santos heaved himself up to stand barefoot on the boom, trotted along, swung himself into the shrouds and ran down to land catlike on the deck. He was grinning hugely and seemed to be enjoying himself, James noted with approval.

'Promote that man to lamptrimmer, Mr Baines,' he called as his brain busied itself with the complications of watch-keeping duties. Lamptrimmer was second in rating only to the bos'n—but that position must be reserved for one of the blacks—one who spoke English and could both accept and give orders. One Portuguese to each watch, he decided; and at that they would need to double as quartermasters. He and Mr Baines must also share wheel watches; and train this rabble. Looking at them standing helplessly in the positions they had been allocated James's spirits sank. Knocking a crew of landlubbers into shape was problem enough, but at least they did show a certain willingness to learn even if only from a sense of self-preservation. But a slave, treated like an animal and trained like an animal to perform certain tasks and none other, lacked initiative, the ability to think for himself.

The task seemed hopeless. The eyes in the dulled faces were blank and he doubted that even Baines, for all his boasting, could make seamen from this herd of black sheep.

James came out of his reverie to see the tug fulminating

across the river, smoke and sparks belching from its funnel, driving beams rising and falling so that it seemed to progress across the water like some ungainly monstrous insect. Its iron bows crunched into the ice then rose high while the stern paddle thrashed and tore at the water. Then the ice creaked and groaned, stretched and finally gave beneath the weight of the vessel. The paddle stopped, churned astern, and the tug charged once more. Long fissures split across the ice field in a series of sharp explosions and the *Pampero* rocked and heaved, her mooring lines humming and twanging like giant bowstrings. A figure on the tug swung a heaving line and threw it expertly. The group on the fo'c'sle head caught the weighted end and, urged by the excitable Portuguese, Ramon, hauled until the bight of the massive hawser, stiff with freezing water, jammed itself between the fairleads. Ramon whooped and cursed and then Baines was driving his own group forward to lend a hand.

The black bodies bent almost double as, feet slithering on the icy deck, they hauled and heaved at the thin manilla line. James watched Baines quickly bend on a traveller—a two-inch manilla rope with a breaking strain of two tons. Again they threw their weight forward, sweating and heaving, but not yet in unison.

'Heave!' roared Baines. 'Stamp and go! Stamp and go!' he chanted, giving them the time, and raised his hoarse voice in a chantyman's roundelay:

'Was you ever down Mobile way,
Pickin' cotton all the day?
Hey-ho! Stamp and go!
Stamp and go! Stamp and go!'

The deep African voices picked up the rhythm, giving to the seafarers' chanty a strange rich dark melody, a haunting threnody of nostalgic longing.

The massive eyelet squeezed tight to emerge suddenly like a cork from a bottle. The straining bodies surged aft to tumble into a writhing heap of waving arms and legs. The black faces split into wide grins of delight and black mouths opened to vent roars of laughter; and there was Baines in among them, slapping, hugging and guffawing, and all the time urging them to fresh efforts, to drag the hawser further inboard and finally loop the eye over the bitts.

There was no doubt about it, James considered; Baines had an enviable ability to extract the best from the worst of men. He could be kicking and cuffing one moment and laughing and joking the next, and no one ever seemed to bear him ill will. Such a virtuoso was worth his weight in gold to any shipmaster.

Baines waved his arms at the tug then turned and bawled for the waiting longshoremen to cast off.

The newly promoted Santos self-importantly directed his group to haul in the sternline as the tug leaned back and took the strain. Its engines banged and clanked, steam hissed from leaking joints, the paddle churned slowly and acrid black smoke swept across to engulf the *Pampero* in a sulphurous cloud of hot cinders and fumes.

The great coir hawser tautened to throw off a fine spray as the enormous pressures squeezed it like a sponge. The *Pampero*'s bows slowly turned, groaning protestation as the shifting ice twisted and cracked, lifting and turning until black water boiled and spouted between rending fissures and grinding vortices. Ice fountains rose and fell and geysers of spume roared through suddenly opening blow-holes. The bows continued to push and strain, widening a channel until the bowsprit pointed the way to clear water.

Quite suddenly the ship bobbed free, the stern scraped against the jetty, splintering the taffrail and shattering the starboard trailboard like so much matchwood; then the deck canted and James felt beneath his feet the familiar slow pitch and sway of a ship once again at one with the sea.

The tug hauled the *Pampero* clear of the near ice-bound Patapsco and into the clearer waters of Chesapeake Bay before casting off and wheezing an asthmatic farewell on her steam whistle. The last they saw of her was a straggle-tail plume of smoke and a fountain of spray thrown up by the churning paddle as she chomped her way back through the fast-closing ice field.

Baines had the main topsail spread and driver and jib hoisted when James belatedly rang eight bells and sent the hands to breakfast.

The women had been allowed to come out and join the menfolk sitting on the forehatch where, laughing and joking, Baines among them, they wolfed down Jão's attempt at mutton-broth pie.

James ordered the fo'c'sle door unpadlocked and the remainder emerged blinking and shivering to stare in wonder at the broken ice drifting and bobbing past the slow-moving vessel. Their eyes, he noticed, soon turned with sick longing toward the heavily wooded shorelines on either hand where trees plumed with snow nodded and beckoned a spurious promise of freedom.

But soon they were mingling with their fellows while Baines's chosen few, warm in heavy guernseys and canvas trousers, strutted and pointed aloft boasting of feats of valour and daring.

Anne and Guthrie came to join him. Her eyes were red and tired lines pulled her face into triangular planes of bitterness. A little of Guthrie's urbanity seemed to have left him and his manner held a contained edge of irritability. James permitted himself a private grin. No doubt the slave-catcher had been subjected to the sharp edge of Anne's tongue, an experience no man would willingly undergo or easily forget.

'Why are only a few of those unfortunates attired in warm clothing?' was her opening greeting.

'To give the others an incentive,' he told her. 'In this

temperature I doubt there'll be any lack of volunteers.'

Guthrie snorted. 'Volunteers! A slave does not have the disposition to proffer his services; nor is he expected to; a slave, sir, obeys, and the master commands.' His brow came down in a frown of disapproval at the sight of Baines surrounded by the group on the hatch chattering and cawing with laughter. 'Furthermore, sir, it is not seemly for a white man to frolic with niggers. It makes them into uppity backtalkers.'

'I would be obliged, Mr Guthrie,' said James icily, 'if in future you would keep to your quarters and your opinions to yourself.'

'Those blacks are my property,' snapped Guthrie. 'And worth twenty dollars a head travelling money.'

'Oh, they're worth a great deal more than that,' said James ambiguously; and wondered if it were possible to give Anne just a hint of his scheme, if only to take the look of the hurt animal from her eyes. He extinguished the thought before it could flicker into life; there was too much at stake and if he must walk a dangerous tightrope he preferred to walk it alone. Even now he had said too much; he caught a haze of suspicion clouding Guthrie's eyes and decided to adopt a conciliatory attitude.

'I apprehend your concern,' he said. 'But you must accept my assurance that your negroes will come to no harm. I need them to crew the ship and I have complete confidence in Mr Baines's ability to train them in at least the rudiments of seamanship.'

Guthrie considered a moment then nodded approval. 'I apologise, Captain Onedin. My suspicions were unworthy.' He shrugged and smiled thinly. 'In any event under the circumstances I am entirely in your hands. If it were in your heart to make off with my property there is nothing I could do to prevent it.' He bowed to Anne. 'You will excuse me, ma'am? I have no wish to add to the offence of my presence the affliction of tobacco smoke and will therefore retire to take my cigar below.'

'I don't trust that man,' said Anne after he had left them alone.

'No more do I,' said James with more truth than he cared to admit. Something lay behind that thin smile; it had almost twisted itself into a smirk of triumph. Guthrie, he was sure, had a trick up his sleeve, but its precise nature completely eluded him. There simply hadn't been time for Guthrie to formulate, much less act upon, chicanery. On the face of it there was nothing whatever to prevent James from freeing the slaves and making a run for it across the Atlantic.

Anne had developed an uncanny, and often uncomfortable, knack of seeming to read his mind.

'Why don't we?' she asked.

'What?' He was still musing over the problem of Guthrie's unreasonable confidence.

'Free those miserable wretches and flee to England with them. They would crew the ship with a will,' she urged, eyes shining. 'And you would be striking a blow for freedom.'

'Whose freedom?' he demanded. 'Not mine, nor yours. Such a scatterbrain scheme could have but one outcome—we should finish our days in a Yankee jail. You seem to forget, Anne, that this voyage has but one purpose—to deliver one hundred thousand vines to Senhor Braganza without delay.'

'Then why not head directly for Lisbon?' she tried coaxingly. 'Ignore calling at Charleston which surely can only waste valuable time.'

James turned the wheel a spoke or two, checking the tendency of the head to pull to starboard, then looked up to the topsail barely drawing in the light wind. The clinging ice had melted and the weak winter sun was drying the canvas into patches of light and shade. A light breeze ruffled the water and carried the sweet scent of pines from the forests of Delaware. He drew in a deep breath and became aware of the faint but unmistakable aroma of cigar smoke and knew without turning his head that it came from the bell-mouthed ventilator leading to the saloon below. He smiled sourly and pitched his voice a shade higher for the benefit of the unseen listener.

'My obligation to Mr Guthrie is to conform to the terms of our contract. If I were to act upon your suggestion I should be guilty of conniving to steal another man's property—merchandise entrusted to my care—and for which crime I could be prosecuted in any British or United States court. Would you scruple to make me a criminal, little Anne?' he asked as lightly as he could.

She shook her head bemusedly: 'I don't understand. All I know is that those poor creatures are at the mercy of profit and wicked laws.'

Guthrie climbed down from his perch on the settee, drew deeply on his cigar and paced thoughtfully about the saloon. The woman was a Tartar, of that there was no doubt, but the Englishman seemed prepared to honour his part of the undertaking. Nevertheless for all his high-sounding talk of law and obligations the man was sharp, very sharp and probably knew six ways to skin a cat without raising a squeal. There was a calculating brain behind those hard blue eyes and every instinct warned Guthrie that somehow a trap had been set and was only waiting the opportunity to be sprung. He continued his restless pacing, mulling over the past events but finding no flaw. He had tried to tempt Onedin into a false move by insinuating that he was powerless and that Onedin could make off with the blacks at will. But all he had received for his trouble was a flat stare from those bleak eyes and a smooth-tongued assurance that they would come to no harm. By God, they'd better not come to harm! They were prime niggers and that big buck Henry alone was worth five hundred dollars. A troublemaker, that one, a real spoiled nigger, a house servant that some fool had taught to read and write. Considered himself educated.

Well, his master would educate him some on his return. Take a yard or two of meat off him with a raw-hide and probably break an ankle or a leg into the bargain—no one runs far with a crippled leg. Yes, that Henry would certainly bear watching and he was pleased to note that Onedin had sense enough to go armed. If those blacks were to rise their lives wouldn't be worth a bent dime. Fortunately he had taken care of that eventuality. Whatever his schemes Onedin was in for a sharp surprise before he was much older.

He was still musing when Anne appeared, stared down her nose and stalked off in the direction of the chartroom.

Guthrie sighed. There was simply no reasoning with the woman. She had a closed mind and a venomous tongue. A formidable combination. Her kind were responsible for most of the ills of the world. Heaven alone knew what drove them to be eternally poking their noses into other folk's business. It was such busybodies that were driving the United States to the brink of civil war. He shivered at the thought. War itself was a bloody enough business, but there was the additional nightmare that with the young men away the blacks might rise in a fury of burning and slaughter. And no doubt that damned woman would be satisfied, look down her long nose, sniff, and say 'I told you so'. Fortunately Onedin seemed to be master in his own house. They made an odd pair by any account, she prim-faced and his senior by a year or two for certain sure, and he stiff-necked and slippery as an eel. He wondered what the devil she was doing in the chartroom; navigation was surely her husband's business? Guthrie gave up the profitless speculation, snuffed out his cigar and took himself off to his stateroom, there to ruminate in peace.

Anne unrolled the chart, stared at it and tried to read James's mind. She felt almost light-hearted. Totally without reason, she kept assuring herself, as though any other thought would be a betrayal of her principles. But

James, that remarkable man, was planning something. He had a scheme. She had seen it in his eyes and read it in the inflection of his voice. He surely *must* be plotting to keep the slaves as crew, and in some way manage the business so that he stayed within the framework of the law. And for some reason he would not, could not enlighten her.

She studied the chart with fierce concentration, trying to wrest some significance from the carefully marked shoals and promontories of Chesapeake Bay.

The inlet ran two hundred miles south before meeting the grey waters of the Atlantic at Hampton Roads. To the east the Delaware peninsula resembled a half-submerged beaver swimming toward Baltimore with the tip of its tail wagging in the direction of Norfolk and the Gosport Navy Yard across the Elizabeth River. To the west were the bordering states of Maryland and Virginia. The bay varied in width from 30 miles to a few thousand yards with sounds and islets making navigation a hazardous problem.

The key, she decided, must lie in the fact that a ship in the Chesapeake was like a ship in a bottle with federal gunboats ready to act as effective stoppers at the narrow neck between Cape Charles and Newport News. James was no doubt biding his time, waiting until he was clear of the trap before running for the open sea. It must, she concluded, be that infernal Fugitive Slave Law that was dictating his actions. Doubtless word had been telegraphed ahead and the ship's progress closely observed from the shore. But once clear of the Chesapeake surely James would show his hand? She frowned again in perplexity. Guthrie? The man's presence brooded over the ship like an evil presence and yet they could hardly put him ashore in an American port if they hoped to keep the negroes. Again she was assailed with doubts: James was such a stickler for the letter of the law.

The *Pampero* sailed steadily south beneath a washed-blue sky as Baines strove to work the blacks into the semblance of a crew. Slowly, to the groaning creak of yards clumsily hoisted, sails blossomed like so many petals reaching to the sun.

James had handed the wheel over to Santos and busied himself with taking cross-bearings of points of land while his mind gnawed at the same problem. What the devil was he to do with Guthrie? To keep him aboard for the duration of the voyage meant that the man would naturally raise a hullabaloo at their first port of call. On the other hand he could not very well maroon him like some latter-day Robinson Crusoe. He had toyed with the notion of casting the nuisance adrift in the ship's dory while land was close, but that would simply result in finding a wrathful federal gunboat awaiting their arrival at Hampton Roads. James shook his head, no nearer to a solution than when he had first formulated his plan.

He looked up as Baines approached, hoarse-voiced from mouthing torrents of threats and cajolery. But the big man seemed pleased enough with his work.

'I reckon they'll do,' he said. 'A few more days and they'll be scampering around like organ-grinders' monkeys. I've set 'em into two watches and picked out the sharpest as topmen. And I've got me a bosun.' He pointed. 'That big buck with the whiskers.'

James looked toward where a tall negro, well-muscled and lithe as a cat and with a couple of weeks' growth of dark beard, was haranguing a group gathered about the mainmast fiferail.

'His name's Henry,' Baines told him. 'He's a Sambo and the talkingest nigger I ever did see, but when he says jump, they all jump.'

'A Sambo?' James eyed Baines with interest. The man was an unfailing mine of curious information.

'Jambo is the Swahili way of saying how d'ye do? so blacks from Africa got to be called Sambos. This feller

Henry says he was brought across on a slave-runner when he was no more'n an eight-year-old piccaninny. His folks died on the middle passage but he managed to survive. He's a Mandingo from Gambia and his tribal name is Enory which is Mandingo for number one, meaning he was the eldest.' Baines paused for breath, hauled a pigtail of tobacco from his pocket, cut off a sizeable hunk and wedged it into the side of his cheek.

'Where did you learn all this?' asked James.

Baines first walked to the shipside to spit reflectively into the pale drifting water.

'He's a talking Sambo, y'see. Of course they jabber away in their own lingo when they have anything important to say. Luckily Swahili is the only common langwidge they got; although they batter away too fast for me; but I reckon I can follow the set and drift ready enough.'

'You speak that heathen lingo?' James, no linguist, could never comprehend Baines's almost childlike facility for rapidly understanding the tongues of others.

'I picked up a smattering when shipping out of the Ivory Coast,' Baines said casually as though that were explanation enough for any sensible man. He shifted the quid of tobacco into the other cheek. 'The thing is,' he added, 'they're planning to take over the ship.'

'When?' asked James sharply.

Baines shrugged. 'Not yet awhile. They think the Chesapeake's a river. Some of 'em are even of the opinion that it's the top end of the Mississippi. Henry's advised 'em to bide their time. He'll give the word. Our passenger's in for a rough time. They're going to hang him from the yard-arm by one leg and let him dry out in the sun after a few other pleasantries. Can't say I blame 'em,' Baines added philosophically. 'They're in for a rough handling once their masters lay 'em by the heels again. It'll be a flogging for all, leg irons and spiked collars for some, and a few ringleaders like Henry'll probably have their tongues slit for talking too much and their eardrums burst for listening. 'Course,' he said, eyeing James speculatively, 'if we could persuade 'em that we weren't putting into a Yankee port . . . ?'

James was tempted but thought the better of it. Give them but a whiff of freedom and their entire attitude would change and hardly go unobserved by a nincompoop, much less a man as shrewd as Guthrie. He shook his head decisively.

'I cannot give such an undertaking, Mr Baines. Keep a close watch on them. And plenty of sail drill,' he added testily, irritated by a reproachful look in Baines's eye. Was there no end to people questioning his motives! He sniffed and walked away to the weather side thereby ending the conversation.

Baines grunted acknowledgement, rolled away, spat once more over the side and in a few moments the black figures were clumsily scurrying about the deck to the cry of 'Jib sheets and halliards,' while others clambered gingerly out along the jib-boom to gather in the wildly flapping sail.

James watched sourly and prayed that they would not be caught in a sudden squall.

The sun ran like molten gold behind the western snow line and day turned into night with stars hanging like crystals in the dark cavern of the sky. The temperature dropped to twenty below and the moon rose like a lantern to sharpen the outlines of forest and hills with a strange unreal clarity.

Sound seemed to die with the sun and soon the stillness of the ship was broken only by the slap of water and the steady monotonous creak of yards and cordage. Occasionally a rumble of voices and a rare burst of deep-throated laughter would issue from the fo'c'sle. Once the door opened to release a shaft of yellow light to blend with the blanched whiteness of moonlight and a shapeless figure padded across to the women's quarters. Periodically the lookout repeated the strokes of the ship's bell and his sonorous call of 'All's well' rose and fell in melancholy cadence. Then with each turn of the hour-glass silence became more and more absolute until sound itself became a concentrated distillation of hearing.

The *Pampero* ghosted through the night. At two a.m. she was abeam of the Potomac where dark waters sluiced into the bay and currents eddied and swirled to carry fairy ice to twist and bob on the surface. The eldritch shriek of an owl haunting the woodlands raised the hairs on the back of James's neck. He was lightly holding the wheel spokes and, half-hypnotised by the up-thrusting light from the compass binnacle, had not heard Baines's soft footfall until the owl's cry brought him to his senses and he became aware of the mate standing beside him.

Baines yawned, stretched, and rasped a hand across a days' stubble of beard. James relinquished the wheel to him and jerked a thumb shorewards.

'Virginia,' he said. 'It might be as well to remind them that that is a slave state. It could serve as a warning not to start any nonsense yet.' He did not wait for an answer but dragged out his canvas reclining chair, shook the rime from his blankets and stretched out to rest. 'Tomorrow,' he murmured drowsily, 'Santos and Ramon will share the wheel watches. At first light we'll have the royals on her. Sail drill, Mr Baines,' was the last thing he remembered saying, 'plenty of sail drill,' and was asleep before he could catch Baines's reply.

Fingers of light, reaching across the eastern sky, drew aside the curtain of darkness and by noon they were through the narrows and off the Rappahannock. Here and there curls of smoke reached to a cloudless sky and once they heard the mournful wail of a distant train whistle. Otherwise the land seemed dead and lifeless, buried beneath a shroud of snow.

The ship steadily worked her way south and as the

temperature rose imperceptibly the patches of ice became more scattered and shimmered with wax-like translucence.

Henry, the newly appointed bos'n, seemed to be everywhere, jabbering away at his fellow blacks sometimes in English, sometimes in their heathen tongue. Never once did they voice a word of complaint, but worked doggedly, untiringly; practising hour by hour; taking in sail; shaking out sail; up aloft and down again and up yet again. They seemed to work with a combined will as though there was some underlying purpose . . . The conclusion leapt into James's mind—of course! They were training themselves in readiness for seizing the ship!

He sent for Jão, Ramon and Santos, armed all three and bade them take up their quarters aft. They were to remain aft and on no account to set foot forrard. In future there would be two men on watch and one at the wheel, day and night. Jão delightedly returned to his duties as steward while Baines paired off the females to replace him as cooks and fetchers and carriers.

Guthrie noted James's precautions with approval but offered no comment.

The day passed uneventfully. By nightfall they had crossed the mouth of the Pamunkey river and at the first light of false dawn they were abeam of the York river and Hampton Roads was a bank of smoke fine on their starboard bow.

James swung himself into the mizzen shrouds, looped an arm around the backstay and steadied the telescope. Dockyards and buildings leapt sharply into view and a forest of masts indicated the presence of a mass of shipping. He focused carefully, scanning the rig of each individual vessel. Mostly merchantmen but a few bore the unmistakable outlines of United States ships of war. Three were large side-wheelers, one of which had steam up and it was the smoke belching from its funnel which had spread into the thin dark drifting cloud that hung over the town in an ominous black layer.

The *Pampero*'s recognition signals broke from the yard in a splash of bright colours and Baines dipped the ensign in acknowledgement of the Stars and Stripes flying above the Navy Yard as the ship's bows met the first of the long grey Atlantic rollers surging into the mouth of the bay. The ship lifted and pitched and the wind freshened, veering a little to blow steadily from north and west; then they were between Old Point Comfort and Newport News and the land fell astern to leave nothing before them but a wilderness of white-flecked water.

Guthrie stood on the poop looking astern and eventually saw the sign he had been waiting for. The big side-wheeler, detaching itself from the surrounding ships and slipping out of Hampton Roads to stalk the *Pampero*. He continued watching the steamer's progress for a few minutes then, satisfied, he returned below.

The activity of the overtaking gunboat had not gone unnoticed, but at first neither James nor Baines paid it particular attention—the Chesapeake was a busy waterway and with Navy Yards at Newport News and Norfolk, the presence of a patrolling warship gave little cause for concern. To the southward a brigantine was clawing its way north almost into the teeth of the wind, seas breaking over her head as the bows dipped into the long Atlantic troughs. A pair of small fishing craft bobbed like corks, and a couple of miles to port a big Yankee barque drove down on them, wind abeam, braced hard on the starboard tack, her sails almost bursting from the press of wind. Baines watched admiringly as she bore down, crossed the *Pampero*'s stern, then almost spun on her heels as the yards came smartly round. With canvas booming and thundering she hauled her wind to arrogantly cross the bows of the oncoming steamer and beat up channel to the derisive jeers of her crew as the paddleboat, hooting anger, swung across to port, almost broaching in the heavy sea. Baines laughed as the gunboat rolled heavily, its starboard paddle threshing madly in the air while spick-

and-span officers climbed red-faced to their feet to shake affronted fists at the barque's insolent stern.

The *Pampero* stood on course until she had the weather of the north-bound brigantine, then James brought her round to steer south-east by south. With the wind on the starboard quarter and the sea rolling in upon the port bow the *Pampero* was in her element. She tossed a white mane of water over her head, leaned forward and commenced to show her paces.

Baines looked astern, grinned and gloated.

'We'll soon leave that firecracker standing. She's making heavy weather of it already. Shipping 'em green. Shall I set stays'ls and royals?' he suggested hopefully. 'Show that converted kettle what a thoroughbred can do?'

'Wait,' said James thoughtfully. He watched the paddler turning, manoeuvring to take station off the *Pampero*'s port quarter. Smoke was belching from its smokestack and its paddles were turning furiously, chopping and hacking at the heaving water. Even as James watched scurrying figures began to race aloft. In a moment canvas billowed from her yards. The gunboat steadied on course and slowly began to close the gap.

Baines ran an expert eye over the ship. 'A converted frigate. Boston rig, I reckon.' He watched their efforts at clapping on all sail and spat his contempt over the side. 'Gimme a couple of stuns'ls and a pocket handkercher and we'll leave that floating frying-pan to choke in its own smoke.'

James came to a decision. 'Keep her snapping at our heels, Mr Baines. I want her astern, in sight, but on no account ahead of us.'

'Aye, aye,' said Baines, puzzled, and waddled amidships to shake up his blacks, many of whom were beginning to take on a grey pallor as the ship met the deep Atlantic swell, rising and falling with stomach-churning suddenness so unlike the slow comfortable roll of the Chesapeake.

'Hoo-ray and up she rises!' sang Baines, thrusting the

staysail halyards into unwilling hands. 'Haul away!' he roared. 'Heave away, you big buck Sambos. All together now: Hoo-ray and hup she rises. Hoo-ray and hup she rises ...'

'Hoo-ray and up she rises,' they chanted weakly, and the main topmast staysail jerked aloft to boom and strain in the wind, and the *Pampero* responded by thundering her bows into the next roller and throwing a cascade of white water high in the air to hiss across the foredeck like a miniature rain storm.

James, balancing easily against the pitch and roll, continued to watch the antics of the gunboat floundering astern. Her captain must be a worried man; by now it must be only too evident that the *Pampero* had the advantage of speed. His intentions were patently obvious: to position his ship to seaward in order to trap the *Pampero* between himself and the land.

Through the telescope the blur of faces became distinct. One face acquired a distinction entirely its own. Squint-eyed, liver-featured, it looked in anguish straight at James. James snapped the telescope shut as Guthrie lurched to grip the taffrail at his side.

'Your friend Harman,' said James.

Guthrie's eyes rolled in his head as the *Pampero*'s stern rose high and then sank dizzily into the trough of a wave. His face was greasy with perspiration and his jaws clenched as he fought to contain a rising nausea.

'You lied,' continued James. 'I thought it unlikely that a man as experienced as Harman would allow himself to be trapped by a half-witted mob. He telegraphed ahead, of course; then took the train to Hampton Roads where he invoked the Fugitive Slave Law and persuaded the Navy to escort us to Charleston.'

Guthrie essayed a sick smile. 'Just protecting my interests, Captain Onedin.'

'You're a fool,' said James and walked away leaving the slave-catcher to retch agonisingly over the side.

For an hour he paced the poopdeck, head bowed, his brain rearranging the jigsaw of his plan, seeking to fit the new piece—the gunboat—into the overall picture. As long as the wind held the *Pampero* was in no danger. She could outstrip the cumbrous steamer at will; but should the wind drop the advantage would immediately lie with her pursuer. On the other hand it might be possible to exploit its very presence. . . . The pieces began to drop into place and a slightly new picture emerged; on the whole rather better than his original scheme, he thought. He looked again at his adversary wallowing astern, paddles churning, blunt bows crashing into the wild sea, the clamorous din of its engines rising above the keening of the wind. Much would depend upon the temperament of her Captain. James decided to give him a run for his money.

The *Pampero* ran steadily south and east, holding to the land and keeping the long yellow spit guarding Albemarle Sound close on her starboard hand. The paddle steamer had given up all attempt to keep station and doggedly ploughed in the wake of the *Pampero.*

By sunset they were off Cape Hatteras with the wind gusting fiercely and squalls of rain blotting out vision. James waited until the beam of the lighthouse scythed its warning, then put the helm down and stood out to sea. When by his calculations they were ten miles out he shortened sail, dowsed all lights and waited patiently for the warship to fume past in the darkness.

At midnight they saw the sparks from her funnel and caught a glimpse of the winking ruby eye of her sidelight as she rolled and trundled after her elusive prey.

James waited until the gunboat's sternlight disappeared over the black horizon then under jib and lower courses the *Pampero* crept after her.

At daybreak the wind backed, shifted to east nor'east, the sea flattened into an oily swell and veils of rain hung from a marbled sky. The mainland was a dark streak on the horizon with the port of Wilmington almost abeam. Far ahead a smudge of smoke betrayed the position of the gunboat.

'Set the royals, if you please, Mr Baines, and take after her. Keep her well to starboard. In American waters,' he added with a lopsided grin, 'I want the freedom of the seas for myself.'

His brain was dulled with lack of sleep and he was grateful when Jão pattered up with a mug of steaming hot coffee. His legs ached and the muscles of his calves seemed to be bound with iron. Dull-eyed he only half-watched Baines chasing up the blacks. They were unusually lethargic this morning and a group, pushed and shoved, reluctantly made their way to the weather shrouds. Suddenly there was a scuffle. Baines lashed out and a man tumbled over. Then a swarm of black bodies bore the giant to the deck. It seemed to be a signal for suddenly the ship was alive with running figures. They poured aft like a black tide. Some, James had time to notice, had armed themselves with knives and cleavers from the galley, others carried belaying pins and capstan bars. He drew his pistol and fired a warning shot into the air. They paused for a moment. Ramon clung to the wheel, round-eyed with fear. Then Santos, Jão and Guthrie were beside him and together they faced the mob.

The big black, Henry, held Baines's pistol loosely at arm's length. He pointed at Guthrie.

'We want him and the ship,' he said.

James heard a click as Guthrie thumbed back the hammer.

'Go below, Mr Guthrie. At once,' he snapped as Guthrie raised an arm to take aim. 'Lower your arm, damn you. Do you want us all butchered?'

Guthrie spoke between his teeth. 'We've got enough fire-power here to stop 'em in their tracks. I'm taking that big black.'

James ground his teeth with anger. If the idiot pulled the trigger nothing would prevent a bloody slaughter. Silently he cursed himself for a fool. He should have kept close to that escorting vessel instead of being so damned clever in trying to outguess everyone. He raised his eyes and looked ahead. Already the smudge had become a column. No doubt her lookout had sighted the *Pampero*'s topsails and she was on her way to investigate. It gave little time to save the remnants of his scheme.

'I shall parley with them,' he told Guthrie. 'I would be obliged, sir, if you would go below and offer your protection to my wife.'

The request seemed to appeal to the man's sense of histrionics. He lowered his pistol. 'You will learn, sir, that you cannot discuss terms with a slave. Kill the ringleaders and the rest will obey. You have my word upon it. In the meantime you may rest assured that I will protect the lady with my life.' He bowed and strutted away stiff-backed.

Henry again pointed to Guthrie.

'We take him and the ship. You other folk will be unharmed.'

'You'll take neither,' James told him flatly. He handed his pistol to Santos. 'A word with you, Mr Henry, if you please.'

He swung over the poop rail and dropped down to deck.

The big negro waited. His eyes were calm and he seemed, James thought thankfully, to be in control of his wits. The others were gathered in angry groups ready to rush at a signal. They had obviously been schooled for this moment; their grouping would make all but the foremost difficult targets. James doubted that the pistols would be a sufficient deterrent. He could understand their position. For them it was now or never.

'Without someone to navigate,' he said, 'the ship is useless.'

'We'll take our chance,' said Henry. 'It's the only one we got.'

Out of the corner of his eye James saw that Baines had come to his feet. Blood was trickling down the side of his face. A thin gangling man with a nervous tic at one side of his mouth stood beside him waving a butcher's knife threateningly. Baines shook his head like a bull and growled deep in his throat.

James concentrated his attention upon the big negro. His face bore the scar of a deep whip lash from eye to chin, one ear had been sliced off at some time and his wrists still showed the marks of the imprisoning gyves. He had a hard but intelligent face, strong in character and with the calm reposed features of the thinker.

'You don't want a ship,' said James. 'Your prime need is for freedom.'

'We can't hardly have the one without the other, Massa.' Henry's voice held a mocking note. ' 'less, of course, you is proposing to put us poor niggers ashore over there . . .' He pointed toward the distant haze of coastline. 'Because according to Massa Baines, that there is the port of Wilmington in the state of No'th Carolina; and we ain't of no mind to be humped ashore in no slave state, Massa.'

James breathed a sigh of relief. At least they weren't planning to beach the ship and take their chances ashore. He shook his head.

'I have a better idea.'

They all heard the sound. The faint thin wail of the gunboat's steam whistle.

'You'd better listen to me before that gunboat lays alongside.'

A man clambered into the shrouds, pointed a shaking hand.

'She's a-coming,' he bawled. 'Chimney afire and blowing out clouds o' smoke.'

Henry eyed James for a moment. 'What's in your mind?' he asked.

'To make British seamen of you,' said James. 'Mr Baines,' he called. 'Open ship's articles, if you please.'

The gunboat fussed around the *Pampero* like a sheepdog finding an errant ewe, then escorted them south until thirty hours later they stood off Charleston harbour.

From his perch high on the mizzen crosstrees James viewed the harbour approaches stretching away before him like a relief map.

The town stood at the junction of the Ashley and Cooper rivers. To the south James and Morris islands pushed out into the sea. Except for the fishhook of Cummins Point guarding the harbour mouth Morris was a false island of saw-grass and mangrove swamp intersected with a labyrinth of waterways. The entrance to the harbour was narrow and protected by batteries at Cummins Point and at Fort Moultrie on the tip of Sullivan's Island opposite. On a shoal in the middle of the channel, halfway between Cummins and Moultrie, stood Fort Sumter, an isolated fortification of brick and masonry rising sixty feet above sea level.

The harbour seemed to be in a fever of activity, its calm waters criss-crossed with the wake of small boats plying forwards and backwards, loaded with stores, oars rising and falling like so many spider legs. A tugboat chuntered out from Charleston and headed toward Fort Johnson at the tip of James Island. James scanned the harbour through the smaller and handier spyglass. Labouring parties were hard at work erecting defences on the various bastions and from this distance the murmur of voices and chink of hammers fell upon his ears like the chirping of crickets. Hostile preparations were visible everywhere. On James Island and on the slopes of Mount Pleasant opposite recruits clumsily marched and countermarched. With the exception of Fort Sumter all the shore batteries were defiantly flying the Palmetto flag of South Carolina. At Cummins Point and Moultrie worried artillery officers had their glasses focused upon the federal gunboat lying well out to sea. Sweeping the glass across the narrow entrance James saw the pilot cutter make a long tack to pass Sumter and then head toward them. He snapped the spyglass shut, tucked it into his belt and slid down to deck. It was time to put his plan into effect.

Baines had kept the *Pampero* alternately beating and then bearing away across the harbour entrance. To an observer on the distant gunboat she presented an innocent enough picture of a ship tacking back and forth while awaiting the tardy arrival of her pilot. It also gave a valid reason for the hands working aloft.

James eyed the gunboat. She lay about a mile distant and about four miles off-shore. No doubt her commander was more concerned with the activities ashore than with the *Pampero* idling about the harbour mouth, even though each time she bore away the distance between ship and shore gradually increased.

If the newspaper reports were to be believed, a little more than a month ago Fort Moultrie had opened fire and scored two hits upon the United States merchant ship *Star of the West* bound for Fort Sumter with reinforcements. James imagined the terms of the Captain's orders: 'To escort the British vessel *Pampero* to Charleston, ensure that the said vessel enters harbour, garner such intelligence as possible by standing off-shore out of range of coastal batteries and on no account engage in any overt act of war.' That Captain, he decided, must be in an acute state of nervous tension by now, anxious only to be rid of his charge before some madman ashore lost his head and opened fire.

The *Pampero*, under lower courses and jib, lazily came round and headed away from the land. It was a manoeuvre she had carried out half a dozen times before and to which those aboard the gunboat paid scant attention.

James bent his eye to the compass pelorus, checked their heading and scrupulously entered the bearing on the chart. They were three-and-a-quarter miles off shore and steadily gaining sea room. He straightened, coughed drily.

'Very well, Mr Baines. Set lower t'gallants and tops'ls, if you please.'

There was no need for Baines to raise his voice; the crew had practised until they were near perfection. He simply waved his arms and the topmen, strung out along the yards, cast off the gaskets. The buntlines hissed through the blocks and the lower yards rattled down. With a series of sharp thunderous claps the *Pampero*'s sails bellied in the wind and inner and outer jibs raced up the stays to be sheeted home. Suddenly the *Pampero* seemed to bloom into a cloud of straining white canvas that lifted the bows high and hurled the ship through the water with the wake creaming and foaming behind her. The sharp clipper bows sliced into the green water and gulls, dozing on the surface, awoke to throw themselves into the sky in a volley of clamorous white furies.

James surveyed the work appreciatively as Anne came to stand beside him. He grinned at her. 'I told you we'd make seamen of 'em.'

'British seamen,' she emphasised and touched his arm. 'I should not have mistrusted you, James.' Her eyes held a hint of reproach. 'But was I not worthy of your confidence.'

He smiled and put a protective arm about her thin shoulders.

'You have no talent for dissembling, little Anne. You would have given the game away. Believe me it was better that you should remain in ignorance. If things went awry there was little point in us both languishing in a Yankee prison.'

The steamer seemed to have gone mad with rage. She went astern, toot-tooting throatily on the whistle, turned in her own length, then, paddles churning furiously, ploughed in pursuit of the fleeing *Pampero*.

The wind blew a strand of hair across Anne's face. She brushed it aside impatiently.

'Will we escape them?' she asked breathlessly.

'I hope not,' said James. 'I want her Captain aboard. I have some points of maritime law to discuss with him.'

Guthrie, white-faced with anger, strode up to James.

'What the devil do you think you're about?' he demanded. 'Turn back this instant, or by the Holy I'll see you rot in jail!'

James did not turn his head. 'Mr Henry,' he called. The big negro trotted up and knuckled his forehead.

'Yas, sah?'

'You will oblige me by escorting this gentleman to his cabin. He is to remain there until I give contrary instructions.'

The scarred face split into a grin. 'Yas, sah!' He bowed extravagantly to Guthrie. 'This way, Mr Guthrie, Massa, sah.'

Guthrie looked at James, then toward the fast approaching gunboat. He nodded his head slowly.

'You will pay for this outrage.'

'Someone will,' said James. 'Good day to you, Mr Guthrie.'

The steamer was closing fast. 'Starboard a point,' James told the helmsman.

The *Pampero* answered the helm easily and nosed away from the converging paddleship until they were running on parallel courses.

Anne watched the giant paddle turning like an enormous waterwheel. The steady thunk-thunk-thunk of the blades biting deep into the sea and thrusting the ship forward with a seemingly irresistible impetus gave her a frightening glimpse of the power of steam. From a distance the ship looked like a squat ungainly box, but now she was close enough to display something of the forces at work. From the raging demonic fires in her belly to the roar of flames and smoke from the tall funnel; the venomous hiss of steam; the tireless rhythm of pistons and the battering-ram strokes of the massive driving beams: all combined to give the ship the appearance of a fearsome mechanical sea-monster from the realms of nightmare. The sea between the two vessels began to boil like a cauldron. The *Pampero* quivered and sheered away like a high-strung thoroughbred shying in alarm.

The two paddle boxes were connected by a bridge-like structure with a pilot house amidships. A red-faced man in the uniform of a United States naval commander leaned dangerously out over the yawning gap of water. He raised a speaking trumpet to his lips and bawled imperatives that Anne could not distinguish above the tumult. But James seemed to understand for he raised an arm in acknowledgement.

'Bring her round and heave to, Mr Baines,' he said.

She heard the ting of a bell aboard the steamer. The paddles stopped churning, allowing the *Pampero* to forge ahead, then turn, come up into the wind to forereach with the sails shivering delicately. Then the job watch hauled on spilling lines and downhauls, the topgallants and topsails flapped, the yards squeaked up and the topmen hauled in the drooping canvas. The ship's head came round until the bowsprit pointed directly into the wind, the fore and main courses were backed, and the ship lay to, rocking quietly on the long slow ocean swell.

The paddler lay abeam, puffing and gasping as though from over-exertion. The lean snouts of guns poked through the after gun ports and a boat was lowered swiftly from a pair of davits.

James watched for a moment as the red-faced man clambered down the shipside followed by the squat figure of Harman.

'My compliments to her commander, Mr Baines,' he said. 'And ask for the favour of his company below.' He smiled down at Anne and she noticed that he seemed to be enjoying the situation. He put a hand to her shoulder. 'Come along, Anne, you may join our discussion.' He pulled his face into mock-mournful lines. 'Otherwise I feel sure you will die of curiosity.'

She followed him below, quite convinced this remarkable man could work miracles.

He laid out the chart on the saloon table, placed the ship's papers in two neat piles, and called for Henry to release Guthrie. Then he sat back in his chair to await calmly the arrival of outraged authority.

Guthrie stamped in, flung himself into a chair and puffed furiously upon a cigar—without, Anne noticed, so much as a by-your-leave. She sniffed and ostentatiously fanned the air, but the creature was evidently in too much of a bate to consider the civilities. So much the worse for him, she thought, knowing from experience that James liked nothing better than to deal with men on the verge of losing self-control. At such times men spoke rashly and without heed; the more they raged, the calmer James became. She settled herself to listen and learn.

Henry was about to leave. 'I would prefer you to stay, Mr Henry. You can be a valuable witness to our proceedings and'—he smiled sardonically—'later report back to your fellows that there has been no subterfuge. But you will take no part in the discussion unless called upon to do so. Is that clearly understood?'

'Yas, sah,' said Henry.

'You are a seaman,' said James. 'In future remember to say "aye", not "yes".'

'Aye, sah,' grinned Henry, and stood politely to one side as Harman and the naval commander erupted into the saloon.

'By George!' expostulated Harman, clapping eyes upon Guthrie. 'Am I glad to see you safe and sound! I had a fear this rogue might have knocked you on the head and disposed you over the side.'

'Be quiet, if you please, Mr Harman,' snapped the commander. 'I will conduct this business. This, I take it, is your partner, Mr Guthrie?' He then looked at James with the contempt of a dyed-in-the-wool abolitionist. 'And you, sir, I take it, are Captain of this—slave-runner?'

'And who are you?' asked James coldly.

'I am Commander Nicholas of the United States steam-frigate *Susquehanna* under orders to escort you and your infamous cargo to Charleston.'

'I doubt your orders contained instructions to stop a British ship about her lawful business on the high seas.' James swept a hand across the chart. 'I assume your navigation to be at least the equal of mine. Perhaps you would confirm that this is our position. By my reckoning we are one-and-a-half-miles outside the limits of American jurisdiction.'

Commander Nicholas was a thickset man, ruddy of feature and of wide hard mouth. There was a harsh grating quality to his voice and he spoke with the clipped accents of Boston. His eyes narrowed. 'So that's the way of it? You would do well to reconsider, Captain, before taking a stand upon that plank. A slave-runner on the high seas is subject to seizure by British or American ships of war.'

'There are no slaves aboard this ship,' said James flatly.

Harman's face empurpled and his onion eyes almost started from his head. He pointed a shaking finger at Henry.

'That—that grinning crittur is a slave! I know him for sure! His name is Henry and he's the property of Mr George Mander of Greenville, Alabama. You'll find a circle M branded on his right shoulder.'

'Once a man signs articles of agreement he is bound to me, and none other, for the duration of the voyage. I have no interest in his antecedents.' James looked across at the big negro. 'What is your occupation, Mr Henry?'

'Ship's bos'n, Cap'n, sah,' said Henry promptly.

James opened the wide pages of the crew list for Nicholas's inspection. 'I opened articles thirty-six hours ago, Commander. These men are British seamen.'

Nicholas ran a cursory glance down the list of names, the majority signed by the cross, mark or thumbprint of the illiterate, each neatly countersigned by James and Baines. He sighed. 'A bold try, Captain, but it does not make them British subjects.'

'But it does make them subject to British law,' said James.

They stared at him.

'My country does not recognise the institution of slavery. On the contrary it has enacted that any slave setting foot on British soil automatically obtains his freedom.'

'Damme, sir,' Guthrie burst out. 'A British ship is not British soil . . . !'

Nicholas held up a hand. 'I do not care to enter upon those waters, I prefer to stand by the law of contract.' He picked up the charterparty and read it through carefully. 'This document makes it perfectly clear, Captain, that you entered into an agreement with Mr Guthrie to ship his property from Baltimore to Charleston. Slaves are property. I regret the law, but there it is.'

'Cargo,' said James. 'Subject to the usages of the sea.'

Nicholas frowned. 'I don't follow you, sir?'

James thumbed through a well-worn, shabby-looking volume with dog-eared pages and close print. He cleared his throat. 'A morsel of law for you gentlemen to chew over: "A charterparty is subject to the laws of the country whose flag the ship flies." ' He looked up and blinked at them. 'If the document does not comply with those laws it is held to be void. Item: "The object of the enterprise must be legal." It is an illegal act to transport slaves by a British vessel. This document, sirs, is not worth the paper it is written on.'

Harman glared at Nicholas. 'You'll not let him get

away with that tarradiddle? By God, if you should, sir, I'll see you broken.'

'Don't threaten me, Mr Harman,' said Nicholas coldly. He turned to James. 'You put up a good case, Captain Onedin, but my instructions are clear and admit of no equivocation. I am to escort you to the port of Charleston.'

James humped his shoulders in a portrayal of resignation.

'Very well, Commander, I accept your decision.' He leaned back in his chair, steepled the tips of his fingers and smiled his lop-sided smile. 'Provided,' he added carefully, 'that you lead the way.'

There was a fleeting look of embarrassment on Nicholas's face. He harrumphed, flourished a fine white handkerchief and dabbed at his nose.

'That, I am afraid, is not possible,' he began.

James sat up abruptly and pointed a lean finger at him. 'Exactly,' he said, silently praying that he had read the situation aright. 'I have no doubt but that your orders are as plain as any circumlocutory quill-pushing cleric can make 'em. South Carolina is in a state of insurrection and you are on no account to try conclusions with her coastal batteries.' He slapped a copy of the newspaper on the table. 'There it is in black and white: "On December 20 the state convention passed an ordinance of secession, declaring South Carolina a separate, sovereign, free and independent state".'

He turned his bleak gaze upon Guthrie and Harman. 'It could hardly be surprising news to you gentlemen.'

'Of course we knew!' exploded Guthrie. 'It is public knowledge.'

'And the rest of the Southern states will not be long in following suit,' growled Harman. 'Alabama, Mississippi, Georgia, Florida have already declared.'

'And knowing that,' asked James softly, 'you, Mr Guthrie, freely signed this document?' He picked up the charterparty and allowed it to flutter to the table.

Guthrie frowned uneasily. 'What of it?'

James picked it up and read: 'Clause: "In the event of any riot, insurrection, revolution or war, the Owner has the option of cancelling this charter or if any cargo has been loaded the right to proceed on the voyage with the cargo so loaded." Now, Mr Guthrie, either slaves are property, and therefore cargo; or they are not property in which event you have no claim upon them.'

There was a prolonged silence while Guthrie and Harman digested the implications. Then Nicholas began to wheeze and quake with laughter. 'By God, Mr Guthrie, but he has you there!' He dabbed his eyes. 'A beautiful trap, beautiful. I shall dine out on this story for months to come, damme if I don't.'

'I invoke the Fugitive Slave Law,' grated Guthrie.

Nicholas grinned. 'Not on the high seas, you don't.'

'Now that this nonsense is settled,' said James, 'I would be obliged to be permitted to be about my business, I have lost time enough as it is. Perhaps, Commander, you would be kind enough to offer Mr Guthrie a return passage?' He held out a hand palm up and looked flintily at Guthrie. 'After he has paid his twenty dollars.'

Guthrie gaped at him.

'What?'

'Passage money,' said James.

'I'll be damned if I do,' snapped Guthrie.

James shrugged. 'Suit yourself. You may stay aboard if you wish and try your luck in a British court. I shall add a dollar a day expenses for the voyage home.'

Guthrie held his gaze for a long moment, then broke.

'Pay him,' he snarled at Harman, pushed his way roughly past Nicholas and stamped out.

James carefully counted the money, shook hands with Nicholas and ushered them on to deck.

Anne stood by his side watching the small boat crossing the gap between the two ships. She squeezed his hand.

'Thank you, James,' she said.

He was staring dreamily at the paddle steamer. 'Mm?' he grunted absently.

They watched the boat hoisted inboard.

'On behalf of the negroes,' she said.

A bell ting-tinged on the steamer. The great paddles slowly began to churn. The ship moved easily through the water.

He had already forgotten.

'Steam power—just look at her—heading directly into the wind.' His eyes were lost, looking into a future beyond her ken. 'Albert was right. There's money in steam for those with the notion to take it.' He sniffed, harrumphed and cleared his throat. 'Mr Baines!' he called harshly. 'What the devil are we waiting for? Liven them up, there. No idlers. I want a fast passage. Senhor Braganza is awaiting his vines!'

He really was a most remarkable man, Anne thought.

Chapter Six

The spring sun frolicked from behind a wisp of cloud to draw the chill from the early morning air and chase lingering shadows of night across the grimy brickwork and granite bastions guarding the perimeter of Frazers' shipyards.

The heavy wooden gates were opened wide to admit a tide of carpenters and shipwrights, riggers and riveters, painters and sailmakers. Ironshod boots rang and clattered over cobblestones and a ragged stammer of voices rose and fell to dip to respectful silence as they herded past the unbending figure of old man Frazer himself, standing at his customary post, heavy silver watch in hand, counting in his work force. Foremen and gangers mumbled hasty 'good mornings' and thought themselves fortunate to receive a nod of recognition in return. With unvarying regularity, fair weather or foul, at five minutes before the hour, Iron Jack Frazer would take up his position, and it was popularly held that one day he would put in an appearance at the gates of Hell clocking in the devil and his legions.

The shipyard steam whistle cleared its throat before howling its hated final imperative. The laggards at the rear began to push and shove those in front until the whole crowd was surging into the yards at a stumbling trot. The whistle's wail died away. Frazer kept his eyes upon the tiny ticking second-hand of his watch and two late-comers rounded the corner, breath rasping in their lungs, eyes straining, boots pounding the pavement. Frazer snapped the watch case shut.

'Close the gates, Perkins.'

The gateman, a one-eyed seneschal with the self-important servility of his kind, swung the enormous oaken doors together and, as the breathless runners threw themselves against the closing barrier, triumphantly dropped the heavy bar into place.

The smaller of the two men sank to his knees, the breath whistling in his thoat. Saliva ran from his mouth as he coughed and retched and the high red spots of the consumptive flared upon his pale cheeks. His companion beat his fists in a frenzy of frustration against the 'Frazer' of the legend '*John Frazer & Son. Shipbuilders and Repairers*' spread in golden curlicues across the gates.

'You bastard!' he sobbed. 'You penny-pinching, hard-hearted bastard!'

Mr Frazer walked past the skeleton of a brig taking shape on the stocks and paused for a moment to watch a carpenter and his mate trimming and trueing the raw timber of a topmast yard. They worked with the calm unhurried speed of craftsmen, plane and drawknife whispering along the wood to deposit curls of shavings about their feet. Frazer nodded approval and then turned in the direction of his office, a three-storey building of red sandstone stained and weathered by the eroding winds of the sea.

The porter, brass-buttons agleam on olive-green coat, leaped to yank open the door. He bowed deeply, bid 'good morning, sir' and not receiving his customary due of '’morning, Pepiss' concluded that the Old Man must be in a foul temper today.

Frazer crossed the mosaic-tiled floor and climbed the marble stairway to march along the first-floor corridor on his regular tour of inspection. The magpie chatter of a group of messenger boys congregated at the far end of the corridor stopped as though their vocal cords had been severed. Offices were open for inspection with the chief clerks waiting on the thresholds. Frazer received their bows and marched straight ahead without so much as a glance of recognition. He turned at the end of the corridor and climbed the stairway to the second floor which accommodated the draughtsmen's offices. One door at the end bearing the gold-lettered superscription, '*Mr A. Frazer. Private*', was closed. He pushed it open and poked his head inside Albert's private sanctum to find it untenanted. The room was cluttered but tidy, as though the occupant knew exactly where to lay his hands upon whatever piece he might require. There was a specimen link from an anchor cable, samples of iron and copper tubing, a steam valve and, propped in one corner, a full-size brass porthole. Shelves held models of steamships, some only half-completed, some with one side removed to show the position of machinery and bunker space. There were sketches and pen-and-ink drawings of Sam Cunard's western ocean paddleships, of steam tugs and excursion steamers. The large desk had been pushed beneath the window and an incomprehensible design for new-fangled machinery lay open for study, the drawing paper held flat by lead weights.

Frazer snorted disapproval, pointedly left the door wide open and stalked off to his own office on the floor above.

His confidential secretary, the fox-featured Benson, was waiting as usual and as usual meticulously arranging and rearranging papers on the desk as though his hands could never be satisfied with less than perfection itself.

Frazer grunted acknowledgement of Benson's greeting, hung up his top hat and overcoat and warmed his hands at the cheerfully blazing fire.

Benson cleared his throat. A faint dry whisper of an introductory cough.

'I am to remind you, sir, of your three o'clock appointment.'

Frazer twisted his face into the semblance of a grin. 'I am not likely to forget. It is not every day that a man has the opportunity of attending a christening. At least,' he added drily, 'that of his own grandson.'

'May I add my felicitations to those of the staff, sir?' Benson fidgeted with the papers. 'There is one outstanding account which requires your attention. Long overdue. Mr Onedin, sir. You may recollect that we granted a four month extension of credit. It is now rather more than six months.' His voice held a note of reproach.

'Yes,' said Frazer. 'I remember.' Disappointment stole like a thief into his memory. He had had high hopes of that young man. James Onedin had brazenly walked into his office after putting Callon's nose out of joint and . . . A suspicion grew in Frazer's mind. He looked sharply at Benson.

'Did George Callon have a hand in this?'

Benson coughed delicately. 'Mr Callon did take the opportunity of asking me to remind you of the matter, yes, sir.'

'The devil he did!' Frazer scowled at the bland secretary. 'Are you Callon's man, or mine?'

Benson readjusted the inkwell stand fractionally. 'I am devoted entirely to your service, sir. I should consider myself remiss in my duty if I had ignored . . .'

'Yes, yes, yes,' snapped Frazer testily, cutting him short.

The bill was for something under two hundred and fifty pounds for work carried out on the *Charlotte Rhodes*. A trifling sum to Frazers' but, at the time, life or death to Onedin. Confound the man! It wasn't the money, it was the sense of being let down that rankled. Dammit, he'd trusted the rogue! And yet he could have sworn Onedin to be a man of his word.

He walked to the tall mullioned windows overlooking the yards and beyond to the busy waterways of the Mersey. The yards were active and his order books full. Long-familiar sounds filtered up through the mild spring air and a lone pigeon stepped on to the window sill, softly flapped its wings and cocked an inquiring eye at this intrusion into its private world. He could hear the thud of hammers and the rasp of saws and away to his left the clamour of riveters at work on one of Albert's pet projects, a steam tug; a squat ungainly brutish thing of cantankerous smoke stack and enormous paddles. He lifted his gaze. The river was busy this morning. It was the time of slack water with the flood tide on the turn. The lock gates of Coburg and Queen's were open and back-pedalling tugs were straining to heave a couple of heavily-laden barquentines out into mid-river. Three topsail schooners in line astern scudded downstream from the direction of Runcorn, and fuliginous steam ferries fussed across river while a flag-bedecked excursion steamer ploughed white furrows on its way to the Welsh holiday resorts of Llandudno and Colwyn Bay. A big white clipper, weather-stained paintwork and loaded to the gunwales, flew up river to meet a tug snorting out of George's Basin. To Frazer's professional eye she was of unmistakable Yankee rig, with slender lines and a gold-painted figurehead. Her yards snapped around and her sails reefed in with typical American smartness. Her master, with the arrogance of his kind, refrained from dropping anchor but calmly brought his ship into the wind so that she now sat on the water like some great disdainful white bird.

The pigeon drew its head into a ruff of feathers and gargled softly to itself. Frazer turned away: Benson was right; he had procrastinated long enough.

'What assets does he have?' he asked.

'Only the *Charlotte Rhodes*, sir, and she appears to be operated by his brother, Robert, during Mr Onedin's absence.'

Frazer slumped into his desk chair and drummed his fingertips upon the arm. 'Where the devil is the man?'

Benson shrugged. 'I have no idea, sir. But I venture that the *Charlotte Rhodes* is showing little in the way of profit. My information is that she is employed principally upon the Irish immigrant trade.'

Frazer snorted. 'The man's a blockhead, the ship will barely recover her costs. Very well, Benson, you may proceed. We'll put his ship up for auction.'

A gleam of satisfaction showed in Benson's eyes. 'Yes, sir,' he said. 'Immediately, sir.'

Robert shaved and dressed with care. He bobbed his head beneath the low beam crossing their bedroom ceiling and surveyed himself with satisfaction in a cheval glass propped in the corner between the marble-topped washstand and a cane knick-knack table beside the bed. He had, in his considered opinion, just cause to commend himself; and the mirror-image stroked moustache and side-whiskers and winked a fleshy eyelid in agreement. His high-buttoned cutaway coat sat very well he thought; his shirt collar was perhaps a shade on the tight side, but no bad thing, it indicated that he was putting on a little weight—the hallmark of the successful businessman; indeed, by turning sideways he could see that his stomach was distinctly rotund and showed to perfection the heavy gold Albert looped across his waistcoat. His boots were new and strenuously polished and tended to creak as he walked but, as he oft-times pronounced, he was never a believer in spoiling the ship for a ha-porth of tar. Yes, all things considered he should cut quite a figure—it was true that his trousers drooped a little and no amount of scrubbing with carbolic could quite remove workaday grime from his hands, but he would wear gloves as long as decently possible and at other times try to remember to keep his fingers curled towards his palms.

Robert finally tore his gaze from the narcissistic mirror, left the bedroom and made a stately descent of the narrow stairs to the back parlour below.

Sarah had ironed his kid gloves and brushed his top hat until the nap lay smooth as silk. His silver-headed walking stick lay on the table beside them. They had debated the point long into the night, consulting *Enquire Within Upon Everything* and the *Cyclopaedia of Household Hints*, but now, faced with the decision, he came to the conclusion that Sarah was correct. A gentleman would not walk, but drive to church, therefore a stick, be it ever so handsome, would be superfluous. An umbrella, yes; a walking stick, no. He picked up the stick, swung it between forefinger and thumb, then reluctantly replaced it. There was something manly about a good, solid, well-fashioned, silver-headed walking stick, it had a satisfying 'get-out-of-my-way-fellow' feel to it. He poured himself a small medicinal whisky to settle a mild queasiness of the stomach, but before he could raise the glass to his lips Sarah bustled in from the shop. Her eyes widened and her nose compressed itself into a sharp point of disapproval.

'Really, Robert! Surely it cannot be your intention to attend a place of worship with your breath reeking of intoxicants.'

Robert felt like a child caught with its fingers in the sweet jar. 'My stomach,' he explained weakly.

She adjusted his tie and dusted a speck or two of dandruff from his shoulder. 'After the ceremony,' she pronounced, offering a crumb of comfort, 'it is customary for a small reception to be held at the home of the happy parents. Albert will undoubtedly provide a sufficiency of refreshments, and you will be expected to toast the child and make a short but telling speech.'

Robert groaned. 'I have had but little practice in speech-making.'

'You have a mellifluous voice, my dear, and if you eschew vulgarisms and tedious narrative I am sure you will be listened to most attentively. Remember, the Frazers are quality and it must be considered quite an honour to be asked to stand as godfather.'

Robert had no illusions on that score. 'Elizabeth's doing. She couldn't think of anyone else.' He carefully poured the whisky back into the decanter. 'I wish you were coming,' he added unhappily, his self-confidence oozing away at the thought of hob-nobbing with Albert's society friends and being called upon to address the company to boot.

'So do I, dearest,' said Sarah. 'But the business will not run itself. I have Jenny Carpenter to help and I daresay we shall manage quite comfortably; then, of course, there is our little Samuel to be considered—and although Maggie is a treasure in her way she is not quite the person to whom one could entrust the care and well-being of a beloved child.'

Robert agreed wholeheartedly. Maggie was the slavey who slept in the attic by night and flitted about the house by day, scurrying from room to room, turning beds, black-leading grates, dusting, polishing brass, washing pots and pans, carrying scuttles of coal and, in Sarah's words, generally making herself useful. She couldn't have been more than seventeen years of age, a wan, greasy-complexioned mouse of large frightened eyes and voracious appetite.

Sarah handed him a beribboned rectangular parcel containing their gift offering—a silver christening mug pleasingly embellished with winged angels guarding a kneeling child. Robert, by a happy chance, had discovered it only the other day among a pile of junk in the corner marine store. Once the verdigris and grime had been removed and the mug given a vigorous polishing it looked, in his considered opinion, as good as new.

'You shall recount every detail on your return,' Sarah was saying. 'And, by the by, you might take the opportunity of remarking—quite discreetly—that an invitation to take tea would not be unwelcome.' She helped him into his cape of melton cloth and deposited upon his cheek a token of wifely duty before adding tartly: 'I do think that Elizabeth would have had the grace to send a card of her own volition without the necessity for an enjoinder. After all, she is your sister.'

Robert drew on his gloves, picked up his hat, grunted acknowledgement of his mission, finally took his leave and with further admonishments not to step in puddles, remember to give her regards to dear Albert, and that Mr and Mrs Frazer would always be welcome, ringing in his ears he thankfully left the shop behind him and stepped smartly out in the direction of St Bride's Church. There was no doubt about it, none whatever, Sarah was a splendid wife and helpmeet. But she did upon occasion display a somewhat splenetic humour and had an unhappy knack of implying by some womanish necromancy that he was responsible for the ills of the world.

A hansom mooched along the kerbside touting for a fare. Robert fished out his watch, made a quick calculation of time, intercepted the driver's hopeful look, climbed in and ordered the man to take him to the Porthole tavern. If that sorry-looking sack of drumsticks plodding between the shafts could be persuaded to break into a trot he would have a good fifteen minutes to spare for a hot medicinal whisky with a slice of remedial lemon. He rapped upon the box, promised the driver a bonus and as the whip cracked across the lean haunches and the hooves broke into a cloppity-clop, he sat back in contemplation of his speech.

Captain Joshua Webster carefully closed the door on an empty cottage and pocketed the key before walking smartly down the steep cobbled street to the bustle and hubbub of the dock road. Drays with streamers of urchins clinging to the tailboards rumbled over the cobbles, carters thrashed their whips and horses squealed and neighed as they tried to force a way through a maelstrom of traffic. A group of aproned women, voices raised in anger like gulls squalling over a school of herring, surged about two of their number who, clawing and shrieking, fought for possession of a sack of rubbish.

Webster, his head filled with the thunder of ancient battles, was scarcely aware of their presence. He passed beneath the overhanging jib-booms of clippers, whalers, Yankee blood-boats, and sleek China birds bound for Whampoa, Foochow or Shanghai to load with tea. Ninety days out and ninety days back. The fastest ships in the world. He could remember quite clearly the arrival of the first ever Liverpool ship from China with a full cargo of tea. Then only the rich could afford to drink it, nowadays every Tom, Dick or Harry seemed to be gulping the stuff down as though tea were a weed grown in a back garden.

In Clarence dock one of the new-fangled steamships was building up a head of steam and belching clouds of acrid smoke along the length of Waterloo Road. It was a presage of things to come and Webster paused a moment—a squat bullfrog figure leaning heavily upon a silver-topped ebony walking stick; an old man staring into the past. He turned his head slowly and looked at the forest of masts. They seemed to shiver before his gaze and he was a boy again and war with the Frenchies was raging. King's ships and privateersmen crossed yards with

Guineamen and merchantmen, and little midshipman Webster, eleven years of age, had sat on his sea chest and wept in lonely misery.

That was 1804, and just a twelvemonth later Nelson had caught the combined French and Spanish fleets off Cape Trafalgar. Webster sighed. People laughed at his tales and thought him a garrulous old liar. But he'd been there. He'd stood on the quarterdeck of the first-rater *Bellerophon* locked in battle with the French *Aigle*. Captain Cooke had been shot through the chest in the opening engagement and died instantly. A moment later a cannon ball had shattered the sailing master's leg. Webster was always proud of the fact that he had kept his head, run down to the gundeck to report to Lieutenant Cumby and then to the cockpit for the surgeon. When he returned the Frenchies were swarming aboard and little Midshipman Webster had cut and thrust with the rest. And all the time the guns had never stopped pounding and red carnage had raged all around. Yes, he had reason for pride remembering that twelve-year-old boy stabbing away at a gigantic French Grenadier and killing his man.

In truth the incident had long disappeared into a ragbag of memories until the day he first saw the beggar. He was an old man blasted with age, squatting on his haunches, back against the wall, lean shanks twitching and rheumy eyes fixed hopefully upon the approaching figure.

Webster would have passed him by for beggars were as thick as fleas and their impudent impostures passed all belief. A placard hung about his neck read simply: 'A Survivor of Trafalgar. Take Pity'.

The man had rattled his tin cup and Webster had at first been affronted and of a mind to call a constable. The wretch surely must be an impostor.

'What's your name and rank, my man?' he had barked.

The scarecrow had hoisted itself to its feet and cupped a hand to one ear. The eyes were fixed on Webster's mouth and he had understood that the man was trying to lip-read.

'Name and rank,' he repeated slowly and distinctly.

The beggar knuckled his forehead. 'Gunner Allspice, Cap'n, sir.'

It had been the instant recognition of the lower deck, not the play-acting of a rogue. And what was more the man bore the indelible characteristics of his trade: the stunted growth, the stooped shoulders and bowed legs acquired through a lifetime spent below decks where even a medium-sized man could never stand upright. The deafness, too, was an occupational hazard of guncrews; in the confined space of a gundeck the concussion of a broadside could shatter a man's eardrums. But it was the face that clinched it. It still bore the dark mottling of flash burns and the blue tattooing of gunpowder; the trade-marks of a man-o'-war's gunner.

Webster had fumbled in his pocket and given the man all the coppers he could spare—little enough, but a crumb of comfort was worth a loaf of misery. Then each day thereafter he found the path of his regular constitutional leading invariably in the same direction and he would hand over a sixpence, or a threepenny piece, one day rather shame-facedly two ha'pennies. But old men lived off the charity of others and he himself was no exception. The ancient tatterdemalion was Webster's only living link with the past and he had come to dread the day when the beggar would no longer be patiently waiting. He had come to look upon his act of charity as a sop to mortality—that grinning spectre never far from his own shoulder these days.

He continued his journey, crossed the Goree Piazzas and headed toward the Custom's House.

The beggar was waiting. He gave the man a sixpenny piece, exchanged ceremonial salutes, crossed the road and headed for the Porthole tavern. He would just have time to take a hot rum toddy before continuing his journey to church. Webster touched his pocket where the gold half-sovereign nestled snugly against the engraved invitation. It had been a kindly thought, an act of open-hearted generosity. He must remember to thank the wench—Mrs Frazer he must remember to call her now. She'd certainly shown more Christian charity than either of those penny-pinching brothers of hers. As miserly and mean-mouthed a pair of sanctimonious back-sliders as he'd ever clapped eyes upon. Particularly that rogue Robert with his shopkeeper's eyes and pickthank servility doling out a weekly florin—to which he was entitled; Anne, bless her heart, had made provision for him before setting off with that other rogue—and what could a man do with two shillings a week except seek consolation in rum? Robbed of ship and daughter in one blow and not enough money to mix with gentlemen! Tears of self-pity welled in the old man's eyes as he pushed open the doors and marched inside to find that villain Robert propping up the bar . . .

The child asleep was softly blowing bubbles. It bore not the slightest resemblance to Daniel Fogarty, Elizabeth decided for the thousandth time. In fact it looked like nothing other than a common or garden variety of baby. A minute mannikin, plump and pudgy with tiny doll-hands like an imitation human being. He was palely soft and his strange old-man pate was covered with a thatch of black hair. It was the one feature that alarmed Elizabeth, she and Albert each being fair-haired and blue-eyed. Daily she would closely examine the infant, searching for tell-tale signs of Daniel's features—heavier brows, a square jaw instead of the somewhat Mephistophelian point displayed by Albert, a short nose, and in particular, the eyes. Sometimes when the chubby arms reached out to her the eyes would widen like deep purple saucers and she had a growing conviction that each day they turned a shade darker. Night was the worst. Possibly by some illusory trick of gaslight the round orbs seemed to change to a smoky sable and her heart churned at the memory of Daniel and her pet name for him. Monkey-eyes, she had called him. Brown monkey-eyes.

The baby, wrapped in a christening robe of hand-embroidered silk, lay in its cot while they waited for Albert to finish dressing. She moved away and walking to the window dreamily stared through her reflection to the waiting carriage in the street below.

Today was yet another day she had come to dread. Albert and the Reverend Mr Magnus—an owl-eyed young man of rotund vowels and omniscent bearing—had tried unsuccessfully to argue, cajole, browbeat and admonish her to recant, to modify her obstinate determination to have the child baptised on a weekday. The Reverend Mr Magnus had wrung his hands and quoted ecclesiastic rubrics from canon law, but she had remained obstinate, defiantly and obtrusively quoting as precedent the fact that the Queen herself had been christened on a Monday. Was her baby due no less consideration? At which the Reverend Mr Magnus's vowels had taken flight to emerge from the roof of his mouth as though from the nave of a cathedral. 'It is mahst convenient,' he had bayed, 'thet the chaild be received into the charch when the most numbah of people come togethah, thet is to say upon Sahndays and other Holy-days, and to thet end it has long been established prahctice to present the chaild to the congregation ahfter the lahst lesson at morning prayer or the lahst lesson at evening prayer.'

'If necessity so require, children may be baptised upon any other day,' she had countered and thrust her prayer book beneath his nose in triumphant refutation.

In vain they had united in protesting that necessity did not mean a passing whim. She was adamant and appealed to Albert with inflexible logic: was it his wish to expose their dear child to all manner of disease from verminous riff-raff come solely to gape and gossip? Which utterance did the mercantile congregation of St Bride's a grave disservice.

Albert, the weaker vessel, had eventually tired of argument, taken Mr Magnus to one side and offered a bribe in the shape of a handsome donation to the church funds, and the matter had been settled.

Naturally she had been quite unable to explain to Albert the reason for her bout of pertinacious obduracy; but in truth she had been terrified out of her wits of standing before a packed congregation with a child of sin in her arms. The roof might fall upon her as it had upon poor Mrs Coney in *The Vengeance of the Lord*; or an ogre from the past rise from the body of the church to raise an accusing arm and claim the child as his own—as in *The Trials of Sister Slater*; nor did it take much effort of imagination to replace the ogre with the spectral vision of Daniel Fogarty come to claim his due. If only she had never written that damnable letter! There were times when she had half-convinced herself that the missive had gone astray, or perhaps Daniel's ship had foundered. Then she had had a fit of the horrors at the possibility of Daniel returning to haunt her, glowing green and covered in seaweed, like Jack Foliot in *The Return from the Grave*.

Albert emerged from his dressing-room to break into her reverie. He was resplendent in soft turned-down collar, flowing tie, and bright yellow waistcoat almost concealed by a high-buttoned pearl-grey cutaway coat. It pleasantly complimented, she thought, her own lavender crinoline with its froth of rose-coloured lace almost hiding dainty little cloth boots with silken laces and patent leather toe-caps. Even the flowers in his silver buttonhole exactly matched the roses of her diminutive bonnet.

He beamed at her. 'Don't look so mournful,' he said. 'It's a christening, not a wake,' and rang the bell for Marie the buxom French nursemaid on call on the landing outside.

Harris, their coachman, doffed his beribboned top hat and bowed them into the barouche. At a flourish of his whip Nomad arched her neck and stepped forward proudly while the gatekeeper at the end of the square swung open the wrought-iron gates that protected the residents from such undesirables as street musicians, loafers, vendors and beggars.

From Abercromby Square to St Bride's was about a four-minute ride and Elizabeth's heart almost stopped at the sight of a line of carriages drawn up in array before the church, and a colourful group of floriated ladies and top-hatted gentlemen milling and haw-hawing on the pavement outside.

A space had been left for their carriage. She stepped down weakly and escorted by Albert and followed by Marie with the baby crooked in her arms made her way through the blur of unfamiliar faces to be greeted by the sonorous-voiced Mr Magnus at the church door.

She thought she caught a glimpse of Albert's sister Harriet and her husband, Mr Fowler Dickson, but the rest were nothing but featureless heads swaying and bobbing as though on stalks. She looked in vain for sight of Robert and Captain Webster then, near to panic, found herself in the lofty echoing coolness of the church.

They were ushered to a front pew by the verger, a stoop-shouldered attenuated man with a broad bill of a nose and stilted heron-like walk. Behind them dry coughs and sibilant whispers rose to the vaulted roof like a long-forgotten medieval chant as the congregation rustled and shuffled to their places along polished oaken stalls.

Elizabeth stole a sideways glance across the aisle to the pew reserved for the godparents. She received a nod and a smile of encouragment from Harriet, and a young man seated next to her dipped a fiery head and fiery complexion into cupped hands in an attitude of prayer. But of Robert there was no sign. Her mouth dried and she peeped into her prayer book to refresh her memory. Yes, there it was in Holy Writ! 'For every male-child to be baptised there shall be two godfathers and one godmother.' She sneaked another glance around a segment of the communicants. Where the devil was that cursed fool? Probably, she thought furiously, still serving in that damned shop! Or, miserly as ever, had decided to walk! She perspired in an agony of apprehension that the dolt would arrive too late and shame her before the entire congregation. Another thought prickled. She nudged Albert.

'Where are your parents?' she whispered.

Albert was seated with folded arms, staring rigidly ahead. He leaned toward her.

'Immediately behind us,' he muttered out of the side of his mouth.

Elizabeth felt the back of her neck turning brick red. In a moment she knew she would swoon with embarrassment. She had not yet met Albert's parents. After their runaway marriage her newly-acquired in-laws had flatly refused to acknowledge her existence and the old man had threatened to cut off his son without a shilling. Not that the prospect seemed to disturb Albert. He had, he claimed, a sufficient income of his own and in any event he and his father had been at loggerheads for years; his defiance of parental authority by eloping with a shopkeeper's daughter had simply brought matters to a head.

She had never believed for one moment that they would come although she had written a most civil letter expressed in terms of heartfelt contrition and penitence, adding—in a moment of inspiration—that 'everyone exclaimed at the dear child's uncanny resemblance to its grandfather'. She had splashed a few tears on the letter as makeweight and sent it off complete with engraved invitations. A curt acknowledgement by return of post had alerted her to the suddenly frightening possibility, and she and Albert had sat up late that night drafting fresh invitations. Albert's list had seemed endless and required drastic pruning, but she could think of no one beyond

Robert and Sarah and Cousin Wilberforce Onedin—whom she could now hear whooping into his handkerchief from the back of the church. Uncle Will Perkins, of course was out of the question; he would be roasted on a griddle rather than set foot in a priest-ridden Anglican temple of idolatory. Then she had thought of Anne's father, that funny old man Captain Webster—he at least should be used to mixing with the gentry—so she had sent off a card and enclosed a newly minted half-sovereign with the cunningly worded hope that he would be in no way affronted by this small token of inexpressible gratitude which he might choose to wear upon his watch chain as a memento of the occasion.

Albert touched her arm. 'Who are all these people?' he whispered.

She frowned in perplexity, having imagined them to be friends of the family—his family—then she caught a faint smirk of triumph flitting across Mr Magnus's face as he mounted the steps to the pulpit. The inexplicable became explicable: that worthy pastor had evidently been active in shepherding his flock to the sacramental fold. Weekday or no weekday the rites of baptism were going to be witnessed by as large a congregation as could be mustered beneath one roof, and as the organ droned into the opening bars of 'Blessed Jesu, here we stand', Elizabeth realised that she had been out-generalled by a superior tactician and they were to be subjected to full ceremonials instead of a simple turning out of the guard.

They sang, bowed their heads in prayer, sang and prayed again. Then the Reverend Mr Magnus cleared his throat and embarked on a long and tortuously reasoned sermon based on the parable of the sower and the seed in which he exhorted his congregation to invest wisely that the fruits of their labours might multiply, to eschew the perils of the flesh and the promptings of the devil and to remember that the tallest tree was only as strong as its roots. Mr Magnus was no spellbinder, but what he lost in fire he more than compensated for in sheer tedium. Once or twice she heard the church door open to admit late-comers, and once there was a muted commotion accompanied by the clumping and squeaking of boots and a general shuffle along a pew as room was made for the interlopers. Then the good burghers of Liverpool settled down again to continue their somnolent appraisal of Mr Magnus's convoluted pastoral. Even a dissident snore from the back of the church did no more than add counterpoint to the fluting tones of dissertation and when it seemed that Mr Magnus, like a mighty river, was likely to flow on for ever, his voice eventually broke over the shoals and shallows of the broader reaches of time. To the accompaniment of an opening and snapping shut of watch cases, some intermittent coughing and a frenzied whoop from Cousin Wilberforce, the river at last found its way to the sea and the sermon to its end.

As the organist led into 'Lead, Kindly Light', Albert whispered anxiously, 'Where the deuce is Robert?' Elizabeth shook her head in a gesture of non-comprehension, took the infant from Marie and followed Mr Magnus to the font. Harriet and the red-haired young man took their places in the procession and the verger filled the basin with water from a silver jug as the child awoke to raise its voice in a piercing wail of private lamentation.

Mr Magnus reminded all present that man was conceived and born in sin, and an imperfectly suppressed burst of hiccups rose from the back of the church like a series of punctuation marks.

Elizabeth's immediate relief at the vision of Robert lurching to his feet from the seclusion of a rear pew was quickly dispelled by the sight of his perspiring moon-face and a convulsion of hup-hup-hups popping from his lips. His tie was askew and he tried to tip-toe with exaggerated care down the aisle, his boots squeaking protest at each carefully plotted step. He swayed once, lost his balance, dropped a parcel he was carrying and paused to apologise profusely to a severe-looking dowager overflowing an end pew.

Elizabeth closed her eyes and silently prayed with more fervour than the mechanical braying of Mr Magnus. When she opened her eyes again it seemed that her prayer had been answered for Robert had disappeared as though the floor had truly opened to swallow him. She tried to concentrate again upon the service and became aware of Mr Magnus demanding of the godparents: 'Dost thou, in the name of this Child, renounce the devil and all his works, the vain pomp and glory of the world, with all covetous desires of the same, and the carnal desires of the flesh, so that thou wilt not follow, nor be led by them?'

'I renounce them all,' responded Harriet and the red-haired godfather.

'I renounce them all,' said a sepulchral voice at her side and for one heart-stopping moment she thought that a shade from the nether world had taken Robert's place, then turning her head she saw James grinning down at her and felt the pressure of his supporting arm beneath her elbow. She mouthed: 'James!' and he grinned again and winked and jerked his head toward a row of pews where Robert sat puffing and hiccupping next to Anne who looked as brown as a berry and nodded and smiled recognition. James put his lips to her ear and murmured across Mr Magnus's melodious cadences: 'Robert is as drunk as a fish.'

Elizabeth struggled to suppress a fit of giggling behind the baby's strident mewling and felt positively light-hearted as she relinquished the child to Mr Magnus's outstretched arms.

'Name this child.'

'William Albert John,' responded Harriet and the fiery young man.

'William Albert John,' parroted James, and William Albert John's wails rose to a shriek of protest as Mr Magnus dunked his pate into the cold water.

'William Albert John, I baptise thee in the Name of the Father, and of the Son, and of the Holy Ghost. Amen.' he added hastily and quickly passed the child back to Elizabeth.

They made their way out into the sunlight through a crowd of admirers and a tall granite-faced man poked a finger as thick as a post at young William's thatch, grunted, 'Aye, he bears the Frazer stamp, there's no denying it,' and Elizabeth found herself staring into the hard eyes and stern features of Albert's father.

As Albert ceremoniously introduced his parents, Mr Callon joined the group. He doffed his hat and smiled an avuncular smile at Elizabeth.

'My congratulations,' he said. 'No doubt you will be gratified to know that the *Barracuda* has entered port.'

Chapter Seven

Daniel Fogarty left Callon's office and swung left along Strand Street, past enormous blank-faced warehouses bulging with merchandise and reeking of hides, bones, indigo and saltpetre, guano, oil, pitchpine and musk. Bales of wool and cotton whipped up from waiting drays swung precariously from the outstretched arms of iron davits high above the heads of passers-by. A pair of massive Shire horses leaned into their harness, steam rising from their flanks, iron-shod hooves striking sparks as they struggled to draw to the sawmills a long lumber cart groaning beneath the weight of a massive baulk of Spanish mahogany. A pony and light trap with a load of jangling empty milk churns threaded its way through the traffic, and a man waving a red flag walked ahead of a locomotive engine hissing and belching clouds of steam, its caravan of trucks clanking and banging on their way to the coal tips at Canning Dock.

Thoughts buzzed through his head like bees in a hive.

Elizabeth's letter had followed him to Australia and he had, by the greatest good fortune, received it the day before sailing. It would, therefore, have been absurd to attempt to reply, the *Barracuda* being the fastest ship out of Melbourne. He had returned with grain, wool, gold and forty passengers in the record time of sixty-nine days, and were it not for a gnawing anxiety about Elizabeth had every reason to congratulate himself.

The child would be born by now. It must be. There was no escaping the damning logic of figures. He cursed himself again for making a tardy outward voyage. But there had been no great urgency and, as it had been his first command, he had had no intention of running unnecessary risks. The Doldrums had delayed them for a day or two but that was only to be expected. Once south of the Cape and deep into the Roaring Forties the *Barracuda*, built for wind, had covered 6,000 miles in 21 days to arrive at Melbourne 110 days out from Liverpool. No record, but a fair passage.

They had discharged and then sailed as far north as Brisbane, picking up part-cargoes here and there before returning to Melbourne to lie in idleness for six weeks before topping off for Liverpool. By the time she was finally battened down and ready to sail the *Barracuda* had spent four months in Australian waters.

Homeward bound around the Horn he had driven the ship like a demon, almost tearing the masts out of her in his urgency to hurry to her distress. But drive as he would he could no more prevent day following day than he could stop the inexorable ticking of the ship's chronometer.

A ship at sea was the centre of a private universe in which time itself became timeless and memories froze like flies in amber. Her last remembered image remained vivid and changeless: the soft mounds of her breasts, her wide open mouth and furiously wagging head as her belly arched and leaped beneath him; her final wild cry in the anguish of delirium as their bodies flowed together; and then she had lain still and quiet until asking: 'Do you love me? Really and truly love me?'

By night her image, like some tormenting succubus, devoured his sleep. By day she was a beckoning ghost calling, 'Hurry, hurry, hurry . . .'

And now he was home and didn't know whether she was alive or dead, been safely delivered of a son or daughter.

Not finding her waiting on the quay had again raised the spectre of fear that she had been taken from him forever. He had reported to Callon's office as duty demanded and learned only that Mr Callon had taken himself off to some damned reception, left his compliments and required Captain Fogarty to present himself at nine o'clock tomorrow morning.

He ignored a newsboy shrilling his wares, thought of taking a cab but changed his mind considering the walk would both help to find his shore legs and keen the edge of a resurgent excitement at the prospect of seeing her again.

A two-storey warehouse of crumbling stonework sagged in the dilapidated misery of old age. One shoulder propped by enormous wooden crutches leaned toward its more well-to-do neighbours with a mendicant air of supplication. The ground floor was occupied by the premises of Groter's Marine Store, a down-at-heel Aladdin's cave of junk—the detritus of a more affluent society whose ripples barely touched these shores of poverty. A Jew old-clothes seller followed by a horde of ragamuffins pushed his cartload of evil-smelling rags, broken boots and sacks of bottles into the dark cavern of the building and left his plaintive call of 'Ol'clo, ol'clo' ', fluttering on the air like the cry of a wild seabird tossed by the wind.

Robert's shop was but a street away. Outwardly at least it hadn't changed. The signboard: 'R. Onedin. Ship Chandler & Provision Merchant' was perhaps rather more weather-stained than he remembered and there was an air of affluence about the rows of seaboots and oilskins hanging from a rail above the windows. The step, worn shallow by the tread of countless feet, had recently been white-stoned and the pavement outside scrubbed clean. He remembered how Elizabeth had hated the work and wondered if Robert still drove her out with brush and pail in the icy cold of winter mornings. If so, that would smartly come to an end, by God!

He sucked in a deep breath, straightened his shoulders and pushed open the door.

A gaunt pasty-faced woman looked up from behind the counter at the jangle of the shop door bell and bid him an adenoidal 'G'd afternoon, sir?'

Fogarty paused, for a moment unable to comprehend the shop without the expected presence of Robert or Sarah. Recovering he asked politely for Mr Onedin.

'Izzout.' The wax face relapsed into an habitual melancholy. 'Gone to a do,' she finally vouchsafed as though the information had been dragged from her by hot pincers.

Fogarty's heart sank, then rose again as the squawl of a baby pierced through the house. 'Miss Onedin?' he enquired.

The woman must have misunderstood for, parting the curtain drawn across the doorway leading to the back premises, she called through: 'Missus! Yer wanted.' Then on an explanatory note, 'Gent to see yer.'

The curtain opened again and Sarah's questing head appeared. Her jaw dropped as though on a hinge. 'D-D-Daniel . . . !' she stuttered, then unaccountably bent from the knees to subside in a heap as though her bones had turned to sawdust.

Daniel brushed aside the ineffective ministrations of the gaunt creature, scooped Sarah up in his arms and shouldered his way through to the living-room.

It hadn't changed. The Welsh dresser with its trembling array of cups and saucers still leaned uneasily against the wall. Dark green cloth still covered the table and even the bowl of artificial flowers stood in the precise centre exactly as he had remembered. One change was a cradle beside an armchair with a red-faced baby squawling as though its lungs would burst.

He laid Sarah upon the horsehair sofa, rubbed her hands and looked around helplessly for means of succour. The shop woman had followed him, eyes bulging with excitement at this sensational turn of events; she lit a spill from the fire, blew out the flame and held the smouldering end beneath Sarah's nose. The remedy was crude but efficacious for Sarah opened her eyes to sit up choking and spluttering and wave away the offending fumes. A mouselike creature appeared in the kitchen doorway, stood for a moment wringing her hands in an agony of indecision, then suddenly scurried forward, seized a bottle of smelling salts from a crowded knick-knack table and presented it shakily toward her mistress.

Sarah took the bottle, inhaled until her eyes watered and her head began to clear and she was enabled to make a rapid assessment of the situation. Mercifully at that moment the shop door bell tinkled, thereby demanding the immediate absence of the more dangerous tattler.

'When you have served the customer,' said Sarah, 'you may clean the outside of the windows, Mrs Carpenter.'

Mrs Carpenter squinted spitefully at Sarah for this treacherous banishment from a prime source of gossip, and stalked from the room with the pursed lips and stiff-backed stance of one whose probity had been called into question.

Sarah smiled wanly. 'I do apologise, Mr Fogarty. A momentary indisposition. A womanish fit of the vapours. Thank you, Maggie, you may go. To your room,' she added firmly.

'Yes'm,' said the maid of all work, and fled to the sanctuary of her attic.

Daniel stole a glance at the cot. The child seemed to

have lapsed into an uneasy slumber. He knew little about babies but this one did seem uncommonly large for one of such tender age. And where the deuce was Elizabeth?

Sarah dabbed eau-de-cologne upon her forehead and settled the first unspoken question.

'Our little Samuel,' she told him. 'Born a week or two after you sailed, as I remember. He's turned nine months and already showing his first teeth. Such a well-developed little man. Everybody remarks upon it.'

'Ah,' said Daniel, enlightened. Of course! He should have remembered—something else had changed—Sarah's figure. 'My congratulations.' He paused and shuffled awkwardly before asking: 'Elizabeth is not at home?' and he felt his mouth dry in anticipation of the answer.

'Do sit down, Daniel,' said Sarah, determining to settle the matter as quickly as possible.

'Thank you,' said Daniel, wondering why the infernal woman seemed so bent on evading the issue. 'Elizabeth?' he prompted as Sarah composed her features into the grimace of a smile.

'You would, I am sure, have been the first to congratulate her upon such a splendid match. She is the most fortunate and blessed of women.'

He stared in total incomprehension. Sarah, surely, had taken leave of her senses? Splendid match . . . ? Who on earth was the fool babbling about?

Sarah's tongue, once given rein, leaped into full gallop. 'Dear Albert. Such a cavalier! Quite swept her off her feet. A runaway marriage, no less. So romantic! Took us all quite unawares. They were joined in the sight of God at Gretna Green. With benefit of clergy, of course,' she added emphatically, that there might be no illusions as to the strength of the bond.

'Elizabeth . . . ?' she was mad! There was no other explanation. The woman was raving mad! Elizabeth married? It simply wasn't possible! She couldn't . . . ! It was unthinkable!

Sarah reached out a comforting hand. 'Dear Daniel,' she murmured. 'The intelligence has no doubt come as something of a surprise, but the prolonged absence of a loved one does play havoc with a young girl's affections, and—I must say it, Daniel, even at the risk of incurring your censure—Elizabeth was ever of a somewhat unstable temperament. After your departure she was so given to morbid fancies and frequent distempers of the spirit that I do assure you we quite feared for the lucidity of her mind.'

Of course, he thought, the baby—the poor child must have been demented with worry. 'I quite understand,' he said. 'I had a letter . . .'

'A letter . . . ?' Sarah repeated, warily.

He hesitated and then blurted it out. 'She said she was with child.'

Sarah compressed her lips. It was worse, much worse than she could have imagined. She looked across at Daniel. He had lowered his eyes in embarrassment and was unhappily rubbing the palms of his hands together. Sarah regained her composure and again summoned up the vestige of a sympathetic smile.

'I am so glad,' she said, 'that dear Elizabeth took the opportunity of breaking the news to you herself. No doubt the disclosure of her marriage caused you considerable pain and anguish of heart but, believe me, Time the Great Healer will bring solace and consolation . . .'

Daniel Fogarty raised his head and stared at her blankly. The woman seemed intent on wilfully misunderstanding him. 'You don't understand,' he said harshly. 'The child is mine!'

Sarah drew herself erect. 'Really, Mr Fogarty, you overstep all bounds of common decency. That is a most dreadful accusation, a scandalous imputation of the honour of my dear sister-in-law and a most culpable self-condemnation from a man with pretensions to gentility. No, hear me out,' she continued sharply as Daniel opened his lips to protest. 'While I can readily comprehend that a distraught heart is not the wisest of counsellors, I cannot possibly countenance such slanderous observations under this roof; and you would do well, sir, to guard your tongue when outside. The Frazers,' she added—and the warning was unmistakable—'are a rich and powerful family and unlikely to forget or forgive such a calumny. You have the letter?'

He nodded mutely and put his hand to his pocket.

'I do not wish to be acquainted with its contents,' she said quickly. 'Take my advice: burn it and forget it.'

He shook his head.

Sarah felt she was gaining the upper hand and pressed home her advantage. 'You could not have arrived at a more inopportune moment. The child is being christened today. The boy is said to be the perfect image of his parents.' She held his gaze and spoke slowly. 'Everyone remarks upon it.'

Daniel looked into her eyes, read the lie, and at last understood the enormity of the betrayal.

He came to his feet and towered above Sarah. 'Where are they living?' he demanded thickly.

'Albert and Elizabeth have taken up residence in a most superior establishment. In Abercromby Square,' she added impressively. 'One of the most select quarters of the town . . .'

'I know it,' said Daniel, shortly. 'Thank you, Sarah. I shall trouble you no more.'

'But you must not call uninvited,' she wailed after his departing back. 'They are holding a reception. *Everybody* will be there . . . !'

Daniel, too full of black anger to formulate any coherent plan of action, strode through the busy thoroughfares heedless of the expostulations of outraged citizens as he bumped and bored his way toward his goal.

At the wrought-iron barrier he barked 'Frazer's house?'

and the gateman respectfully touched his hat, swung open the wicket gate and pointed to an open door with a liveried servant lounging on the steps and a line of carriages drawn up before a residence of imposing respectability.

The house was one of a row of stucco-fronted Georgian terraces, each with its pillared entrance, tall windows and overhanging balcony. The Frazers' was as like its fellows as one of a pair of well-bred peas. It stood a little off-centre and on the more desirable northern side.

Daniel had entered the square through the south-side gate and was therefore forced to cross the well-tended gardens of the small private park in the centre of the square. He marched across briskly, discovered that the path wound in arabesques and curlicues about flower-beds and shrubberies, so stepped on to the grass and directly across to the north side. A gardener, red-faced with anger, rose to his feet. 'Get orf me grass,' he yelled and added a low obscenity that brought a blush to the cheeks of a passing nursemaid and a chorus of condemnatory 'oooh's' from her charges.

Daniel's gaze was fixed upon the first floor where tall casement windows were thrown wide open to admit the cool airs of late afternoon. He could hear the muted murmur of voices, a babble of conversation that purled and rippled to break into sudden rapids of laughter. Figures moved like shadows into shadow. Once he paused in mid-stride as the sun, creeping from its hiding place behind a chimney stack, directed a beam of golden light straight into the room, and Elizabeth chose that very moment, as though conjured by some black art, to appear at the open window. She seemed to be bathed in a halo of light, and he imagined for one unnerving moment that she looked straight at him. But she had screwed up her eyes against the glare, then turned her head to speak to someone behind her. The chimney gouted a cloud of smoke, the sunlight wavered and she was gone.

Daniel crossed the road, pushed in front of a horse nuzzling greedily into its feedbag, mounted the steps and irritably waved away the guardian footman holding out a hand for his invitation card.

The hall was lofty and cool with hangings of green and gold. It had been decorated by someone with expensive but frivolous tastes: the umbrella stand was a bashful maiden rising from the uncovered frame of her crinoline, and a large gold-framed painting of 'The Babylonian Marriage Market' met the eye of the beholder as he crossed the threshold. The stair well was hung with allegorical paintings, 'The Bath of Psyche' having pride of place next to 'Venus and Adonis' and 'The Sleep of Sorrow and Dream of Joy'. Small statuettes of Parian marble stood on heavy stands, while a plaster frieze of fat cupids chased one another endlessly around the walls.

A liveried footman stood in possession of an array of hats and coats, and female servants scurried back and forth with trays of delicacies. Daniel took the stairs two at a time. On the first floor landing a group of gentlemen, taking their cigars, glanced at him with idle curiosity before returning to their weighty discussion.

The door to the upstairs withdrawing room stood open and the rat-a-tat-tat of conversation drummed on the air. He took a glass of wine from a tray proferred by a lank housemaid in starched dress and ribboned cap, and lounged across to lean against the door jamb while he took his bearings.

He still had no clear idea as to his course of action. His sense of outrage and headlong rush had left him perspiring and trembling; but his anger was now contained. He concentrated his attention upon the crowded room. The majority were strangers to him: a red-haired young man was bleating to a horse-faced lady of impeccable respectability, and a tall pale-complexioned man of thinning hair stood in a corner engaged in a muffled paroxysm of coughing into a large white handkerchief. He caught a glimpse of Iron Jack Frazer, his back as stiff as a ramrod, talking in low measured tones to an owl-faced clergyman all smooth attention. He heard a braying laugh followed by a short burst of hiccups and Robert's moon face drifted from behind a screen of chatterers. Mr Callon stood with his back to him, bull head thrust forward, his voice a hiss of expostulation as he rasped angrily at a lean and sardonic James . . . then he caught sight of her. Her tinkling laughter was unmistakable. She had moved from the window and, holding a glass of champagne, was talking animatedly to Anne. He took a step into the room and Elizabeth turned her head and looked straight at him. Her eyes widened in alarm and her mouth made a moué of surprise; then she swayed, touched the curtain for support and he saw the glass tilt and tremble in her hand.

She was more beautiful than he had ever remembered. He had wanted to rant and roar at her, shake her, strike her; but now his anger melted as wax before a flame. A mirror above the marble fireplace threw back a multiplicity of images and she seemed to swim toward him from near and yet from afar. He stood like a fool, unable to speak or move, afflicted with a complete paralysis of the senses; yet he had a heightened awareness of her presence: the delicate fragrance of her perfume, the swishing susurration of her dress, and her form rising like some exotic flower from the swaying bell of her crinoline. She laid a gloved hand lightly upon his arm and her touch ran through him like a blade of fire.

'Why, Daniel?' she said. 'How nice of you to call.'

Her voice was soft and cool, a barely audible whisper as though the commonplace was destined for his ears alone. But her smile was that of an automaton and he realised that his sudden appearance must have come as a blinding shock and that she was holding herself in control with an effort of will that rasped the breath in her throat and replaced the early flush of confusion with the pallor of fear.

He found his tongue at last. 'I received your letter and came as quickly as I could.' He could not keep the bitterness from his voice. 'In the event I was evidently too late.' He was about to swing on his heel and walk away when a hand slapped his shoulder and a hateful drawling voice bade him welcome.

'Fogarty, my dear fellow!' said Albert, cheerfully. 'You could not have timed a better entrance had you been a Thespian!'

Daniel wanted to smash the vacuous grinning idiot to the floor. Elizabeth's grip tightened upon his arm and he turned his head to discover that her eyes were brimming with tears. 'Dear, thoughtful Daniel,' she said and, weeping openly, leaned forward to kiss him upon the cheek.

Albert smiled and put an arm about her shoulder. 'Crocodile tears. Come, Daniel, you must pay your respects to our guest of honour.'

Daniel followed them along the corridor to the white-painted door of the nursery.

Inside, weak sunlight filtered through bunched lace curtains to slant a honey-coloured tracery of light and shade across the room. A plump nursemaid rose respectfully from the quiet seclusion beside the crib, put an admonitory finger to her lips and drew aside the muslin drapes at the cot head.

Daniel Forgarty peered down at the sleeping child and was immediately convinced that the tiny elf-face was an exact miniature of himself. Elizabeth surely could not hope to continue the pretence much longer? He took a perverse pleasure in the knowledge of a shared secret and for a moment found it in his heart to pity the poor dupe standing beside him.

They had not heard the soft footfalls behind them and it was a rumbling burp that betrayed Robert's presence.

He weaved unsteadily toward them, leaned perilously over the crib, hiccupped once more, then dug Fogarty in the ribs to wink knowingly and enunciate thickly: 'Like father, like son, eh, Daniel?'

In another room a clock struck five silver notes. They hung on the air, trembled, fell away to silence.

'Every inch a Frazer,' said Robert uncertainly, vaguely aware that something was wrong. He looked hopefully at their faces. No one believed him.

They lay side by side in the darkness and Albert's brain pecked at the bones of memory like some scavenging bird of ill-omen. True, Elizabeth had approached the altar in something less than a state of grace, but for that situation he had always held himself entirely accountable. Had he not seduced her? 'Or been seduced?' The thought rose unbidden from some dark recess of his mind. No, the elopement had been his idea. Or had it? James had first put the notion into his head: something to the effect 'With Fogarty away you will never have a better opportunity'. Was it possible? Could brother and sister have connived to father another man's child upon him? He groaned in the anguish of misery and Elizabeth stirred beside him. He wondered irritably how she could sleep so soundly. She must either be innocent or totally devoid of conscience. The faint musk of her perfume reached him and his thoughts took a new direction to twist and tumble through the corridors of the past. He remembered the turbulence of their love-making in the shabby bedroom of that seedy Scottish hotel, and her trust and companionship throughout the long dreary wait in that dismal little town forever whipped by winds and enshrouded in rain.

He remembered clearly the first time. Just before taking her she had whispered: 'Do you want children?' 'Yes,' he'd replied. 'You shall have a son, I promise,' she had answered softly. Her subsequent storm of passion had taken him by surprise. In truth, he thought wryly, it had so embarrassed him at the time that he had put a hand across her mouth fearing that her moans and cries might rouse the hotel. She had learned quickly, become docile and compliant to his wishes, and their love-making had been slow and sensuous. Best of all he liked to take her by stealth, when she was asleep and would give a drowsy little moan of pleasure before awakening to murmur endearments in their private secret code. He relaxed and felt a need for her. Then a bat of doubt rose suddenly from the abyss of unreason: 'You shall have a son. I promise'. Was it guile, or innocence, that had prompted her? He suppressed the thought and gently reached out for her.

Elizabeth had been lying awake as quiet and still as a mouse, her mind a hotch-potch of fears and doubts. In this realm of uncertainty there was but one verity of which she was gospel-sure: Albert had no proof. Though he might have suspicions by the bucketful there were no grounds upon which he could successfully challenge her. Daniel, of course, was the fly-in-the-ointment; his temper was always of an uncertain quantity and his jealousy knew no bounds. His sudden appearance at the reception had terrified her almost out of her wits and then when that intoxicated fool Robert had blurted out his sly innuendo she had seen the suffusion of rage on Daniel's face and for one heart-stopping moment believed that he would strike that loud-mouthed ninny and defiantly claim the child as his own. But in the event he had swallowed his anger and passed it off with a weak and uncertain laugh. If only she had been able to compose herself! But the strain had been too much and she knew that guilt had stamped its indelible attestation upon her features and that Albert had read the evidence as though she had brayed her sin from the housetops. Nevertheless from that moment he had neither spoken nor hinted of the doubts which must have tormented him, but had continued to treat her with his usual cool courtesy and consideration, and their guests with politeness and civility. It was only after all had left that he had lapsed into a black humour of silent introspection.

She knew instinctively that never under any circumstances must she imply by deed or word that she had any awareness of his suspicions. The first move in this dangerous game must come from him. Dear Albert. She loved him. Really and truly loved him. . . .

Her heart stumbled at his touch. She lay for a moment in the pretended bewitchment of sleep then curled over opening to receive him. Loving him she murmured, 'Mmmmmm-Albert, Albert, my love,' and raised her hips in response. She would make it nice, so nice for him, she promised.

'Be quiet!' he snapped. 'Keep still, damn you!'

She opened her eyes wide in a shock of alarm. His face loomed above her, cold and implacable, his eyes flecks of blue anger.

'You strumpet!'

She tried to wriggle free, hurt and hating, but he pinned down her arms and thrust deeper.

'Are you a wife or a harlot?' he demanded.

Tears filled her eyes, ran down her cheeks in scalding streams of self-pity.

He shook her. 'Answer me, damn you! Wife or harlot?'

His fierce anger robbed her of resistance. 'W-wife. I am your wife,' she sobbed.

'Then behave like a wife and not a trollop. You will remain still. Do you understand?'

She sniffed and sobbed, but lay obediently supine until he had finished. Then she rolled away, loathing him, until, wrapped in a cloak of unbearable misery, she fell into a sleep of despair.

Chapter Eight

Daniel Fogarty presented himself at Head Office punctually at nine only to be informed by a hand-wringing, unctuous-voiced Agnew that Mr Callon desired Captain Fogarty to present himself at the Company dock office with all despatch. Agnew, who invariably knew in what direction the wind was blowing, ordered a cab and personally bowed and scraped him to the street door.

The dock office was a small lime-washed single-storey structure with the monastic look of a stone cell. It stood four-square to wind and rain and a pair of small-paned blank-eyed windows stared across the dock at the *Barracuda* discharging her cargo alongside the quay.

The door was half open and Daniel could hear Callon's harsh voice issuing a stream of orders to the master stevedore standing at the threshold. Daniel knew him well and raised a hand in greeting. ''morning, Mr Jarvis.'

Mr Jarvis was a short, squat, liver-featured man of gravel voice and red-rimmed eyes. He wore corduroy trousers, bottle-green coat and a short, stubby, hard hat clamped to his head. His jaws chomped methodically as he listened to Callon, occasionally nodding his head in accord. ''morning to you, Cap'n Fogarty,' he replied, briefly saluted Callon and stumped away toward the *Barracuda*, his voice already raised in the first of a torrent of instructions to his work force.

Daniel politely tapped at the door.

'Come in, come in, my boy,' called Callon with unexpected affability.

Daniel stepped inside. Long familiar with the office he merely glanced out of habit at the worn and battered furnishings. The desk sloped beneath one of the grimy windows. The pigeon-holes with their litter of invoices, despatch notes, bills of lading. Out-of-date Notices to Mariners pinned to the wall. The hoop-backed swivel chair with the worn leather seat. The bare boards of the floor and the pot-bellied cast-iron stove radiating unaccustomed heat.

Callon stood warming his backside against the stove. He tossed the *Barracuda*'s cargo manifest on to the desk and held out a welcoming hand. 'Congratulations upon a most successful voyage, Captain Fogarty,' he crowed, jerking the surprised Daniel's arm up and down like a pump handle. 'Profitable. Most profitable; and a record-breaker to boot. For a first command you have more than justified my high opinion of your ability. An emphatic endorsement of my decision in promoting you over older heads. You'll go far, my boy. Mark my words, you'll go far.'

'Thank you, sir,' said Daniel, overwhelmed. His employer was unusually complimentary today. Daniel felt a sense of relief. At least he would be assured of retaining command of the *Barracuda* and with luck he could be off to sea again within a week or two and put that other distressing business out of his mind once and for all. 'Flying topsails paid all debts' was the popular saying, and there was, he concluded, more than a grain of truth in the adage.

Callon plumped himself into the chair and Daniel noticed that his eyes were pouched and his flesh sagged. He looked grey and old. Old and lonely, thought Daniel, remembering that Callon's wife had not long survived the loss of their only son. Edmund, in the prime of young manhood, had been taken from them, flushed away in the ocean's swirl when one of those damned steam packets, thundering out of the fog, had sliced the sailing ship in half. Four years since, almost to the day.

'Have you read this morning's newspaper?' asked Callon.

'No, sir. I came straight to the office.'

Callon picked up a copy of *The Liverpool Mercury* and passed it across.

The columns of the centre pages bore a series of headlines: 'War Between The States?' 'Issue of Slavery.' 'Fall of Fort Sumter.' 'President Lincoln's Inaugural Address.' Daniel's eyes flowed down the closely packed columns of print, his brain barely understanding a word. Where the devil was Fort Sumter? And who the deuce was President Lincoln? He gathered that some southern American states had seceded from the Union. Did it really mean civil war? He turned to the next page. 'Federal Government Announces Blockade.' Blockade? Small wonder Callon was showing his years. The American trade was the heart and life blood of Callon's business. Emigrants out, cotton back. Sixteen ships. Fifty thousand emigrants, one hundred and fifty thousands tons of cargo a year.

'Well?' demanded Callon impatiently. 'What do you make of it?'

Disaster, thought Daniel. 'I have not yet digested all the facts, sir,' he began.

'We'll be ruined,' said Callon, flatly.

'A temporary disruption, sir. I am sure it will be over quickly.'

'I expect more from you than soothing words,' snapped Callon irritably. He fished out his watch, glowered at the face as though defying it to disagree with him, snapped it shut decisively.

'I would appreciate your opinion, Daniel. Take time to reflect. You will perhaps oblige me with your company at lunch?' It wasn't so much a question as a command.

'I should be honoured, sir,' said Daniel, politely.

Callon rose from the chair, galvanised once again into a semblance of his old energetic self. 'Use this office as though it were your own. See to it that the *Barracuda* is discharged as shortly as possible. Agnew will send you the manifests for her outward cargo. I want that ship cleared for Melbourne within the week. One o'clock, at my club,' he growled, and was gone.

Daniel reflected broodingly for a few moments over

Callon's parting words. 'I would appreciate your opinion,' he'd said; and called him Daniel into the bargain. It was odd. Decidedly odd. He gave up the puzzle, spread the newspaper on the desk and immersed himself in reading the news items. Concentration became increasingly difficult as fragmented images interposed themselves between his vision and the printed word until the type resembled nothing other than files of black soldiers marching across plains of white paper. How could she possibly have brought herself to marry that insufferable popinjay! Sadly he recognised the answer as being only too obvious; and it brought little credit on himself. His temper hardened. If she could live with the knowledge, so be it; so could he. Robert's idiotic heavy-handed humour rasped across his consciousness and he recollected the responsive shock of alarm which seemed to stifle all sound; the open confession in her eyes and the instant sick understanding in Albert's. Blue eye sounding the depths of blue eye across a child with orbs like pools of jet. Guilt rising to overshadow them all with a hood of infamy. And that blabbermouthed, lard-brained fool Robert hiccupping his weak excuses...

A cold wind whisked dust clouds from the cobbles outside and rushed through the open door to be greeted by the red grin of the firebox. Papers lifted on the desk and the door squeaked and banged fully open. He shivered and walked to the threshold to stare toward the *Barracuda*. The steam cranes hammered and roared, turning and dipping giraffe necks over the ship's hold, extruding long thin tongues to lick up the contents of the *Barracuda*'s storehouse. Slingloads of grain that had ripened under faraway skies were landed on the quayside to be manhandled into the waiting drays. Fully laden wagons lurched and creaked away to a loud crack of whips and jangle of harness while other empty carts rumbled up to take their place. A tempest of dust and straw whirled along the quay, scurrying from nowhere to nowhere. He turned his head away from the wind and saw her standing there like a mirage. She had bowed her head and held a protective arm across her face. The wind passed her by, tugging playfully at her skirts and flirting with the ribbons of her hat. She raised her head and saw him at the same instant and her mouth made a round O of surprise.

He walked toward her and conducted her to the office. Her eyes were buried in pits of despair and she shivered as though in a fever.

'What are you doing here?'

She looked into his puzzled brown eyes, took out a wisp of handkerchief and dabbed at her nose. 'Looking for you,' she said. 'I thought to find you aboard ship.' She sniffed and to his horror burst into tears. 'I don't know what to do,' she wailed. 'I don't know what to do.'

He looked at her in alarm and quickly closed the door, turning the office into a tiny cubicle of private confession.

'Is it Albert?' he asked. Callon, he thought, Callon was such a stickler for the proprieties. The scandal would destroy him. His promising career would be ruined. Why the devil couldn't she have held her tongue for another week?

'He suspects,' she wept.

His heart rose. If that was all . . . ?

'He can suspect until eternity,' he told her harshly. 'But unless you admit of your deception there is nothing he can do.'

Elizabeth stopped sniffling and stared at him in disbelief. '*My* deception?' she shrilled. 'You have the temerity to stand there bold-faced and accuse *me* of deception! You infamous, lying, hypocritical—seducer!' She lowered her head and snuffled bitterly into her handkerchief. 'And to think I came to you for help and consideration. I have been wronged!' she declaimed dramatically like Miriam Candlemass in *The Crime of Lady Carstairs*, adding for good measure, 'Wronged and shamed in my husband's eyes!'

She was speaking like someone deranged. He took her hands protectively. 'I didn't mean it, my love,' he said as gently as possible. 'Not in that way. Believe me,' he stressed, 'were it in my power to undo the harm I would do so without hesitation. But you must accept that such a course is not possible. Albert has no evidence beyond the merest breath of suspicion. Only you know the truth.'

'You don't understand.' Tears of self-pity welled in her eyes. 'He treats me abominably.'

He could well believe it. A man corroded with suspicions of infidelity would be the very devil to live with.

'He has utterly convinced himself,' she was saying, 'and nothing I can say or do will alter that conviction. The man is beyond all reason.' She looked so helpless in her distress. 'Oh, Daniel,' she said. 'I am so unhappy,' and drifted into his arms like a child pleading for comfort. The musk of her fragrance invaded his nostrils and her slender warmth branded his flesh with her imprint. He would do anything for her, anything. He patted her shoulder. 'There, there . . .' he said idiotically. She moved her head from its hiding place on his shoulder. 'Take me away,' she pleaded. 'Take me away.'

'I can't,' he answered desperately. 'I can't.'

'On the *Barracuda*,' she said. 'We could sail to Australia together. Start anew. I want—I've always wanted—to be your wife, Daniel. Not his!' She hissed the final word with the venom of a serpent.

Australia was as far away and remote as the moon. She was a child trying to escape the miseries of the world by running away to a never-never land, a sugar-plum fairyland where troubles were banished at the wave of a magic wand.

The cold wind whistled a sharp warning under the door.

'It isn't possible,' he said.

'I don't see why not. Not if you really and truly loved me.' She spoke petulantly now and broke away from him. The distance between them was a bridge yawning across a widening chasm. 'Captains do take their wives.'

'But not their . . .' He fumbled for a word.

'Mistresses?'

He shook his head

'I could sail as a passenger,' she urged. 'Who is to know?'

Who indeed but the whole world? His world. The world of Callon and Company. Her name on the passenger list? Unthinkable.

'You would never be allowed to set foot on board,' he told her bluntly

The magician had failed her. Her features crumpled into an apex of woe.

'You don't love me. You've never loved me. You didn't care. You never cared. You seduced me and left me with child. Had it not been for Albert I would have been thrown out into the street and left to die in the gutter. And you did not care!'

The accusation was unjust and both knew it. He wished she would not dramatise so, and her once endearing trait of speaking as though straight from the pages of a tuppenny novel now grated like a rasp on raw nerves. He thought of the wild rush of ship and canvas across the oceans of the world, the man-killing hours, straining every rope and spar in his urgency to answer her appeal for help. Not care! He wanted to shake her until the teeth rattled in her head.

'Nonsense,' he snapped. 'You promised to wait, but instead enticed Albert to elope with you.'

'I?' she screeched. 'I enticed Albert? I did nothing of the sort. He begged and prayed and pleaded with me to run away with him. Furthermore I doubt the notion occurred to him until James put the idea into his head.'

'James?'

'What could I do?' she wailed. 'I was with child and going out of my mind with worry. Robert and Sarah wanted to pack me off to a hovel in the country. I'd have died,' she sobbed. 'Died.'

'James persuaded Albert . . . ?' The black enormity staggered him.

She shrugged. 'What does it matter? You don't care any more and Albert hates me. I don't know what to do. Tell me what to do, Daniel. Tell me what to do.'

Over her shoulder and through the fly-specked window the *Barracuda* waited, tall masts raking a wind-torn sky.

'You must make your peace with Albert,' he said.

Her shoulders slumped in defeat. 'He will never forgive me,' she said hopelessly. 'Never.'

He opened the door. 'You must try, Elizabeth. You are his wife. He will believe you because he must.'

She dried her eyes. 'Run away in your big ship, Daniel Fogarty,' she said. 'And never come back!'

She stepped past him, out on to the quay and he watched the busy wind hustle her away.

He kicked the door shut and cursed Albert and Robert and Sarah and James, and above all himself . . .

'The Owners' was a select club for the select. A building of awesome respectability from the outside and of cosseted luxury inside. The diners sat in secluded alcoves, the tables covered in napery stiff and starched. Heavy silverware gleamed to reflect the light of crystal chandeliers suspended by wrought iron chains from the lofty ceiling. The service was soft-footed and soundless as waiters glided across the deep-piled Turkey carpet. The walls were panelled in smoked oak and every bay held a large gilt-framed oil painting: in the main of storm and wrack at sea where waves unnaturally high licked rock-bound wooden ships of tattered sails and bursting timbers. Daniel glanced at the paintings as he was ushered to Callon's table and privately wondered what strange impulse impelled shipowners to surround themselves with intimations of disaster. He also considered that any master who put his ship into such danger should be stripped of rank and sent back to sea as a cabin boy.

Callon had already tucked a napkin beneath his chin and his nose was buried in the menu. He looked up and fished out his watch as the tower clock chimed one.

'Sit you down, my boy,' he commanded. 'Sit you down.' He snapped the menu shut and glowered at the waiter. 'We'll start with the soup. Beefsteak pie to follow. With cabbage and boiled potatoes. And send that wine feller across.'

Thus dismissed the waiter flicked an imaginary crumb from the spotless tablecloth, bowed, intoned: 'Instantly, Mr Callon, sir,' and departed like a liveried shade.

'You'll not do better than the pie,' grunted Callon. 'Rich pastry, plenty of kidney, first rate beef. Soup's rich. Plenty of body.'

'Thank you, sir,' replied Daniel who would willingly have followed his employer's example had he ordered horse and harness.

Callon picked at his nose. 'Come to a conclusion yet?'

'Yes, sir,' replied Daniel. 'If,'—he took care to stress the conjunction—'If the blockade can be rigorously enforced . . .'

'It will be,' said Callon.

'If the Confederate States succeed in sending out privateers . . .'

'They will,' said Callon flatly. 'You can take it from me—they will.'

'In which event, sir,' Daniel began carefully, only to be interrupted by the appearance of the aproned sommelier hung about with cellar keys and silver tasting cup.

Callon impatiently waved away the gravely presented wine list. 'A bottle of your best red,' he demanded. 'French, mind. I'll have none of your Portuguee muck.'

Dumping his heavy chin on his fist he returned his full attention to Daniel.

'We must seek new markets, sir,' said Daniel lamely, cursing the interruption. He had taken a deal of trouble in formulating and marshalling his opinions and prepared his arguments with care. Now he found himself floundering. 'A period of high risk, increased insurance rates, too many ships chasing too few cargoes. Other Owners will be faced with the same problems. Competition for new markets will be fierce.' He paused and to his surprise found Callon to be listening intently, nodding in complete agreement.

'A fair assessment, Captain Fogarty. Now let's hear your solution.'

Thus encouraged Daniel warmed to his task. He leaned forward and spoke with emphasis. 'We prepare for the worst and hope for the best. The worst is a long-drawn-out war. Say two years. We have sixteen ships on the north American trade. I should advise taking ten out of service immediately and transferring them to the Australian wool trade, calling at Spain, Portugal, South America.'

Callon grinned. 'We'll wipe Onedin's nose.'

'He has but two ships,' said Daniel contemptuously. 'We'll run him off the seas.' The memory of James Onedin's perfidy stung his memory and his voice must have betrayed a little of the strength of his feelings for Callon looked at him sharply.

'You have little regard for that upstart, I take it?'

'I care not a button for James Onedin,' Daniel replied. 'And furthermore I wouldn't trust the man an inch.'

'You are a man after my own heart.' Callon twisted his face into the grimace of a smile. 'And what of the remaining six ships?'

'We switch to Canada. Emigrants to Quebec in summer, Halifax in winter. If the war is over quickly, or if the Federal government can keep the northern ports open, we creep down the coast—New York, Philadelphia, Boston. A country at war with itself will shortly be in dire need of supplies: they'll sell cheap and buy dear.' He sat back waiting for Callon's reaction. He was quite confident. He had thought the business out carefully, and, he considered, stated his exposition clearly.

Callon was evidently of the same opinion. He pulled at his lower lip and nodded slowly. 'You echo my own views exactly. You have a sharp head on your shoulders, Daniel, my boy.'

'Daniel, my boy.' There it was again. He was mulling over Callon's unexpected warmth, the singular honour of lunching at the great man's club as the waiter arrived with their first course. The soup was a rich mulligatawny contained in a porcelain-lined silver tureen. Callon liberally dosed his helping with pepper, slurped greedily, dabbed his lips with his napkin then leaned back, face glistening with perspiration.

'A drop of good soup,' he pronounced. 'Strong enough to scorch leather. Ha-ha,' he added unexpectedly.

He did seem to be in uncommon good humour. Daniel sipped and savoured and wondered again what was in the wind. He had not long to wait. Callon blew out his cheeks. 'A question or two, my boy. I shall require straight answers, mind. No trimming, you sail full and by, is that clear?'

'Aye, sir,' responded Daniel. Full and by? If that meant anything at all it indicated that Callon's questions were going to be pretty close to the wind. Something of a personal nature? Callon had been at the reception. Could he possibly have picked up a hint of gossip? He choked on the thought and reached for the pitcher of water just as the wine waiter arrived tenderly holding the bottle as though it were a new-born babe. He presented the label to Callon who flapped the offering away.

'Draw the damned cork and leave us,' he snapped peevishly.

The cork came out with a soft 'phlup'. The waiter leaned across with the intention of dribbling half an inch of wine into Callon's glass. Callon ignored the fool, seized the bottle and snarled, 'If it's foul you'll be the first to hear about it. Now take yerself off.'

He filled their glasses brim full and took a deep and satisfying draught of his own. 'All this Frenchified sniffing and sipping, I've no patience with it. Wine was made for drinking, not praying over. My father drank a tankard of claret every day of his life, at a shilling a bottle. Now they charge half a crown and dispense the stuff like apothecaries.' Having disposed of family reminiscences he changed tack and bore straight down on Daniel. 'This Elizabeth Onedin—married young Albert Frazer. You and she had an—um—understanding once?'

'It is over,' said Daniel shortly. 'The lady is now Mrs Frazer ...'

'And mother to a fine bouncing boy-child.' Callon laughed coarsely. 'Young Albert would seem to have lost no time in removing his boots, eh?'

Daniel flushed with anger. 'Really, sir,' he protested.

Callon grinned. 'I think you leap to the lady's defence a shade too quickly for one who claims to have dampened the fires of ardour. What is your attitude of mind in regard to Mr Frazer?'

Daniel could not for the life of him see where this inquisition was leading. 'I envy him his good fortune,' he replied stiffly.

Callon grunted. 'Then I can accept that there is no likelihood of a renewal of that—um—entanglement?'

'Such a suggestion is unworthy of you, sir. I hold both Mr and Mrs Frazer in the highest regard!' He spoke indignantly, uneasily aware that the statement was far from the truth. At the moment he despised the pair of them.

But Callon seemed satisfied with the answer. He crumbled a piece of bread. 'The fool married beneath him,' he grumbled.

'I do not follow the direction of your questions, sir.'

'They are pertinent, my boy. Pertinent to your future. I am not in the habit,' he added testily, 'of questioning my employees out of idle curiosity. He married beneath him,' he repeated. 'That marriage caused a breach between father and son—but with the advent of the child that breach shows every sign of being healed. Old John Frazer playing the proud grandfather—I never thought I'd live to see the day. But a man must have sons, Daniel. Sons and grandsons—otherwise—where's the purpose?'

He felt sorry for the man. Callon's eyes had the haunted look of a man staring into an empty future.

'I'm left with a daughter.' Callon sighed heavily. 'It's not the same, Daniel, it's not the same. She asked after you, by-the-by,' he added like someone suddenly recollecting a trivial message. 'Sends her regards.'

'Thank you, sir,' Daniel responded politely. 'My compliments to Miss Emma.' He vaguely remembered her. He'd met her once or twice—on one occasion she had been leaving Callon's office; on a second occasion she had been sitting waiting in her carriage caught in a log jam of traffic. He had raised his hat and bid her a formal 'Good day' and she had stared down her patrician nose at him. She had had the best education that money could buy and spoke nasally with a speech affection which was a continuing insult to northern ears.

Callon waited brooding until they had been served with the famous beefsteak pie. It was all that Callon had claimed. The pastry was short and crisp, melting in the mouth like butter. The meat and kidneys were tender and the gravy rich and savoury. The cabbage was green and finely chopped and the boiled potatoes large and floury, breaking open at the touch of a fork. Callon helped himself to a spoonful of salt from the bow-legged silver salt cellar, dusted the dish with pepper, drained his glass of wine and plied knife and fork with a will.

Between mouthfuls he continued: 'We are more than

business acquaintances, me and John Frazer. The two families have been friends for more years than I care to remember. A breath of scandal would touch us both, d'ye understand?'

'You have my assurance on that score, sir,' said Daniel firmly. 'If Mr and Mrs Frazer care to honour me with their acquaintance nothing would persuade me to disregard the obligations of our relative positions.'

'Then we can come to the point,' said Callon. He put down knife and fork and rubbed his eyes tiredly. 'I am growing old, Daniel. Too old to go crawling through ship's bilges, sounding ship's timbers, checking stores against the venal habits of shipmasters—oh, you know that side of the business well enough, my boy. I need a ship's husband. Someone of sharp wits; loyal, trustworthy, honest. Someone who knows that his best interests are my best interests. Someone who knows ships and can handle men. A captain of captains. The modern title is Marine Superintendent, if you care for it?'

Daniel's fork remained poised half way to his mouth. He stared at Callon, unable to believe his ears. This was promotion with a vengeance! He began to understand the purpose behind Callon's probing questions.

'Well, young man? Lost your tongue?'

'I have indeed, sir,' replied Daniel. 'But only because I am overwhelmed by the honour you do me.'

'That, I take it, means you accept?' said Callon drily. 'And perhaps now you understand the nature of my inquisitiveness?'

Daniel nodded. 'I shall be stationed ashore.'

'More to the point you will move in the same social circles as the Frazers. I therefore expect you to take care to meet only on the most formal of occasions.'

'That has always been my intention, sir.'

'Very well, Captain Fogarty, I will see to it that your appointment is confirmed this afternoon. You will take up your new duties immediately.' He picked up his knife and jabbed it toward Daniel. 'But remember—one sniff of scandal and out you go.'

'Yes, sir,' said Daniel.

Chapter Nine

Empty wine casks were stacked in the storeroom above the shop. Robert, wincing unhappily, wished with all his heart that James would stop talking. His head ached abominably and his tongue was furred and felted like a piece of old carpet. His stomach lurched and bile rose into his throat at the memory of exchanging civilities with that rum-soaked old villain Captain Webster. He had but the haziest recollection of succeeding events beyond a nagging impression that he had made a fool of himself. And now James's tongue was clacking away taking him to task for misuse of the *Charlotte Rhodes.*

'I left you in charge with clear instructions,' James was snapping. 'And what do I find on my return? The *Charlotte Rhodes* filled with Irish riff-raff and running at a loss!'

'They cover expenses,' Robert protested weakly.

'The business of a ship is to turn a profit, not recover its costs,' said James tartly. He wagged an accusing finger. 'Furthermore I have heard of your arrangement with that damned lodging-house keeper. You can put an end to it here and now. Senhor Braganza is awaiting his casks. The *Charlotte Rhodes* sails for Lisbon the minute she's loaded.'

'But . . .' began Robert, with the vision of a golden future melting away like spring snow.

'But?' James raged. 'There are no "buts" about it! You'd scald a cat to get its fur, you cheapjack chandler! I gave my word to Senhor Braganza and I've no intention of breaking it in order that you may turn a penny or two selling broken biscuits to a parcel of Papist ragamuffins!

Look around you . . .' He waved an arm taking in the tiered stacks of round-bellied barrels. He thumped one and it rang like a drum.

'I was coming to that,' explained Robert nervously. 'Waiting until we had a full cargo, you see? And for your return,' he added petulantly. 'I know nothing of shipping. I have more than enough to do looking after the shop without puzzling my brains over Bills of Lading, clearance papers and the rest of the mumbo-jumbo.' He puffed out his chest. 'I have a business to attend to, James. A business.'

James eyed him sourly. 'Business? What do you know of business with your penn'orths of this and ha'porths of that? The *Pampero* has just returned me a profit of two and a half thousand pounds!'

Robert's eyes bulged. 'Two and a half thousand . . .?'

'Sovereigns,' said James. 'If you were one half the businessman you claim to be, a fair proportion of that profit would be yours. But no, you knew best and dissolved the partnership. I owe you nothing and you have no claim upon the *Charlotte Rhodes*.'

Robert licked his lips. 'Perhaps I acted hastily, but you must admit, James, that the venture was full of risk. It brought me near the edge of bankruptcy. I have a wife and family to think of,' he added plaintively.

James walked to the grimed and cobwebbed skylight. Clasping his hands behind him he stared out at banners of cloud waving across the sky. He had a problem. Two ships in operation inflicted a gnawing anxiety to be in two places at once. What he required was a base for operations. But he was sure he would go mad if left to sit at home twiddling his thumbs awaiting their return. And to whom could he entrust the *Pampero* but himself? Two thousand pounds odd was burning a hole in his pocket. Money sitting in a bank was wasteful, he needed to put it to work. He turned away from the window and looked at Robert. Robert would always rise to the bait of avarice. He remembered an item of news on the financial pages of the *Morning Post* and suddenly found the key that would unlock the door to the future.

'You could learn,' he said.

Robert's mouth opened like a fat somnolent fish. 'What?'

James's brain was racing ahead. 'I'll have a cooper knock down the casks, bundle staves and hoops together. Mr Purdy, the shipbroker, will find cargo. I'll put master and crew aboard the *Charlotte Rhodes*—one man and four hands should be sufficient—I'll attend to that side of the business. You arrange with your friend Mr Miles to ship his emigrants aboard the *Pampero*—we'll help ourselves to a slice of Callon's emigrant trade. The Americans are busy killing one another—they'll require boots, blankets, cloth for uniforms—that sort of thing. You have connections in the trade—you can be a great help there, Robert. This can be your office. We'll give you an experienced clerk, move in a desk, a few pieces of furniture—you can store our ships and turn a profit at the same time ...'

Robert, floundering behind the welter of words, stared aghast at the madman. 'What on earth are you proposing?' he demanded. 'Another partnership? No thank you, James—I've been bitten once.'

'Not the sort of partnership you have in mind.' James rubbed his hands together. 'We're going Limited.'

The inner sanctum of Tapscott, Wainwright, Coote & Broadbent, Solicitors at Law & Commissioners of Oaths, was a dusty office of mouldering tomes and long-forgotten briefs. A finger of sunlight haloed Mr Tapscott's balding head and aureole of white hair. Muttonchop whiskers cascaded down plump cheeks to meet the conflux of a double chin. He was a large overflowing man in untidy snuff-stained suit, old-fashioned stock and plum-coloured waistcoat. He waved his visitors to a pair of identical creaking chairs, helped himself to a small mountain of snuff from a silver snuff box, trumpeted into an enormous once-white handkerchief, adjusted gold-rimmed pince-nez, leaned back in his chair and surveyed his clients. The lean hungry-looking one would be Mr James Onedin, the fat perspiring one with the red-rimmed eyes and sickly pallor must be the brother, Robert.

'Yes, gentlemen?' He washed pudgy white hands together. 'Please consider Tapscott and Co. at your service.'

'My brother and myself,' James began carefully, 'are engaged in the business of shipping and we are of a mind to enter into a partnership in which our liabilities may be limited to an initial investment. I came across an item in today's newspaper stating that Parliament has recently promulgated an Act designed to protect investors against loss. If such is the case we would appreciate the benefit of your advice.' He cupped a hand to his chin. 'In plain man's language if you please.'

In Tapscott's estimation the man was as cunning as a fox and as sharp as a weasel; there was little doubt in whose direction the plain speaking was to be aimed. He cleared his throat and spoke directly to Robert. 'As you are no doubt aware, in the past it has been by no means uncommon for unfortunate shareholders of a company, with perhaps no more than a few pounds invested in an enterprise, to suddenly find the company failed and themselves jointly responsible for the total debts of the company—a situation in too many cases leading to bankruptcy and even a debtors' prison.'

Robert nodded and bobbed agonised agreement. His head thumped painfully and he wondered if this lawyer fellow would offer refreshment. He tried to concentrate but the words swam past like a shoal of darting fish.

'The purpose of the new legislation is to protect the smaller investor against misfortune and the follies of others. In essence, Parliament in its wisdom has decreed that a company of limited liability is a body corporate regulated by its Memorandum and Articles of Association and is considered, in law, to be a separate "persona"—that is, it may enter into contracts as a person as distinct from its members, and—most important, gentlemen—the liability of the members is limited to the nominal value of the shares they have taken up.'

Tapscott was amused to note Robert's lips moving in soundless repetition as though mouthing the tenets of an imperfectly understood faith. He paused, steepled his fingers together. 'Before proceeding further—a question.' He addressed himself to the sharp one. 'Joint stock, or private?'

'Private,' said James promptly. 'Just my brother and myself.'

Tapscott nodded. 'Advice: First you must draw up a Memorandum of Association. This document will state the objects of the company. Secondly: The Articles of Association. These are the internal regulations dealing with the operation of the company. Both these documents must be registered with the Board of Trade when the company is formed. You will only then be entitled to the protection of the new Act limiting liabilities.'

'Limiting liabilities,' repeated Robert, like a man grasping at the one absolute in an uncertain world.

'Should the worst happen,' continued the lawyer, 'and the company be forced into liquidation, no further call can be made upon the holders of fully paid-up shares.'

'Fully paid-up shares,' parroted Robert. Alarm showed in his face. 'Shares? What shares?' He turned upon James. 'Does this mean that I am expected to invest good money once again in another of your hare-brained schemes?' He huffed and puffed and reached for his hat. 'Not a penny piece! I've been caught before, remember!'

'You'll not go to the wall, Robert,' said James mildly. 'Retain your seat and listen to Mr Tapscott.'

Tapscott drilled two massive injections of snuff up his nostrils, blew into his handkerchief, then continued soothingly as though the interruption had never occurred. 'You may capitalise the company in any sum you desire. The shares will not be quoted on the market, will not be transferable; dividends to be declared annually and agreed by the directors at an annual general meeting of the shareholders. Directors to be appointed by shareholders.' He smiled genially. 'In your case, gentlemen, I foresee little difficulty there.'

James rubbed his chin. 'Non-transferable shares? Let us suppose that at some future date my brother and myself thought it desirable to introduce another . . .' He spread his hands: 'Partner?'

'Fellow director,' Tapscott corrected. He inclined his head gravely and his double chin hung like dewlaps. 'It is indeed entirely possible. Your solution would be to include the proviso in the Articles of Association.' He scribbled a note with an old-fashioned quill pen then pointed the feathered end at James. 'I would also strongly advise that the right of members to dispose of shares be clearly restricted to other members. Never to outsiders, except as hereunder defined, and only then by a majority vote and only after first giving other members the option of purchase. Do you agree?'

'I insist,' said James, thinking of Callon.

'Yes,' said Robert, thinking of his purse.

'Capital investment?' questioned Tapscott, pen poised.

'One hundred one pound shares,' replied James decisively. 'Of which I take 85 per cent, my brother, 15.'

The lawyer scribbled industriously while Robert worked out sums in his head and calculated that he could not possibly be more than fifteen pounds out of pocket. It could be a worthwhile investment if fifteen pounds meant fifteen per cent of profits. The *Pampero* alone had cleared two and a half thousand pounds. Fifteen per cent of two and a half thousand came to no less than three hundred and seventy-five pounds—a fair sum, a fair sum. He would plough it back into the shop.

Tapscott peered over the top of his spectacles. 'Assets?' he queried.

'The tops'l schooner *Charlotte Rhodes*,' James told him.

'That is all?'

'For the moment.'

'What of the *Pampero*? She should be worth a pretty penny,' demanded Robert suspiciously.

'You seem to be in an infernal hurry to saddle the company with debts,' commented James drily. 'She isn't yet paid for.'

Robert's vision of three hundred and seventy-five pounds vanished like smoke.

'No other assets?' Tapscott's nose twitched in the direction of the snuff box. He flicked back the lid, dipped in forefinger and thumb and inhaled a liberal dosage.

James peered into the future. 'How many companies can I have?' he asked.

A slow smile spread across the lawyer's face. This Onedin was a man after his own heart.

'As many as you choose and your purse will allow, Mr Onedin.'

'I'll bear it in mind,' said James. He stood up. 'In the meantime you will oblige me by drawing up the necessary documents in the name of . . .' He reflected a moment. 'The Onedin Line Shipping Company, Limited.' It had a fine sound to it, he thought. Rang true as a gold piece.

Robert, trying out the swivel chair behind the second-hand desk, thought much the same. The coopers had been in, knocked down and removed the casks ready for shipment by the *Charlotte Rhodes*. Carpenters and painters had been at work transforming the dusty attic into a quite handsome semblance of an office, if you remembered to duck your head as you entered. A partition grained to look like oak separated the private office with desk and firegrate from the clerks' quarters with counters and tall stools. A sign painter was putting the finishing touches to a gold-painted legend on the outer door, reading: ONEDIN LINE SHIPPING COMPANY LTD, HEAD OFFICE. Even Sarah had been impressed, particularly by the brass plate screwed to the wall by the street door. 'R. Onedin. Ship Chandler' it stated for all to see, and, that there may be no mistake, a hand pointed toward the upstairs office. Robert had been somewhat uneasy at first but James, firmly supported by Anne, had pointed out that the sort of customers likely to deal with a bona-fide ship chandler were not likely to be impressed if expected to join a queue of gossiping women in an oil shop. As an added incentive James had placed firm orders for victualling both the *Charlotte Rhodes* and *Pampero*, opened an account at the bank in the name of the company, and set Robert's mind at rest by depositing a considerable sum against the account. All that was required of Robert was that he should place orders at the keenest prices and, in his capacity of director and officer of the company, settle the bills when they fell due, but not a day before nor a day later. Robert was more than satisfied with the arrangement—Mr Simpson had proved only too eager to supply casks of salted beef and pork at competitive prices and with a generous discount which would not be shown on the company's books. Other suppliers had shown a like alacrity in soliciting Mr Onedin's favour, and a few items—a sack of peas, a sack of lentils, a barrel of flour and a flitch of bacon—had already strayed in the direction of the shop. Not that it was all plain sailing: James was ever a hard man to convince, and that shrew of a wife of his was of an unpleasantly suspicious nature and forever poking and prying at the growing mountain of victuals on the quayside. She had even had the temerity to condemn two of Mr Simpson's casks of pork as unfit for human consumption, complained as to the quality of the flour, insisted that the coffee was short measure and demanded—demanded, mark you!

—that those cursed emigrants' supplies be of fair weight and measure. Really, the woman was impossible! A man could not make an honest living. He was astonished at James's forebearance—any man of spirit would have sent the creature packing long ago. When he once complained of her interfering ways James had simply laughed and made one of his rare jokes: 'You have heard of ship's husbands,' he had said. 'Well, the *Pampero* has a ship's wife!' and had slapped Robert good-naturedly upon the shoulder and walked away shaking with laughter. But it was no laughing matter—the confounded woman already had her nose on the scent of the missing stores. Only an hour since she had erupted into the office waving invoices and delivery notes in the air, and clamouring for an investigation into the missing items. He had promised to look into the matter and she had taken herself off, no doubt to pester someone else with a catalogue of plaints.

In the meantime it was pleasant to swing idly from side to side in the swivel chair and survey his new kingdom. If James had one virtue in this world, he reflected, it was that he was never a man for half measures. He looked at the desk top, bare except for pens, inkwells and a sheaf of telegraph forms. An Officer and Director of a Limited Company deserved better. He would have a blotter and a box of cigars. And a small cabinet to hold refreshments —a bottle of medicinal whisky, perhaps; one or two of Madeira; and rum, of course—ships' captains were known to be fond of a tot during the conduct of business.

For a few minutes Robert swung soporifically in his chair, dreaming of a hazy future peopled with generous shipmasters with empty larders and bottomless purses. Then, bored with his own company, he yawned, stretched and made his way through to the outer office with the intention of casting an all-powerful eye upon the industry of his personal clerk, Mr Tupman.

Mr Oliver Tupman was a putty-faced, stoop-shouldered

man of prematurely greying hair, concave chest and the dispirited eyes of one of life's downtrodden. He was, in fact, the firm's only clerk and came without recommendation or character reference. But with a knowledge of book-keeping and half a lifetime spent in shipping offices he could be an undeniable asset to the company. Furthermore, like any shopworn commodity, his value had long since been marked down, Mr Tupman performing his duties for a modest honorarium of twelve shillings a week with the hint of an increase should his employment prove satisfactory.

For his part Mr Tupman was more than satisfied, quite unable to believe his good fortune. He bent his head even lower and scratched away assiduously as Mr Robert's shadow loomed over him. Mr Robert he had already filed away as the firm's looby, a self-important huffer-and-puffer; it was Mr James, the lean one with the hard eyes, who was the decision-maker and who had hired him on the woman's recommendation. It had been odd, decidedly odd. He had returned home after tramping the streets the day long in the usual fruitless search for work—for who could possibly be expected to employ a man without a character? Aching with tiredness, a yawning hunger in the pit of his stomach, misery in his heart and fearful of again facing wife and children with nothing to offer but the spectre of starvation, he had slowly clambered the stairs to their one-room hovel, now almost bereft of furniture—everything of value had long since been pawned. Wearily pushing open the door he had been greeted by a strange long-nosed, sharp-eyed lady in a poke bonnet who, in a harsh corncrake voice, had peremptorily ordered him to sit down and eat his fill. He had looked past her in disbelief. His three round-eyed children were seated at the scrubbed-top deal table, cheeks bulging with massive slices of bread and cheese. His wife, Doris, was in the act of stirring the contents of a kettle of stew simmering on the grate. His first coherent thought was that the lady must have been sent by one of the charity societies and, although he had always been resentful of the notion of accepting the bounty of others, he had been too hungry for such foolish pride. Between mouthfuls he had listened to the tale of miracle: Doris had long tried to supplement their non-existent income by hawking a tray of tapes and cottons. On a good day she might make a shilling profit, more often than not she would return with fourpence or sixpence, on a bad day nothing at all. She had been making her way to her usual pitch when she had been overcome with the dizziness of hunger and fainted at the feet of the lady. This strange creature, instead of passing by, had packed Doris into a cab, escorted her home and immediately taken charge. In next to no time she had produced a seven pound fresh-baked cottage loaf, a monstrous wedge of cheese, a string of sausages, a piece of bacon, potatoes, peas, lentils, stewing meat and even a sack of coal.

'I understand that you are a shipping clerk by profession, Mr Tupman?' the lady had asked and, seemingly not in the least affected by his dejected admission, pursued the subject no further but simply scribbled a note with instructions to take it around to the offices of the Onedin Line Shipping Company, first thing in the morning. 'Where,' she had stated, 'employment will be found.' Not 'Where you may apply for a situation', but 'Employment *will* be found.' Looking into those sharp grey eyes he had known she was not the sort of lady to make promises lightly. Then she had whisked away and was gone as though she had taken off on a broomstick, and it was only then that they had realised that they had no idea of her name or standing in the firm.

He had presented himself promptly the following morning and nervously tendered the lady's note to his future employer—a tall man of sardonic features and cold blue eyes as hard as pebbles. He had read the note quickly, smiled as though at some private humour, screwed the paper into a ball and tossed it carelessly into a waste-paper basket.

'Twelve shillings a week,' the blue-eyed man said without hesitation.

He had nodded dumbly, glad to take anything. Twelve shillings a week meant the difference between falling into that abyss of poverty out of which few men ever climbed, and the security of a regular income however small.

The tall man had thereupon asked a few pertinent questions directed at ascertaining his familiarity with the business of shipping. Here he was on safe ground describing the only world he knew. The man had seemed satisfied and then asked the question he had been dreading: 'Who were your last employers, Mr Tupman?'

'Callon and Company, sir,' he had answered shakily. To his surprise a secret amusement seemed to well up behind the cold eyes.

'You'll do, Mr Tupman,' he had said. 'You'll do,' and had instructed him quickly and lucidly in his duties.

The work, he decided, would not be too arduous. He had a retentive memory, was quick with figures and wrote a neat hand. Once left alone he had contentedly occupied himself by entering up the brand new company ledgers, checking and cross-checking invoices.

He was in the act of making copies of the *Charlotte Rhodes'* cargo manifest when Mr Robert's shadow fell across his vision . . .

Robert picked up a copy of the *Pampero*'s disbursements account, hemmed and hawed officiously, muttered 'Quite so, quite so,' replaced it on the desk and was about to take his leave when Tupman coughed politely to attract his attention.

'Excuse me, sir.' The clerk pointed to an item on the manifest. 'Is this figure correct, sir?'

'What's the matter with it?' demanded Robert.

'Nothing, sir,' said Tupman hastily. 'Except that the freight for empty casks does seem unusually high?'

'And what the devil business is it of yours?' demanded Robert irritably. Really, these pettifogging clerks with their insufferable know-it-all looks and impertinent questions were beyond belief. Heaven alone knew from which dust heap James had dragged this specimen with his threadbare suit and down-at-heel shoes.

'None whatever, sir.' Tupman bowed his head over his papers, cringing from the wrath to come.

'Very well,' grunted Robert and took a step toward the door. Then he paused. When the *Charlotte Rhodes* returned with a cargo of Braganza's wine free of freight no doubt the man would once again be pestering him with questions. He decided to enlighten the fool.

'The fact is, Tupman, we have an arrangement with Senhor Braganza to ship his full casks free in return for full rates on his empties. Is that clear?' He hoped it was. For his part he had never been able to make head nor tail of the business.

'Yes, indeed, sir. Most clear. Thank you, sir,' said Tupman, grasping the essence of the scheme immediately.

'Then carry on with your work. Idle chatter is not welcomed in this office, Mr Tupman, not welcomed at all.' With which parting enjoinder Robert furrowed his brows with matters of weighty importance and strode from the room.

In spite of the royal 'we' Tupman never for one moment doubted as to who was the true author of the scheme. My word, he thought, but Mr James is a warm one. A warm one indeed. His quick clerk's brain had understood the import instantly. A ship carried merchandise to Portugal. Frequently it returned in ballast—a wasteful commodity, expensive to buy, expensive to load and equally expensive to discharge. But by carrying wine as ballast Mr James had succeeded in killing two birds with one stone. Furthermore he had arranged to return the empty casks at full rate—but, as everyone knew, empty casks once knocked down took up but a fraction of the space taken up by full.

So the *Charlotte Rhodes* would make her outward passage with iron rails, coal and cement with the parcelled staves and hoops atop. Then load with wine as ballast and a deck cargo of corkwood as a bonus for the return passage.

Yes, he decided. He would overcome his weakness and, with luck, remain for the rest of his days with the Onedin Line. It should not be too difficult if he applied himself diligently to his work and resolutely turned his face from temptation. He dipped his pen in the ink and immersed himself in the task of making copies of the *Pampero*'s cargo manifest.

Chapter Ten

The narrow country lane was of hard-packed red sand rutted with the broad tracks of farm wagons. Occasionally the light trap's yellow wheels would jolt over a half-buried stone, but in the main it bowled along at a smart pace, the pony, head high, breath snorting from distended nostrils, seeming to enjoy its excursion into the clean fresh air of the country as much as Robert and Sarah.

Steep banks topped by blackthorn hedgerows temporarily obscured their view of softly rolling Cheshire hills already furrowed into dark red channels ready for the spring sowing. White clouds of scavenging gulls rose and fell at the sound of the bird-scarer's rattles. Smoke curled lazily from the pretty white-washed labourers' cottages.

All in all it was a good day to be alive.

They had hired a pony and trap from Mr Jenkins, crossed the river by way of the cattle ferry, then clopped along the Chester Turnpike as far as Backford Cross where they had asked directions of an ancient chawbacon in straw hat and Sunday smock seated upon a dry-stone wall and sucking at an empty short-stemmed clay pipe. He had pointed the way with a hand as brown and gnarled as an oak branch and in barely comprehensible Cheshire dialect had advised them to bind right at fowr fowk. Sarah translated and at a crossroads they turned right.

Soon Sarah was delightedly recognising once-familiar landmarks. 'Miller's Rise!' she exclaimed as the hedge dipped to give a view of a white-painted windmill with a fan of sails slowly churning the air.

The pony slowed to a panting walk as the lane wound its way up Bracken Hill. At the top Robert drew rein to allow the mare regain her wind.

Bracken Hill was a hump-shouldered mound contained within a higher bowl of hills clothed in broom and bracken. A stream, winking in the sunlight, twisted and turned its way through the miniature valley. Canebrake, aspen and elder, oak and ash crowded its banks while a dozen or so cows with bawling calves trampled the bed to a sticky morass of oozing mud. A clown-like magpie flew clumsily overhead to rouse an outraged rabble of hard-swearing rooks. To their right a thatched cottage of rough hewn sandstone with a lean-to byre clung to the side of the hill, with a winding footpath leading to a bridge of stepping stones across the stream below.

Sarah clutched Robert's arm excitedly. 'Look!' she exclaimed. 'Our cottage!'

Robert understood her meaning. 'Our' cottage was her birthplace. Sarah, with not too strict a regard for the truth, often laid claim to come from good farming stock, and—by implication—that her forebears were somewhat grander than plain tillers of the soil. 'When I first met Robert,' she was wont to say, looking down her nose at less-fortunate city dwellers, 'we farmed a couple of hundred acres.' Then, sighing romantically: 'It was love at first sight. I often imagine that Cupid must have been lurking in the branches of that old oak at the foot of our garden.'

Robert let the reins hang limply in his hands as his vision swirled into the past. His father had packed him off on an errand to Chester and the cob was plodding its way home when he came across a tear-stained, bare-legged, mud-bespattered waif weeping at the side of the road. It was Sarah, seventeen years of age, a scrawny, tangle-haired, half-wild creature, mewling with self-pity. She wore a dirt-caked smock and when he went to her assistance he discovered that a midden-like aroma hung about her, an unpleasant effluvia redolent of rotting compost and manure heaps. She had, in fact, been driving pigs to market when a herd of cattle moving in the opposite direction had scattered her charges far and wide, and to add to her woes she had not only twisted an ankle but a sharp pebble had also incised a gash in the sole of her foot. Robert had clucked sympathy, bandaged her foot with his clean linen handkerchief, marshalled her porkers and then, he walking, she riding, had accompanied her to the local market. Later she had washed face and legs at the village pump and joined him for a repast of bread and cheese and a pot of ale. He had been enchanted with her chatter and arranged to meet her again. And again and again and again . . .

The dream faded.

'Yoo-hoo!' called a voice, and there was Kate hurrying down the path to meet them. He jerked the reins and the pony obediently ambled forward until they reached the point where the footpath crossed the track. Robert drew to a halt.

'Well, Kate?' he said.

'My,' said Kate. 'You do look grand.'

Sarah looked down condescendingly at her sister-in-law.

'We thought to take a turn in the country for a breath of fresh air and escape from the demands of business. Then, at the very last moment, dear Robert suggested we pay you a surprise visit. I do hope it is not inconvenient?' she added sweetly.

'God love us all, but you'm allus welcome, Sarah, that you well know; although us have little to offer in the way of cheer.'

Robert clambered down and fished out a large wicker hamper from the trap. 'We brought a bite or two. Just a picnic luncheon. A light repast, which I think we shall take . . . over there.' He pointed to a tall sycamore of wide-spreading branches.

'How is Father?' asked Sarah politely.

Kate shrugged. 'He wor took off with the screws. Us buried un last winter. It was a mercy for one and all.'

'I had no idea,' said Sarah. 'Poor man. Poor dear man.'

'Us'd have wrote, but Jeremy he couldn't afford the price of stamp and paper. Things is hard, Sarah, very hard.'

Sarah clutched her skirts and stepped delicately from the trap. 'I know, I know.' She nodded with the solemnity of one who once shared a common heritage. 'The agricultural walk of life was never one of idleness . . .'

'It's brutish,' said Kate shortly. She turned her head. 'Ask Jeremy.'

'Ask Jeremy, what?' demanded a voice, and to Sarah's annoyance she found her best Sunday garments crushed in a bear-like, rib-crushing hug from that great gangling oaf, her brother. He swung her off the ground, the hard stubble of his chin rasping her complexion as he danced her around like a nursery doll.

'Put me down, you loon!' she gasped and he obediently set her feet firmly upon the earth once again and grinned an inane gap-toothed grin, his yokel face and yokel eyes beaming delight.

'By the bones,' he roared. 'If our Sarah hasn't turned into as pretty a little hen-wife as never was! City life suits you, Sis. Better'n mucking out styes, hey?' and he slapped his great horny hands against leather breeches shiny with grease, and capered like a mountebank.

Sarah straightened her dress and began to wish she had not persuaded Robert to make the journey. But it had truly been years and years since she had last set eyes on her family and it had seemed a brilliant inspiration at the time. Now, looking at Kate with her patched Sunday smock hanging loosely from a bone-sharp thin frame, the too-brilliant eyes and unhealthy skin pallor bespeaking hunger, she was not so sure.

A cloud drifted across the sun and a chill trembled on the air. Sarah shivered and the exuberance of the outing turned in a sudden to a sense of melancholy. She remembered all too vividly the bone-aching drudgery of fieldwork, the cramped muscles and the mind dulled and stupefied with day-long remorseless labour, the whimpering cold of rainlashed winters, the long trudge to work at sunrise, and the weary pilgrimage back to the cottage and a supper of potatoes and cabbage. It had been a mistake to come, she realised. They must make their farewells as quickly as possible and escape from this vexatious abode of irksome memories.

But Jeremy was already helping Robert to unharness the pony. 'Take Sarah up home,' he called to Kate. 'Make un welcome, now.'

So Sarah unhappily trailed after Kate to the cottage. The path was steeper than she remembered and by the time they reached the sagging door she was quite out of breath. She paused, wondering how she had ever managed yoked to two pails of water all those years ago, then Kate was ushering her inside.

The single room was even worse than she remembered. A dirt floor of hard-packed clay. The barest necessities —a rough hewn table, chairs cobbled together from peeled branches, a bed in one corner, a heap of rags in another. A wood ash fire slumbering in the grate. Sacking covering paneless windows. An absence of ornament of any kind. The heap of rags heaved and a child's head poked out. Red-rimmed rat-eyes peered mistrustfully at the newcomer.

'It's your Aunt Sarah, Jenny,' said Kate. 'Come on a visit.'

Jenny wriggled from beneath the mound and stood up,

rubbing sleep from her eyes and gaping idiotically at the visitor. She had an oversize elfin head perched upon a thin parchment-covered skeleton. Hair and pinafore were covered in straw. Her mother walked across and dusted her down. 'Us had five,' she said indifferently. 'T'others was weaklings.'

Sarah felt sick. In her father's day hardship had been their daily lot but made bearable by the knowledge that there would be a tomorrow. You would survive. But this —this was soul-crushing starvation at its lowest level. She wanted to turn and run, back to the security of the shop, the warmth of their hearth; but at that moment Jeremy and Robert stumped in kicking clay from their boots.

Once there had been an old dresser with a few cracked plates. A clock. A bellows that always hung by the fire-place. Pewter tankards. Rush mats on the floor. She stared at Jeremy. 'What happened?'

Jeremy shrugged. 'No work. Old story. Rents up. Wages down. Then the master enclosed. It wor bound to come.'

'A week or two back the pig caught fever and died on us,' Kate added.

'And wi' it went the cost o' fattening. Left us wi' a mound of debt. No work—no credit. No future.' Jeremy's shoulders slumped hopelessly. 'We has nothing. Us is finished.'

Robert stood blinking in the dim half-light. 'What will you do?' he asked.

'Take to the road,' said Jeremy despondently. 'Head for Liverpool, I reckon. They say there's work o' sorts in the towns. There's naught in the country. Take a hare or a rabbit and you're clapped in jail.'

Liverpool! thought Sarah. Oh, no you won't! She had a foreboding of a dreadful future with Jeremy and his family clinging like leeches and eating like locusts. There was little work in the towns for the Jeremys of this world when all they had to offer was their labour. But they were family and therefore could not be turned away from one's own doorstep. She wished, oh, she wished they had never come!

She was searching for a solution when Robert harrumphed, dumped the picnic basket upon the table and announced determinedly: 'We came for a picnic, and a picnic we shall have.'

He unfastened the straps, opened the lid and, like some top-hatted god of plenty, produced a cornucopia of good things. A veal-and-ham pie, a roast chicken, a round of cheese, half a dozen hard-boiled eggs, a dozen of Sarah's home-baked scones, a pot of butter and a couple of bottles of wine.

Jeremy stared in disbelief, found his voice at last. 'Enough to feed an army—and you folks call it picnicking.' He tried to smile but his voice shook. 'By the bones, but you've come up in the world, that you have, Robert.'

'Oh, I haven't done too badly,' said Robert, smugly. He tore a leg from the chicken and passed it to Jenny with the kindly admonition: 'Take care not to swallow the bones, child.' Then added gruffly. 'For heaven's sake sit down and eat, you two.' He busied himself uncorking a bottle while Sarah hacked into the loaf and watched her carefully prepared picnic disappearing down gluttonous throats.

'Robert holds a most important position in the world of commerce,' she announced conversationally.

'Oh, aye?' questioned Jeremy, mouth full.

'A director of a Shipping Company. Limited,' she added importantly.

'Well,' said Robert, modestly. 'In a small way of business.'

'Nonsense,' said Sarah. 'My husband is of far too retiring a disposition. He is a Principal Director.' She spelt it out in approbatory capitals.

Jeremy washed down a hunk of bread with a gulp of wine. He wiped his mouth with the back of his hand. 'Where do these ships travel?' he asked.

'Anywhere they may show profit,' said Robert, uncorking the second bottle.

Sarah sipped from her glass with ladylike delicacy and recollected the *Pampero*'s purpose. 'Have you ever given thought to the prospect of emigrating, Jeremy?' She dropped the question like a stone into a pool and waited for the ripples to widen.

'Us have thought about little else these past twelve month,' said Jeremy. 'But voyaging costs money.'

'Five pound a head,' Robert told him. He topped up his own glass and leaned across the table to slop more wine into Jeremy's and Kate's tin cups.

'Five pounds!' Jeremy drained his cup and held it out for more. 'I've never owned five pounds in the whole of my life.'

'Perhaps,' said Sarah, carefully, 'Robert may be able to help you there. I am sure—if you really do have it in mind to emigrate—that Robert could use his influence. After all, he is a Director of the Company.' She adjusted the starched frills of her blouse and smiled an all-embracing smile of confident assurance.

Robert saw his small store of sovereigns dwindle as he calculated swiftly. Five pounds a head. Add to that sum the cost of the provisions for the voyage. Pots, pans and kettles. He wouldn't get out under twenty-five pounds. What on earth was Sarah thinking of! He caught her eye.

'I'll see what I can do,' he said, weakly.

Webster hunted through the cottage parlour, grunting annoyance, picking up and putting down cushions. Anne sighed and laid aside her sewing.

'What is it, Father?'

'My spectacles,' growled the old man. He glared accusation at the world at large. 'They've been hid from me.'

'Nonsense, Father.' She rose and took the wire-framed spectacles from the mantelshelf. 'Here they are.'

He took them, grumbling, and plumped himsclf into his favourite fireside chair, shaking out the pages of his copy of *The Illustrated London News.*

Anne returned to her placid sewing. The old man was becoming more childish than ever, she thought, biting off the end of a strand of cotton. But in other ways he had improved beyond measure. He now shaved daily and dressed neatly. True, he still drank far too much, but no longer with the desperation of failure. Nothing corroded a man so much as failure. Failure ate a man alive. Nevertheless a secure home, a shilling or two for his pocket, had erased many of the worry-lines from the corners of his eyes. He could hold up his head in the knowledge that he now owed no man a penny piece and could take his rightful place at the corner table of his favourite tavern, standing his turn for a dram with cronies in similar straits to himself. But his hatred for James never diminished. The unreasoning hatred of the weak for the strong. Poor James, she thought, everyone seemed to cling to his coat-tails so that every step he took up the ladder of fortune increased the burden. She smiled wryly to herself at the notion of anyone pitying James. And yet the metaphor suited him. James did tend to see life as a series of ladders to be climbed.

The old man huffed from behind his paper. 'Not the only thing that is being kept from me in this house.'

Anne threaded a button. 'And what might that mean?'

His watery eyes swam behind the heavy lenses. 'Storm clouds brewing is what I mean. I know the signs. Everyone hauling their wind and running for shelter. It'll be that son-in-law of mine that's at the bottom of it, mark my words,' he added darkly and cryptically.

'Rubbish, Father,' she snapped. 'James is solely concerned with business, nothing else.'

'Aye, he's a tradesman's talent for turning a penny,

I'll grant him that,' he grunted and rustled the paper angrily.

'The talent that you are so eager to condemn,' she reminded him sharply, 'has kept us from the poorhouse and brought you a little comfort for your old age.'

The old man snorted. 'It was a bargain—as you so often keep reminding me. Taking ship and daughter . . .'

She cut him short, tired of his tantrums. 'A bargain which James has more than kept. You have a few shillings for your pocket . . .'

'From you,' he interrupted. 'Not from him. From your purse, Daughter, your purse.'

'James's money,' she countered tartly.

'That rascal would not give the time of day without asking ten per cent in return.' His face was beginning to empurple. She laid aside her sewing again and tried to speak evenly.

'We have no debts, a full larder. You have clean linen and a good suit to your back. What more do you want?'

'Grandsons,' he answered unexpectedly. 'What use is a house without children?'

Anne lowered her head, abashed and embarrassed. A flush spread across her features. The old man had touched unerringly upon a tender spot. She knew James hoped for a son and she felt a sense of near-disloyalty at not having provided him with one. Not that he was at all accusatory—on the contrary sometimes she wondered if he ever noticed the omission. Of course, she reasoned, that was one of the less pleasant aspects of marriage which each, by mutual unspoken consent, tended to avoid. But a son he wanted, and a son she was determined he should have.

James chose that moment to march in looking as pleased as a cat that had been at the cream.

The old man hoisted himself to his feet. 'I'm off for me constitutional,' he announced gruffly, scowling at the intruder.

James grinned, bowed him to the door, then in a

moment of unwonted generosity, dipped into his pocket and pressed a golden guinea into Webster's hand. 'Drink my health,' he said.

The old man glowered at the coin, then flung it to the floor. 'Keep yer damn' charity,' he snarled and stumped out.

James looked toward Anne who shrugged. 'He's hopeless,' she said. He bent and picked up the coin, flipping it in the air, then passed it to her. 'He'll accept it from you,' he said lightly, and dropped in to the recently vacated chair, thrusting out his long legs toward the fire. He clasped his hands behind his head and announced his news: 'I've just chartered the *Pampero*.'

A frown of puzzlement puckered her brow. 'The *Pampero*? I thought . . . ?'

He beamed like a schoolboy presenting an exercise for approval. 'She's on charter to the Onedin Line.'

She shook her head. 'I don't understand.'

He grinned at her. 'You will when the profits come in,' he said. 'And so will Robert.'

She gave up. James seemed able to steer his way through the mysterious waters of finance as confidently as he took a ship across the oceans of the world. She bent her head over her sewing once again, content in the knowledge that James had their future well under control.

The emigrants buzzed around the Medical Officers' Office like a swarm of bees.

Robert officiously hustled his protégés to the head of the queue. The buzz rose to an angry hum.

'Perhaps we should wait our turn?' Jeremy suggested in alarm.

'Nonsense,' replied Robert. 'First aboard get the better berths. I have used my influence to get you this far, I see no reason why you should not continue to avail yourself of my good offices. It is the least I can do,' he added, hoping he could bustle through the formalities and smuggle them aboard before James's sharp eye should fall upon his efforts.

A burly Irishman of pugnacious aspect looked for a moment as though he was about to protest at this usurpation of his hard-won place, then in the face of pompous top-hatted and frock-coated authority thought the better of it.

'You know what to do,' Robert instructed them. 'Present your tickets, stick out your tongues and show your hands, then leave by the other door where I shall be waiting.'

Jeremy nodded and moved forward a pace.

The emigrants had been herded behind barriers leading directly to the medical office and separating them from the ship. Their baggage had been delivered by Mr Jenkins and now lay in a mountainous confusion of boxes, baskets, hampers, pots, pans and kettles guarded by an assortment of evil-looking porters who would resolutely refuse to relinquish their charges until the victims had disgorged at least a shilling a parcel.

Robert made his way to where Jeremy's few belongings had been placed in a separate heap. One of Mr Miles's runners respectfully opened the barrier for him and Robert took up his stance beside a shifty-eyed ruffian who had evidently selected Jeremy's baggage as his personal prey. So much the worse for him, thought Robert sourly, and occupied himself once again in calculating the cost. The passage money he had put through the company's books but Mr Miles had insisted upon receiving the pound a head service charge he added to each ticket. Then there were the provisions and the usual travelling necessities plus warm cloaks for Kate and Jenny and an overcoat for Jeremy, all obtained after a deal of unseemly haggling from Groter's Marine Store. All in all he reckoned himself almost ten pounds out of pocket. But at least he had saved fifteen pounds passage money. He looked uneasily toward the *Pampero*. Baines was busily bawling incomprehensible orders to the seamen, James seemed to be fully occupied attending to the last details of cargo stowage, and Mr Tupman had taken up position near the gangway where he could check the number of emigrants against his passenger list.

The two doctors worked in shirtsleeves, chanting hoarsely: 'Ticket. Put out your tongue. Show your hands,' as the emigrants slowly shuffled past the counter. Each doctor stamped the ticket, glanced unseeingly at the stinking piece of human flotsam passing before him, waved them on, called: 'Next. Ticket. Put out your tongue. Show your hands.' They had no time to waste with three hundred emigrants to pass at a fee of two pence a head between ten in the morning and high tide at two o'clock. Then the medical inspection would deal with a later sailing and repeat the procedure. They were tired, red-eyed and irritable and, Jeremy noticed as his turn came, smelled strongly of intoxicating liquor

He shepherded Jenny and Kate before him, only half aware of the Irishman pushing and trampling at his heels. His head was still in a whirl at the rush of events. He'd been to Chester near three years back and she were a fair-sized town that took a man's breath away; but this Liverpool . . . ! Acres of stone houses and cobbled streets and a great flood of a river—and people! He had never thought to see so many people congregated in one place in his whole life. Left to himself he was certain sure he would have remained rooted to the same spot throughout eternity—how in heaven's name did a man venture to cross a road? With a tide of horses and carts and carriages and pairs all going every which way it was more than a life was worth. But Robert seemed to find his way around as comfortable as you like. He'd say one thing for Robert, and challenge any man to deny it—he was a regular harness-horse, all heave and push. Why, they'd barely had time for a shake of the hand before being fitted out with all manner of goods and chattels and hurried away to a lodging-house where Robert had said they would be very comfortable. He had crossed his fingers to ward off the Evil One at the sight of Mr Miles with his squint eye and hump back; then he had been separated from Kate and Jenny and spent the night in a dormitory packed as tight as kippers in a box with a sour-smelling rabble of heathen Irish as dazed and lost as himself.

'Ticket. Stick out your tongue. Show your hands,' intoned the first doctor. As they pushed their tickets across the second doctor dealt with Kate and Jenny. Jeremy raised his eyes and caught sight of a large notice pinned to the wall opposite. 'NOTICE TO EMIGRANTS' it read. 'BEWARE of CHOLERA. SMALLPOX. SHIP FEVERS. Emigrants should provide themselves with warm clothing, soap, and solid and wholesome food. Both clothes and person should be clean before embarking, and kept so during the voyage. It is desirable that emigrants should not go in a ship that is too much crowded, nor one that is not provided with a Medical Man.'

'Move along,' snapped the doctor, testily. 'Next. Ticket. Put out your tongue. Show your hands.'

He followed Kate and Jenny through the exit door and found himself in the blinding light of the day with a surge of porters gripping his arms, plucking at his sleeves and demanding that he should choose his baggage. Then mercifully Robert appeared and guided them to their separate pile of luggage. He reached for his box but the porter snarled, shoved him rudely away and hoisted the box upon his shoulder. Robert, however—that pillar of strength—was, as ever, equal to the occasion. He beckoned to one of Mr Miles's runners, a man called Gruber, armed with a cudgel, a man who—Jeremy had already noticed—seemed to act as Mr Miles's gaffer. Gruber calmly took the box and just as calmly back-handed the porter across the face.

'Mr Miles's pers'nal effecks,' he pronounced, spat a

stream of tobacco juice at the porter's feet and escorted them to the ship.

At the gangway Robert bid a hasty goodbye, wished them a safe voyage, advised them to go below and select suitable berths as quickly as possible, rather shamefacedly pressed a sovereign into Jeremy's palm, then strode away purposefully.

They watched him skirt a crowd of quarrelling porters and Irishers fighting over possession of kit-bags and chests and make his way to the dock gate. Then they showed their stamped tickets to a clerk at the gangway and made their way aboard.

The wooden deck felt strange to their landsmen's feet but they were given little opportunity to linger and wonder at the strange world of ropes and masts and swarthy seamen with the look and confidence of gypsies. A lean cold-eyed man in top hat and frock coat stood upon a railed enclosure above them. He cupped his hands and called ashore. 'Move 'em along. Move 'em along!' Then a couple of barefooted seamen pattered up and hustled them, bag and baggage, to an opening with a ladder leading below to a cavern as dark and noisome as a cellar.

At the foot of the ladder they paused to stare around in dismay. A few lanthorns suspended from the great oaken rafters of the ship's beams threw out a sickly yellow light. Jeremy squinted into the darkness and took a pace forward. In a moment or two his eyes adjusted to the gloom. Tiers of shelves ran away into the darkness, each tier separated from its fellows by a three-feet-wide alleyway. He took another step forward and bumped his head against one of the beams. He could hear a murmur of voices from other shadowy groups moving about seeking their promised berths. A baby's wail cut the air and echoed and re-echoed throughout the length of the hold. He and Kate looked at each other, fear in their eyes. This—this surely could not be true? Not their home for—? How long did Robert say? Six weeks? Jeremy reached out and touched one of the shelves. It must be one of their sleeping places. It was of unplaned timber, about three feet wide and six in length. This must be some sort of dormitory. But where then was their accommodation?

The square of light from the hatchway above their heads momentarily darkened and one of the sailors dropped lightly to his feet and stood grinning at them.

'Pick your berth,' he said. 'Take my tip. Choose a lower berth amidships, not too near the hatch. Stow your dunnage beneath.' He trotted off into the darkness and they followed dragging box and bundles with them. The seaman paused and experimentally shook a pair of the supporting stanchions, tested the plank as though it was a feather mattress.

'That should suit the Queen herself. You'll be snug as bugs in a rug.'

'My wife and child?' hazarded Jeremy. 'Where do they sleep?' The man laughed. 'Where does your missus usually lie? With you, bucko, with you. You're one of the lucky ones. Your ticket entitles you to a bunk to yourselves. Most of 'em only has a quarter share.' He laid a finger to his nose. 'Now I'll tell you the manner in which to make yourselves comfortable. Speak to the sailmaker and for five shillings he'll let you have two of the neatest pieces of canvas you ever did see. Curting for privacy, if you follow? Then if one of you nips ashore you'll pick up a nice donkey's breakfast for half a crown. Unless you'd care for me to render the service for you?' He rubbed forefinger and thumb together in the age-old gesture.

Jeremy clutched the sovereign in his pocket and shook his head. It was all they had. The seaman looked disappointed.

'Wait,' said Kate. She fumbled in the pocket of her skirt and held out a halfcrown and a sixpence. 'Sixpence for your trouble,' she told him, adding firmly. 'On your return.'

The man spat on the coin, touched a forelock and rolled away.

'Where did you get the money?' Jeremy asked her.

'From Sarah. Four halfcrowns for my purse and sixpence for Jenny. Sarah has been very kind, Jeremy. Very kind.'

Jeremy sat wearily on their box He put his head in his hands.

'Very kind,' he said. 'Very kind.'

Mr Tupman rose respectfully to his feet as James and Anne entered the office.

'Everything in order, Mr Tupman?' queried James.

'Yes, sir,' replied Tupman. He shuffled the ship's papers together and handed them to his employer. 'Clearance papers. Cargo manifest. Passenger list. A copy of the time sheet and laytime statement for yourself, as requested, sir.'

'Thank you,' said James. He glanced quickly through the neatly drawn documents. They seemed in perfect order and yet Tupman had a distinct air of unease about him. There were minute beads of perspiration upon his forehead and his hand had trembled as he passed over the papers.

'Is Mr Robert in?' asked Anne.

'Yes, Mrs Onedin. In the private office, I believe.'

'Thank you, Mr Tupman.' She treated him to a friendly smile. 'I will just make my farewells.'

James had re-immersed himself in the papers. 'We sail in half an hour, remember,' he warned.

'Not without the Captain, I trust,' said Anne, and made her way through to Robert's office.

'Everything seems to be in order, Mr Tupman,' said James slowly.

Tupman wilted before the bleak gaze. He wrung his hands. 'There—there is just one small item, sir.' He gulped and then, like a man abandoning all hope, presented his account books. 'It's the accounts, sir. They—they don't quite balance.'

'There is no "not quite" about it. You know better than that, Mr Tupman. Accounts either balance, or they do not. Show me.'

Tupman ran a shaking finger down the register. 'The error is in the passenger accounts, sir. I have checked and re-checked, but three fares are unaccounted for.' He took out his handkerchief and mopped his face.

So that's it, thought James. He imagines he will be held responsible for the discrepancy. There are two hundred and ninety-seven names. He ran a finger down the columns, then paused at an entry. 'This is not your handwriting, Mr Tupman?' There was no need to ask. He recognised Robert's looping scrawl instantly.

Tupman shook his head miserably and James understood the wretch's dilemma. One partner apparently swindling the other, with the unfortunate clerk caught in between.

'Have no fear, Mr Tupman,' he told him. 'I will deal with this.' He tucked the register beneath his arm and marched purposefully through to the inner office.

Robert, seated at the desk, broke off his conversation with Anne as James walked in, head thrust forward like a questing heron. James dumped the account book on the desk and jabbed a finger at three inscribed names.

'Friends of yours?' he asked caustically.

'Oh, that?' said Robert. 'Ah yes, to be sure. The Stirlings. Sarah's brother, you know. Married Kate—er—something-or-other. Jenny is their daughter.' He stared owlishly at James as though considering this tarradiddle to be explanation enough.

'Really?' said James. 'And since when have I undertaken to ship your poor relations free of charge?'

Robert licked his lips. 'They're family.'

'And what of it?'

'Articles of Association,' gabbled Robert suddenly and rapidly.

James stared at the idiot. 'What . . . ?'

Robert hauled open a desk drawer and fished out a much-thumbed copy of the Company Charter. He leafed over a page or two and pointed to a paragraph. 'It's all here in black and white.' He cleared his throat and read aloud as though giving evidence before a wigged judge: ' "Directors and Officers of the Company, their wives and families, shall be entitled to travel free of all charges on vessels, owned by, or chartered by, the Company." Jeremy is family.'

An explosive, hastily suppressed, splutter of laughter burst from Anne's lips.

James glowered. 'It was never intended that any Tom, Dick or Harry with the remotest of claims to kinship should demand free transport and accommodation.'

Anne grinned wickedly at his discomfiture. 'It means precisely what it says. You should read the small print, James. Robert has outsmarted you.'

'In black and white,' Robert reiterated firmly, heartened by the support of an unexpected ally. 'You inserted the clause yourself.'

'I know, I know,' James grumbled. He stood up, admitting defeat. 'I only hope,' he added acidly, 'that you will pay equal attention to detail whilst I am away. The business will not run itself. The *Charlotte Rhodes* will return and . . .'

'Yes, yes, yes.' Robert groaned wearily. 'You've told me a hundred times.'

'Goodbye, Robert,' said Anne. 'My regards to Sarah. Come, James, time is running short.'

'Hrmph,' said James and took his leave.

Robert watched them go, then a smile wreathed his face. It was hard to believe, but he had actually bettered James at his own game. He picked up the register and walked through to the outer office.

Placing the account book on Tupman's desk he said expansively. 'Everything ship-shape and Bristol fashion, Mr Tupman. You've done well, very well, indeed.'

Tupman stared after his departing back. Mr Robert seemed in an uncommon good humour. He breathed a sigh of relief and returned to his work. His job was safe; and what was more he had not touched a drop of spirits since his new employment. Nor would he again. Ever. His nature puzzled him. Others could take a dram or two and be none the worse, but the very taste of alcohol seized him by the throat like a demon and he could no more stop until he had spent every penny and pawned everything he possessed than he could prevent himself breathing. As counterpoint to his resolution he heard a chink of glass and gurgle of liquid as Robert, in the privacy of the inner office, poured himself a celebratory glass of medicinal whisky.

The *Pampero* sailed promptly at two o'clock, her decks crowded with emigrants.

Frazer stood at the window watching the tugs haul her out into midstream. He remembered her now—a white ship with a gold figurehead coming about smartly, sails aback, disdainfully refraining from dropping her anchors as she waited for the tug. He had recognised her then as of Yankee origin, but had never for one moment suspected her to be James Onedin's latest acquisition. Well, Onedin had also cleared his debt in the nearest nick of time and saved the *Charlotte Rhodes* from auction.

An oily calm lay over a Mersey ruffled only by the merest catspaws of wind. There was a splash in the water as the tug cast loose. The *Pampero*'s topsails filled and the blue and white Onedin houseflag drooping at the mast-head suddenly opened and fluttered in the breeze.

Frazer continued to watch musingly, his shipbuilder's eye attracted by the *Pampero*'s trim lines as she slid through the buoyed channel, heading for the open sea, but with part of his mind occupied with other problems. There seemed to be a coolness between Albert and his pretty young wife. A pity. A great pity. He found he rather liked the girl. She had determination and spirit unless he was much mistaken. And of course circumstances had changed. She was no longer only a tradesman's daughter but now sister to a shipowner. Moreover one who was bound to make his mark upon the world. He sighed and turned away from the window.

'He don't let the grass grow under his feet, eh, George?'

'He's a fool,' replied Callon. 'A man cannot be in two places at once. You run a shipping business from an office, not from the deck of a ship at the other side of the world.'

'He'll learn,' said Frazer.

'Aye,' answered Callon. 'He'll learn.' He chewed on the end of his cigar. 'And I'm the man to teach him the lesson, by God!'

Chapter Eleven

There were eighty bunks to be shared between three hundred people packed like herrings in a wooden cellar seventy feet long, thirty-four feet wide, six feet six inches high, discounting deck beams and ribs. The air was foetid. Hot and stuffy, thick with the sour stench of unwashed bodies. Rats squeaked and scuttled in the darkness scavenging for crumbs and droppings. Word quickly spread that the captain would pay sixpence a head for every rat killed or captured and Jeremy soon found himself hunting with the rest.

But first he had to adapt to shipboard life.

The seaman had been as good as his word and brought them the donkey's breakfast—a mattress of coarse sacking filled with straw and at half a crown an exorbitant price. They decided canvas screens to be a luxury they could ill-afford and therefore did not avail themselves of the offer of the sailmaker's services. In the event just as well for they soon realised that there was as little privacy below decks as in a madhouse. To make your way along one of the narrow alleyways between bunks was an adventure in itself, negotiating a litter of bags and boxes, kettles and pans and jealously guarded private stores of potatoes, apples, flour and oatmeal; to be stopped at intervals by a baby in convulsions, an hysterical female passenger or, at worst, a drunken quarrel between a group of men. The companion hatches were at either end, the circulation of air aided in fine weather by the introduction of windsails, a form of ventilator which quickly became known to the passengers as 'elephants' or 'elephants' ears' from their trunk-like structure of long grey snout poking down into the hold and a pair of wide triangular flaps held wide to capture the breeze. From the first they needed all the air they could get. Even before reaching the Bar, with the ship merely pitching slightly in the long greasy swell rolling in ponderously from the Irish Sea, a few unfortunates had taken to their bunks and given way to the onset of seasickness.

'Find your sea legs as quickly as you can,' Robert had advised, so at the first opportunity Jeremy took Kate and Jenny up on to deck with the intention of accommodating themselves to this strange new world.

'Walk briskly up and down,' Robert had told them.

'By this means,' Sarah had added, 'you will rapidly accustom yourselves to the movements of the vessel and thus speedily gain ascendency over the rigours of mal-de-mer.'

The advice was no doubt well-meant, but they found the decks crowded with gaping emigrants and cursing sailors, and without sufficient room to swing a cat much less take a walk. Many of the bolder spirits had found their way to the raised forecastle at the bows to lean over the side fascinated by the foaming water. Then there would be a sudden stampede away from the rail as, amid shouts of laughter from the men and squeals of simulated dismay from the women, fountains of spray rose high in the air to drench all with a shower of spindrift.

Liverpool was a huddled sprawl of buildings lying astern. The land slowly glided past on either side. To their right was a desert of sand dunes, to their left the stubby fort of Perch Rock. Ahead lay a wilderness of water and a sky flaming red. Then the ship crossed the Bar and the chop of the sea became more pronounced. The group on the fo'c'sle head began to drift away as the once playful spray now stung like an icy lash.

Jeremy staggered and clutched at a rope hanging nearby as the deck suddenly seemed to slope away from him. He spun awkwardly hitting his ribs against the ship-side. He grinned uncertainly at Kate and pushed himself away. The deck rose to meet him and for a moment it was like climbing a hill. Then it fell away again and he had a sense of walking on air. He saw the other emigrants slipping and falling and clumsily bumping into each other. Jenny burst into tears and clutched her mother's skirts.

'T'is all right, my poppet,' he comforted her. 'There's naught to fear.' But it was, he thought, the strangest damn' sensation he'd ever known. He turned his head and looked out across the water. The sea was no longer flat but broken into long waves rolling endlessly toward them. He fixed his gaze upon one roller higher than the rest. It seemed to gather speed and height as it approached. For a moment he stood petrified believing that it would sweep the vessel and they would drown like rats. He wanted to shout for the captain, for somebody, to warn them of the danger. Then the shipside rose and the wave had gone to be replaced by another and yet another. And each time the ship rose and fell, rose and fell and not one single drop of the water came aboard. He leaned over the side in an effort to see where the next wave went. His feet promptly left the deck as the ship slid into the trough and had it not been for Kate desperately clutching his coat-tails he would have disappeared for ever. Regaining his balance he looked across to the opposite side of the ship and saw the waves running away. He reasoned it out slowly: the ship floated on water; it was built of timber, and wood as everyone knew would not sink.

He looked out again at the darkening sea. If this was the famed Atlantic, they would survive. Satisfied with his conclusions he looked for the last time at the disappearing shores of England then resolutely conducted Kate and Jenny below.

Daniel Fogarty, feeling desperately uncomfortable in formal evening attire of cutaway coat and high stiff collar threatening to slice off his ears at every turn of the head, chewed stolidly upon his boiled mutton with caper sauce and allowed the conversational politenesses to flow past while he pondered over the implications of Callon's unexpected invitation. His employer, he knew from experience, was not the sort of man to invite an underling to dine in the privacy of his home simply out of an avuncular pleasure at his company. There must be some underlying motive, but for the life of him Daniel could not begin to fathom the why or the wherefore.

He cast a glance around the table. Mr Callon sat as of right at the head, plying knife and fork with excellent appetite and looking the picture of comfort in soft shirt and braided velvet jacket. Conversation was desultory and emanated chiefly from Callon himself who seemed to be at his most jovial. It was a small dinner party and Daniel's fellow guests seemed to be chosen at random as though plucked from a lucky bran tub. There was a nephew of sorts, a sandy-haired, sand-faced young man of protruding teeth and pony-like whinny, who, Daniel had gathered over a pre-dinner stomach-crisper of brandy and water, was in way of being a dealer of grain, flour and feedstuffs. Next came the young man's wife, a thin-chested lady of sallow complexion, a hairy mole on the side of her face, and over-dressed in a most unbecoming gown of magenta-coloured material. Then there was an unattached man of about Daniel's age, of pop-eyes and large cavalry moustaches which he twirled affectionately every few moments to a chorus of self-satisfied honks and grunts. He also had a monocle which he occasionally screwed into his eye with the sole intent, it seemed, of glaring displeasure in Daniel's direction. He styled himself as a Captain Bredin of the Liverpool Volunteers and haw-hawed and ho-hummed throughout the meal, reserving the haw-haws for Miss Emma Callon and the ho-hums for Daniel. Miss Callon, as hostess, naturally occupied the seat at the opposite end of the table to her father, with Daniel to her left and Captain Bredin to her right, leaving Daniel's sole remaining dinner companion a mountainous young lady whose name he had been unable to catch and who uttered never a word but contented herself with chomping her way through every dish placed before her.

He stole a glance toward Miss Emma and thought she looked singularly attractive in a cold, rather distant way. Her hair was as black as jet and of silken softness, parted in the centre and drawn smoothly across the brow to be held in a lace chignon at the nape of her aristocratic neck. Her unblemished skin had an almost transparent quality, a faint dusky pallor stretched over delicate bones. She wore a fashionably low-cut gown of bunched layers of tulle embroidered with a motif of entwined primroses, violets and forget-me-nots.

Her eyes were fixed upon her plate and she seemed to be paying the gravest attention to Captain Bredin's exposition of the American Civil War with particular attention to the manner in which he, Captain Bredin, if given command, would bring the business to a speedy and successful conclusion. The gallant captain made encircling motions with his fork, surrounding vast armies and sacking cities by the dozen.

Miss Emma raised her eyes for a moment and caught Daniel's direct gaze. A damask flush spread over her cheeks and Daniel hastily looked away, but not before he thought he caught a glimpse of a sympathetic smile touching the corners of her mouth, then she lowered her head again and pecked daintily at the food on her plate.

He silently cursed himself for an ill-mannered boor and tried to concentrate upon Captain Bredin's military exercises. That young man, warming to his work, swept troops of dragoons across the tablecloth and in a series of brilliant outflanking movements drove the opposing army into the sea.

Miss Emma pushed away her plate and, cutting across the Captain's discourse, politely inquired of Daniel if he had quite settled into his new position?

'Ah, yes, indeed. Thank you, Miss Callon. I believe so. Thank you, yes,' he found himself stuttering, and wondered why women invariably reduced him to a stammering tongue-tied fool.

'The *Barracuda* was your last command, was it not?' she asked in that cool patrician voice.

'Yes. The *Barracuda*,' was all he could think to answer, and lapsed into silence.

Captain Bredin squeezed his monocle into his eye and brought down his brows to squint ferociously across the table, uttered 'Hum-ha' to put Daniel firmly in his place, and addressed himself to Emma. 'If I may beg your attention for a moment, Miss Emma,' he began.

'Do be quiet, Geoffrey,' she commanded, in that same calm voice. 'I am engaged in conversation with Captain Fogarty.'

The monocle glinted balefully in the candlelight. 'I—ah—yah-haw,' uttered the moustaches peevishly, and returned sulkily to its muttons.

She widened her mouth into an encouraging smile and

addressed herself again to Daniel. 'I have never yet set foot aboard one of our ships. Do you think it would be possible to rectify the omission, Captain Fogarty?'

The invitation was all too clear and nothing would be easier, but he had strong reservations. First and foremost would be the almost certain objections of his employer. He doubted Callon would relish the notion of his well-bred daughter being exposed to the rough humour and ribald comments of the docks. Nor did he look forward to shouldering the responsibility for acting the host to a pampered child of fortune. Elizabeth now, Elizabeth was of an altogether tougher fibre. Born and bred in the area she could give as good as she got. Elizabeth! Her damned image kept forcing its way through his consciousness at the most inconvenient of times. He banished it to limbo and tried to concentrate upon a tactful reply.

'Naturally, I should be delighted, Miss Callon. But I do assure you that a ship alongside is not at its best. It is also an extremely busy time, as your father will no doubt confirm.'

The unease must have shown in his manner for her smile broadened. 'I would not dream of imposing upon you, nor of placing you in such an equivocal position, without first obtaining dear Papa's permission.'

'It is a somewhat rough neighbourhood,' Daniel told her hesitantly.

'Ha,' barked Captain Bredin. 'I would consider it an honour to be permitted to act as your escort, Miss Emma.'

Heaven forbid, thought Daniel sourly. He would have trouble enough with Miss Callon without having to keep an eye on this strutting coxcomb. The dockers would probably throw him into the river.

She gave the man a smile etched in acid. 'I am more than sensible of the honour, Geoffrey, and should I ever express a wish to visit soldiers in their barracks I should unhesitatingly avail myself of your offer; but in the world of the seafarer I am sure that Captain Fogarty's authority alone will be more than sufficient.'

Callon himself put an end to further overtures by pushing back his chair and announcing: 'With your permission, ladies. Ices and cordials will be served in the withdrawing room.'

There was a general shuffle of chairs and a liveried servant opened the wide double doors.

'Captain Bredin,' Callon called. 'If I might beg your indulgence? I have a matter of business to discuss with Mr Armstrong and my Marine Superintendent. Emma, my dear, would you be so kind as to entertain Geoffrey for a few minutes?'

Captain Bredin bent stiffly from the waist, twirled his moustaches, said: 'Hah-yah. Delighted,' and, presenting a triumphant arm to Emma, escorted her to the withdrawing room.

Mr Armstrong, Daniel conjectured, was evidently the buck-toothed nephew, the dealer in grain and feedstuffs. Now, no doubt, his employer would draw aside the veil of mystery which thus far had overhung the proceedings.

Callon left his chair, harrumphed at the servants, grunted: 'You can clear up this mess later. Be off with you,' and on their departure took up a stance by the fireplace. He waved an hospitable arm towards the sideboard. 'Help yourselves to brandy and cigars, gentlemen, and let's to business.'

Mr Armstrong immediately trotted to the sideboard only too eager to fetch and carry like Everyman's valet.

Daniel sipped his brandy and lit a cigar from a taper held out by the accommodating Mr Armstrong. Callon blew out a cloud of smoke. 'Onedin's well on his way, leaving the conduct of the business in the hands of that fool, Robert,' he pronounced. He swirled brandy around his glass and looked over the brim at Daniel. 'Do you think you could persuade him to supply Callon ships with flour? Say a thousand casks? At current prices?'

For a moment Daniel imagined his employer to have taken leave of his senses. He paused before replying, then recollected Callon's qualifying statement. 'At current rates?' he asked.

Callon laughed approvingly. 'Exactly. You've a sharp head on your shoulders, Daniel. A sharp head. I've always said so.' He clapped Armstrong familiarly upon the shoulder. 'Current grain prices, Arthur?'

Mr Armstrong's features were overcome by a look of rat-like cunning. 'Low, Uncle. Very low. But they will shortly rise rapidly. The next shipments . . . ah.' He sucked his teeth knowledgeably.

Callon grinned. 'We place an order when the market is at bottom. At keenest prices and for future delivery. The contract to be handled by Mr Armstrong. A contract which we enforce. At current rates.' He seemed to like the phrase so much that he repeated it. 'At current rates.'

Daniel brooded. It could work and it would not be the first time a man's judgment had been eroded by avarice. A guaranteed price and a named supplier could drive a man to the wall unless he had his wits about him. The ploy was simple enough. If Robert could be persuaded to undertake delivery at such-and-such terms before Armstrong increased the buying price, he would be forced to meet the balance of payment from his own pocket. He thought it through, then regretfully shook his head. 'I don't think it would succeed, sir.'

Callon scowled at his protégé. 'Why not?' he barked. 'If you have doubts as to your ability, young man, I can deuced soon find someone of more confidence.'

'It isn't that, sir,' replied Daniel. 'On the contrary, I would take the greatest satisfaction in pulling Robert's nose. But I understand James to have provided him with a clerk, and any clerk who knows his business would be bound to carefully scrutinise any such contract and advise accordingly.'

'H'mm.' Callon grunted and took a thoughtful pace or

two about the room. 'This clerk—what do you know of him?'

'Nothing beyond his name—a Mr Tupman, I believe.'

Callon stopped his pacing. 'Tupman?' he frowned. 'Tupman? Tupman. Tupman. Now where have I heard that name before?' He dug into the recesses of memory, snapped his fingers. 'I have him! Tupman! The wretch was once in my employ. He was dismissed for . . .' His eyes glinted. 'I know Mr Tupman's weakness. With the clerk out of the way do you think you could manage the business?'

'With pleasure,' said Daniel

'Capital. Capital,' purred Callon, once again all affability. 'Leave Mr Tupman to me, Daniel, my boy. I know that weazen's shortcomings. He'll be on short-commons, soon enough, hey?' and Callon guffawed at the pun in the greatest of good humour.

Daniel laughed dutifully and Armstrong showed his rat teeth in a sycophantic grimace.

'I think we'd best join the ladies, Arthur,' said Callon, putting a hand to Armstrong's elbow and propelling him toward the doorway. 'No, no,' he protested as Daniel rose to his feet. 'If you would oblige me by waiting a few moments I have another matter to discuss with you. The brigantines,' he added mysteriously. 'We'll switch 'em back to the Portuguee run. Clip Onedin's wings, eh? Help yourself to brandy, my boy.' And with that he escorted Armstrong through to the withdrawing room and left Daniel more bewildered than ever. Accepting Callon's invitation he helped himself to a second glass of brandy. It was odd, he thought. Damned odd. This piece of business could have been settled within the space of five minutes during working hours. He let his gaze wander around the room. Callon was comfortable, very comfortable. For the occasion the gas jets had been turned off to be replaced by ornate silver candelabra and girandoles bearing expensive spermaceti candles, gaslight being notoriously fickle in regard to ladies' complexions. A rich, wine-coloured, heavy flock wallpaper covered walls hung with gilt-framed pictures, pride of place being reserved for a large oil painting of Callon in aldermanic robes. Suspended above the fireplace the portrait dominated the room as its owner dominated his business. The furniture was solid, in the Jacobean style but encrusted with Gothic embellishments; towers and pinnacles to the massive sideboard, fluted and convoluted legs to chairs and table. It was the home of a man as solid and stable as society itself.

He turned from his inspection as the door opened. Expecting Callon he was taken a little by surprise at the sight of Emma. She closed the door and walked smiling toward him, her crinoline imparting a strange sensual sway to her progression. It was the largest crinoline he had ever seen, completely circular, and she seemed to move as though drifting on air. Her smile, he noticed, was the mechanical smile of the hostess designed to put him instantly at ease, but perhaps by some trick of the firelight her features seemed unnaturally flushed.

'My father apologises for his absence and has suggested that I indulge myself with the pleasure of your company for a few minutes.' The politeness tripped from her lips as though learned by rote.

Suggested, thought Daniel, sourly. Ordered, she means. But he screwed his face into a semblance of conventional civility and mumbled his gratitude. Her educated nasal drawl accompanied by a well-bred habit of speaking between her teeth put him at a further disadvantage. He became conscious of his own harsh northern accents and so lapsed into an uncomfortable silence.

'Do sit down, Captain Fogarty,' she begged after an eternity of shuffling his feet and avoiding the direct gaze of her eyes. 'I should feel quite discomforted if I thought my presence in any way inconvenienced or embarrassed you.'

She spoke banteringly but he thought he caught a hidden irony in her voice. Obediently he lowered himself into a chair strategically stationed beside the hearth. He looked up at her, felt at a greater disadvantage than ever and wished with all his heart that Callon would put in an appearance.

A crust of glowing coal fell in upon itself to send a shower of sparks hissing and rocketing up the chimney. Although the room was immoderately warm she spread her hands toward the benison of yellow flame and stared pensively at the fire.

'What is your opinion of Captain Bredin?' she asked abruptly.

The unexpectedness of the question took him by surprise. Really, it was quite unreasonable to expect him to criticise a fellow guest. 'He seemed quite a knowledgeable fellow,' he answered cautiously.

'He is horrid,' she said. 'And my father holds him to my head like a loaded pistol.'

'Oh?' He wriggled uncomfortably. Apparently he was to be made her confidant, though why he should be chosen for this singular honour he was at a loss to understand. He waited for her to continue, but she seemed lost in thought again. Somewhere in the house a servant opened a door and a surge of draught made the candles gutter. Their flames sent flickering patterns of light across the room, then steadied again and thin spires of smoke rose like incense. The faint musk of her perfume drifted toward him as she lapsed into sombre brooding silence. Then, as though at last tired of standing, she sank to the floor to crouch beside the fire, the crinoline billowing around her to give the illusion of a melancholic Aphrodite rising from a sea of frozen lace.

He cleared his throat. 'I don't quite follow . . .' he began.

She seemed not to have heard him. 'Ever since the

death of my dear brother, Papa has determined upon finding a surrogate son.'

For a moment the implication quite escaped him, then understanding rose in a tumult of emotion. Callon wanted to marry off this dainty creature to that coarse-grained mincing coxcomb! She could not be serious!

'Unless,' she continued, 'I find a suitor for myself, dear Papa has undertaken to find one for me.'

'But surely, Miss Emma, your father has canvassed your views?'

'My views on that score are perfectly simple, Captain Fogarty. I have not the slightest inclination to marry. In fact, I consider marriage to be a fate worse than . . .' She showed her teeth in a smile of self-mockery: '. . . spinsterhood.'

'You do not welcome Captain Bredin's attentions?'

'I despise the man,' she said venomously. 'And dear Papa, of course, is well aware of the fact. Hence the threat. And hence—this.' She opened her arms in a sad little gesture of resignation.

'This—?' he asked, perplexed. She seemed to speak in riddles.

She shivered in spite of the glowing heat of the fire and folded her arms to enclose herself in a narcissistic hug.

'An example of my father's somewhat clumsy efforts at matchmaking. Leave two young people together and love will find a way.' She spoke spitefully with a curl of irony in her voice.

'Love—?' He stared at her blankly.

'You are the current apple of his eye. He never ceases singing your praises.'

Anger and embarrassment strove for ascendency. He came to his feet, spluttering: 'Really, Miss Callon, I do protest! I had no idea! I will speak to your father immediately!'

He took a half pace toward the door.

'Oh, do sit down!' she commanded, curtly. 'I appreciate your concern and apologise for the necessity of putting you to such disadvantage, but I am sure you have no more wish to be party to this—deception—than I have, myself.'

He remained standing. 'Thank you for your frankness,' he said coldly. 'I will not impose my presence upon you any longer.'

She looked up at him. 'Unless you wish to put an end to a promising career you would do well to remain until our conversazione is tactfully disturbed.' She managed a crooked smile. 'Nor have I said that I find your presence entirely unwelcome.'

'I do not know what to say,' he began.

'Then, pray, do not attempt to say it,' she answered. 'And please, please do sit down, Captain. I find the necessity of looking up to you quite uncomfortable.' She smiled again to take the sting from her words.

Looking down he thought she had the flawless perfection of a piece of Dresden, even to the porcelain-like texture of her skin and an unnatural luminosity to her eyes.

'Thank you,' was all he could think to say, and returned to his chair.

She eyed him thoughtfully for a moment and then began to speak slowly. 'Now that we understand each other, and appreciate the invidious position in which dear Papa's scheming has placed us, we might—if you are agreeable—exploit the situation to our own advantage. It would certainly be no hindrance to your career, and it would save me the further embarrassment of Father's plots and ploys, if—' She bit her lip and this time it was no trick of firelight, she unmistakably blushed, a roseate flush that rapidly spread from her brow to the delicate exposure of bosom. 'If,' she repeated, 'you could see your way to formally paying your addresses to me. Formally,' she added hastily. 'For the sake of convention. I should not expect—. I mean—. You do understand?'

He understood only too clearly. Callon was evidently a tyrant at home as well as at the office. A man so devoid of feeling deserved to have the tables turned upon him. And, as Emma had taken care to point out, it would most assuredly be of no hindrance to his future. On the contrary . . .

She must have mistaken his hesitation for she reached out and touched his hand. 'Believe me,' she said earnestly, 'I would under no circumstances keep you to your implied obligation. I would also undertake to release you at any moment of your choosing.'

He looked at her, gravely. 'Let me say that I deeply honour your confidence and the trust you place in me.'

'Oh, I believe you entirely trustworthy, Captain Fogarty,' she said. 'Otherwise I should never have broached the matter.'

He grinned at her, spread his hands in a gesture of surrender. 'My dear Miss Callon, how could any man refuse so realistic a proposal?'

'I think, Daniel,' she replied, 'you had best start by calling me Emma.'

Chapter Twelve

Overnight the *Pampero* rounded Point Lynas, cleared the Skerries and South Stack, and headed south in a quartering nor'west breeze.

Jeremy awoke with a conviction that he was floating on air. Then the room tilted and unaccountably he seemed to be standing on his head.

He opened his eyes and at the same instant became aware of the hiss and slap of water. In alarm he put out a hand to touch the floor half-expecting to find it awash with the invading sea. But the timber was reassuringly dry, dry as a bone. He lay half-awake for a few moments during which time his head rose higher than his feet.

Jenny, clutched in Kate's arms, murmured plaintively in her sleep. Then, as the slant shifted, Kate rolled toward him and he found himself drowsily pressed against her. He took comfort from her warm proximity. Then the ship rolled slowly, parting them again. His vision accustomed itself to the dim illumination of the few lanthorns swaying gently in the all-enveloping darkness. His hearing began to select and particularise from a fremescent murmuring echo around him. He identified a sonority of snores punctuated by the groans and retching of the seasick; a goblin yell of nightmare howled in the shadows, and somewhere a woman neighed and moaned lost in the throes of rapture. A pale shaft of opalescent light poured from the square of the open hatchway bringing with it a taste of cool night air.

The straw of the mattress itched and scratched at his back. He slid quietly from the shelf, withdrew his woollen shirt from beneath the makeshift pillow and dressed quickly. The air was hot and clammy, sour with the stench of vomit. He picked and shuffled his way toward the ladderway reaching to the deck above.

Once on deck he seemed to have the ship to himself. The air was clean and fresh with a salty tang quite unlike the familiar soft sweetness of trees and grass. Wind whimpered and sobbed in the rigging and the stars hung like tiny jewels embedded in velvet. A double halo of orange and green ringed a gibbous moon and far to the east a faint pearl of light heralded the onset of dawn.

He stood for a while, swaying clumsily, absorbing the sights and sounds of this strange alien world. Beyond the shape of the ship was a rumpled moving darkness heaving with the slop and gulp of the sea. He looked up, his eye following the spidery tracery of rigging. Moonlight painted the bellied sails with a ghostly pallor and the tall masts swung pendulum-like against the stars. In the vastness of the night the ship seemed to sing softly to itself, a threnody of creaks and whispers against a contrapuntal thrumming of taut shrouds and a faraway high-pitched cadence like a child whistling between its teeth.

Someone coughed and he saw a figure move against the background of the sky on the high break of the poop. For a heart-stopping moment a disembodied head aglow with an unearthly light swam in the darkness. Then the ship rolled, his eyes refocused, and he recognised a human shape, its features illuminated by the upthrusting yellow glimmer of the compass binnacle.

The ship lifted and sank and he remembered Robert's admonition: Walk, he had told him. Gain your sea-legs as soon as possible. So Jeremy sucked in a lungful of salt-laden air and set off on an early morning patrol.

It was, in all conscience, difficult to keep your balance, but perseverance brought a measure of success. He took to counting his steps. Twenty-five paces forward and twenty-five paces back. He pondered as he lurched along the deck—a ship must be wondrous built to keep out all that water; he remembered reaching out to touch the floor and finding it dry, and that no more than eighteen inches or so above the gush and swirl of the sea. Jeremy clamped his brows in a frown of conjecture, imagining the ship as a sort of odd-shaped haycart, flat-bottomed and with the sea running beneath. Yes, indeed, a ship must be wondrous built to keep all safe and dry.

Two bells rang sharply and a far-away voice sang 'Two bells and a-all's well.'

There was another thing! He simply could not make head nor tail of this striking of bells. At home the church clock chimed reliable hours, stroke by countable stroke, but this shipboard time-keeping seemed beyond the wit of any man to fathom.

He paused, listening to the purl of water against the hull, and his stomach suddenly griped with hunger. They had had nothing to eat since a breakfast of thin gruel and a slice of bread at Mr Miles's lodging-house yesterday morning, and he wondered when their entitlement of rations would be issued. He had thus far resisted the temptation to break into the contents of Sarah's hamper, even though others, unable to contain the pangs of hunger—or from sheer greed—had opened and devoured their parcels of meagre supplies. They would wait, he had decided obstinately, until they had had the opportunity of testing the quantity and quality of ship's victuals. The extras would supplement their diet. Forty-two days for the crossing, Robert had said. It was a fair old distance and a mighty long time to cover it in.

From ahead a different bell chimed three deeper tones and a voice sang out something incomprehensible to be answered by a chanted hail from the poop deck. Jeremy stared out beyond the sharp bows of the ship and thought he saw a sudden lightening across the sky. Then it darkened again. He fixed his eyes upon the spot and sure enough a pale yellow glow appeared and disappeared. He scratched his head, wondering at this latest manifestation of the mysteries of the sea, when a hoarse voice bawled: 'All hands! All hands!' and he was almost knocked over in an eruption of seamen. Someone turned him roughly by the shoulder, cuffed and kicked him toward the open hatchway and he found himself bustled below once more while above his head bare feet pattered, ropes hissed and whined through blocks, canvas boomed, sails banged and clattered and a voice started to sing:

> 'Clodhopper Joe,
> Come heave and go,
> Clodhopper Joe,
> Clodhopper Joe . . .'

The ship heeled as it altered course and he fell to his knees amid a cascade of falling baggage and pots and pans and a torrent of curses and cries of alarm as sleepers tumbled from their bunks to crash to the floor in a chaos of flailing arms and bodies.

A moan of fear seemed to take all by the throat so that the hold echoed as though from one animal voice. Jeremy slid on to his bunk to avoid being trampled in the sudden mass rush for the ladderway. Women and children screamed and the men bellowed, pushing and shoving in terror of their lives, convinced that the ship was turning over, that they would be drowned like rats in a trap.

A howl of dismay rose from those at the head of the ladder as a grating slammed into place securely imprisoning them below. A voice bawled down to the clawing hands and upturned panic-stricken faces: 'There's no danger! Go back your bunks. There's no danger! We're altering course, is all. Back to your bunks! Back to your bunks!'

Kate clutched Jeremy and Jenny whimpered.

'T'is nothing,' he told them calmly. 'Listen—does that sound like folk aboard a sinking ship?'

Above the tumult they could hear the chant of the seamen as they went about their work:

'Joe, he was no sailor,
So they shipped him aboard a whaler.
Clodhopper Joe,
Clodhopper Joe.

Joe he was a lubber,
No father nor no mother.
Clodhopper Joe,
Clodhopper Joe.
Heave and go,
Heave and go.
Clodhopper Joe . . .'

Jeremy put an arm about Kate and smiled at Jenny.

'Ships is wondrous vessels,' he said, knowledgeably. 'Wondrous built and wondrous dry.'

The flicker of light Jeremy had seen was no more than the loom from the Smalls lighthouse, a lonely one-eyed rock perch blinking into the darkness fifteen miles from the Welsh coast and guarding the narrow neck of the St George's Channel. Away on the starboard quarter Tusker's slower knowing wink protected shipping from the rock-bound shores of Ireland.

The *Pampero* slipped between while the sky turned pink and the sun tore a hole through the curtain of night to burn the horizon furnace red.

James joined Baines on the poop deck, took bearings of the scything lights and plotted their position on his blueback chart. He peered at the compass course, looked aloft to the set of the sails, grunted satisfaction and, nodding approval, said: 'Keep her as she goes, Mr Baines. Call me when we sight Fastnet.' He longed to stay on deck and handle the ship himself but he knew there was nothing more demoralising to the officer of the watch than having the master constantly breathing down his neck. But they had a good slant and the wind held fair. There was nothing he could do that Baines could not handle equally well. Nevertheless he sought for an excuse to linger.

'How is the schooling progressing?' he asked. He took out and lit one of his favourite long thin black cigars, a tactful indication that he was prepared to unbend for a few moments' gossip without the imprint of authority.

'Ah,' said Baines, glad of the company. 'Mrs Onedin reckons I'm making fair progress with the reading and writing. It's figuring that has me baffled, but she's promised to take me in hand during the voyage and instruct me in the method of it.'

'There's nothing to it,' said James, seizing the opportunity to linger a few moments longer. 'You can box the compass, calculate the ship's speed, and I have yet to see you make a mistake in counting your pay-off.'

Baines scratched his head. 'That's different. The one's practice, the other's coin. Cash money. No one needs lettering to know there's twelve pence to a shilling.'

'Good,' said James. 'You've learned your first lesson—

precept and example. For your second we'll induct you into the mysteries of chart work.' He unrolled the chart, laid it flat upon the pulpit and held it down with a pair of lead weights. 'First identify those lights, then plot their bearings.'

Charts were expensive items, the master's personal and private property and, as such, usually kept safely under lock and key. Baines's chest swelled with pride at being accorded this singular privilege. He clasped his hands and bent over the chart in an attitude of prayer.

'Take your time, Mr Baines,' said James grandly, and moved away. 'I'll keep a weather eye open,' he added, elaborately casual.

'Thank you, sir,' responded Baines gratefully. Cap'n Onedin seemed in a fine generous humour this morning, and he determined to make the most of it.

James spent a pleasant hour, trimming a sail here, bowsing tight a halyard there, occasionally taking time off to further Mr Baines's instruction. The sea turned green beneath a cerulean-blue sky and the sun rose higher to bathe the ship in golden light. All too soon the helmsman struck four bells and James saw the second mate rubbing sleep from his eyes as he approached the quarterdeck.

'I think I've got the hang of it now, sir,' said Baines, stepping back from the chart. He pointed astern to a smudge of land. 'I reckon that to be St David's Head, bearing nor' east-a-half-north.'

'Very good,' said James, adding gentle-voiced, 'And what would be the bearing of that ship ahead?'

Baines moved to the weather side and stared ahead. A couple of miles distant a steamer, paddles thrashing, smoke billowing from its twin funnels, was crossing the *Pampero*'s bows. Baines spat reflectively over the side, careless of the quartering wind, and took a sly satisfaction in seeing the second mate duck his head as he climbed the ladder.

Baines understood that James's benignity had run its course. 'I'll bring her round a point,' he said, philosophically.

'Just as well,' said James, caustically. 'Unless it is your intention to cut her in two.' He rolled up his precious chart and tucked it beneath his arm as the second mate tramped on to the poop.

'Yes, Mr Armstrong?'

'Four bells, sir,' said the second mate unhappily. He was a lanky, tousle-haired young man, just out of his time as an apprentice and in mortal fear of his captain and owner. Even now he had a sense of trespassing when taking his lawful place upon that holy of holies, the quarterdeck.

'I am aware of that fact,' said James, malevolently.

'Permission to issue rations, sir?'

'I have already given you your instructions, Mr Armstrong. You require no further permission. Unless,' James added icily, 'it is your intention to seek confirmation of every order given.' It was, he knew, hard on the young man, but he had to learn the meaning of responsibility. The chain of command could not be broken. Armstrong must learn, and quickly, the exercise of authority.

'Aye, sir,' said Armstrong and hurried away.

The carpenter was already ambling along the deck with the slow gait of the privileged P.O.

James leaned over the rail. 'Mr Armstrong,' he snapped. 'Liven them up, there!'

Armstrong gulped and looked about wildly for assistance. He could not afford to fall foul of the P.O.s—bos'n, carpenter and sailmaker—who could make his life a misery; on the other hand he was under the eagle eyes of the master and the mate. Caught between the devil and the deep blue sea, he spied the bos'n, a barrel-chested old shellback with a lifetime's experience and a face that looked as though hacked from granite.

'Bos'n!' His voice almost cracked under the strain.

'Rationing party aft! Move 'em along! Smartly now!'

He had little need for concern. The bos'n had already read the situation. This raw young lobster was backed by the authority of the afterguard and nobody but a fool would cross officialdom in the nature of the *Pampero*'s cold-eyed brassbound master.

The watch on deck were hauling in braces and slackening off sheets and tackle in response to Baines's harsh commands. A small group of the watch below were sitting sunning themselves on the hatch, waiting for breakfast and passing the time with ribald comments on the labours of the job watch. The bos'n rudely interrupted their leisure. 'Ration party, on the double,' he bawled. 'Lay aft and roust out the pilgrims! Smartly now! Jump to it!' he roared ferociously.

Grumbling and cursing their misfortune the group tramped aft to raise the gratings covering the hatchways. The carpenter, a lugubrious Scot of sour and dyspeptic humours and teeth-jarring accent, fished a key from his pocket and leisurely unpadlocked the water casks.

Jeremy scrambled out on to deck to the sound of the sailors' bellow of: 'Rations! Rations! Muster aft for rations! Pots and pans. Bring your pots and pans. Muster aft for rations!'

With the seamen cuffing and pushing the emigrants were herded into the waist of the ship to stand facing the quarterdeck and the figures of authority looking down upon them. Three hundred people stood on this cramped and crowded little world and waited for a voice to tell them what to do. They staggered and swayed with the lurch of the ship and many were green with the pallor of seasickness. But they waited with dumb patience: a huddle of men, women and children, scarecrows with upturned faces, until the tall man stepped forward, gripped the rails with widespread fists and began to speak.

'Pay close attention to what I am about to say, for I will not say it twice.' His voice was sharp and clear, pitched so that even those shuffling and craning at the rear of the crowd could hear every syllable.

'I am the master. On board ship I am the law. This is Mr Baines, second in command only to myself. Below there, is the second mate, Mr Armstrong. You will at all times obey our commands. Without question. Without hesitation. This is for your own safety and for the safety of the ship. There will be times when you are frightened. You will be afraid when faced with your first storm. When that time comes you will be battened down below. This again is for your safety and the safety of the ship, for the decks must be kept clear for the seamen to go about their work. If you were on deck during an Atlantic storm you would certainly be washed overboard and drowned. By the same token if the hatches were left open the ship would fill with water and we should all drown.'

Jeremy nodded to himself. This man spoke sense. No one had as yet mentioned his name but he decided that it must be Robert's brother James, the famous sea-captain. The knowledge brought a renewal of confidence and a sense of kinship. He and Kate and Jenny would be safe in the hands of Robert's brother. He was the master, he had said. It was the same world, whether ashore or afloat. Some were masters and some were men. Masters and men, it was in the nature of things. Once again he paid attention to that clear level voice.

'There are near to three hundred of you,' James was saying. 'And from the appearance of one or two of the ladies we should arrive in America with something in excess of that number.'

There was an appreciative guffaw from the men and blushes and giggles from the women.

'It is my business to see that you arrive safely. Beneath your sleeping quarters lie a thousand tons of cargo. It is also my business to see that that arrives safely, and I have no intention of losing the one or the other in order that some Dismal Jimmy among you may prove me wrong.'

They laughed again and began to relax. The captain wasn't such a bad fellow, after all.

Jeremy frowned in concentration. A thousand tons of cargo! He tried to imagine it. There must be yet another great dark cellar underneath! A ship, then, must be like a floating barn with the passengers inhabiting the hay-loft. There was no doubt about it. A ship must be wondrous built to contain a thousand tons of stuffs and yet float on water. Wondrous built, indeed!

There was a general press forward and a craning of necks as a seaman trundled barrels and dragged bins into view.

'You will receive your provisions once a week, and once a week only. At this time. Remember,' continued the implacable voice, 'if you eat up your stores in three days you will go hungry for the rest of the week. You must arrange among yourselves to take turns at the passengers' galley.'

Their heads turned and their eyes followed his pointing finger as two seamen, with an evident sense of drama, threw aside a canvas cover to reveal a kitchen range of six fires with sliding hooks on rails from which cooking pots could be suspended. It stood in the waist of the ship, open to the weather. Kate tugged at Jeremy's arm.

'What if it rains? Or we be taken with one of them storms and shut up like hens in a coop?' she asked.

Jeremy shrugged. 'Go hungry, I reckon.'

'Fresh water will be issued daily,' said James almost as an afterthought. He leaned over the rail. 'Carry on, Mr Armstrong, if you please.'

Armstrong set up his scales on a small table and as the emigrants surged forward began the long laborious process of weighing and measuring while the seamen, warming to their work, pushed and shoved the mob into some semblance of order.

They had to receive their rations in whatever container was available. Some had pots and pans, some crocks, many of the men used their hats and the women aprons and scarves.

When Jeremy's turn came he discovered their entitlement for each person to be: seven pounds of potatoes, one pound of flour, three pounds of ship's biscuit, two pounds of molasses, four ounces of tea, one pound of sugar, a pint of peas and a pint of lentils. They were also to receive two pounds of salt beef or salt pork twice a week plus their water ration of three quarts each per day.

It seemed a veritable mountain of food but, sitting on the hatch and taking stock, Jeremy realised that though they wouldn't starve, they were not likely to wax fat.

Strands of hair clung dankly to Kate's forehead, beads of perspiration stood upon her skin and her face seemed unnaturally flushed. She swayed dizzily and steadied herself against Jeremy's shoulder.

'What is it, love?' he asked anxiously.

'Naught but hunger, I reckon,' she said weakly. She looked helplessly toward a gaggle of women already squabbling for places at the cooking range. 'I'll make shift with breakfast in a minute.'

'You'll do no such thing,' said Jeremy, firmly. 'Us'll take a morsel or two of packing from the hamper. There'll be time enough for cooking later.' He cocked his countryman's eye up at the blue sky and slanting sun. 'I reckon weather'll hold fair for a day or two yet.'

All afternoon the ship was invaded by the rich smells of cooking and the clatter of pans while the emigrants settled themselves about the ship, chattering and cawing to one another, like a flock of great black birds.

In the lee of the land the wind was soft and the sea calm, and skeins of gulls followed the ship toward the southern tip of Ireland and the wild reaches of the Atlantic.

And out in the Atlantic, far to the south and west, the sky darkened as a whirling mass of cloud began to circle in an ever widening vortex that gathered up the sea and hurried north and east to cross the Western Ocean shipping lanes and destroy everything in its path.

Chapter Thirteen

Mr Tupman was making his way home, his mind pleasantly abstracted with thoughts of the mutton pie and a mug of hot sweet tea awaiting at their lodgings in Kitchen Street behind the railway yards.

He walked along the Dock Road past Wapping and King's wharves where the tobacco warehouses fronted the river. His sharp eyes noted that there seemed to be an unusual number of heavily-sparred, shallow-draughted cotton-traders lying idle. A result of the American war, no doubt. Cotton and tobacco were already feeling the pinch. His clerk's brain assessed the problem in pounds, shillings and pence. Freights would assuredly rise. A couple of barquentines, sheathed in iron, were discharging grain. Alongside these iron monsters lay smart neat ships of delicate lines unloading jute, linseed and indigo from India, tea, musk, bamboo and cinnabar from China. The exotic spice-laden airs of the East, intermingled with the aroma of Mediterranean fruit-ships and the salty tang of fishermen glutted with herrings, added to the all-pervading pungency of tar and hemp.

Seamen of all nationalities paraded before concert and dance halls, grouped about gin-palaces and ale-houses, clustered around covens of parrot-faced prostitutes plumed and feathered in tawdry finery. The strains of a barrel-organ poured from the open door of Ran-Tan Annie's Living Waxworks whose garish posters promised 'Enlightening Tableaus of the Unclothed Female Form in Posées Plastiques'.

He timidly skirted the more rowdy groups, received a cut from a carter's whip for his pains, then passed a skittle-alley sandwiched between two cotton warehouses, a row of slop-merchants and tailors shops, a pawnbroker's and a couple of boarding houses, to thankfully turn off into a quieter thoroughfare.

Here the 'Quarterdeck' rubbed shoulders with the 'Starboard Light', and the 'Captain's Cabin' with the 'Lazarette', taverns of reputedly respectable reputations patronised by Yankee mates in blue cutaways and small-crowned cheese-cutter caps; by ear-ringed dandies from the China trade; and British masters in high beaver hats and square-rig coats; the 'Lazarette' tending to be the reserve of clerks, stewards and other lesser lights.

Abreast of the green glow from the lamps beside the portico of the 'Starboard Light' Tupman was surprised to hear himself hailed by name and a cheerful 'Halloo-there!' from a once-familiar voice.

He looked up, startled out of his reverie, to see Drummond, one of Callon's clerks, advancing toward him with outsretched hand and a smirk of good-fellowship smeared across his pimply face.

'Tupman, my dear fellow!' he brayed, pumping Tupman's arm and clapping him familiarly upon the shoulder. 'How good to see you! How providential!'

Tupman saw nothing particularly providential in their meeting and wondered at Drummond's uncommon bonhomie. To the best of his knowledge he and Drummond had never hit it off in the days when he had worked for Callon. Drummond he remembered as one of Callon's creatures, servile and cunning in the office and boastful and slanderous outside. Nevertheless he summoned up a weak smile and mumbled a greeting in return.

'You remember Blenkinsop?' Drummond extended an arm as a second figure lurched to stand teetering on stilt-like legs.

How could he forget Blenkinsop? Drummond's crony was, he was almost certain, responsible for reporting his weakness to Agnew, resulting in prompt dismissal. He nodded polite acknowledgement and Blenkinsop chirped in high bird-like voice: 'Delighted, old man. Glad to see you on your feet again. Employed by the Onedins, hey? That should take fat Callon down a peg or two, hey? Hey-eh-eh-eh,' and chirruped, as though it were the best news since the relief of Lucknow.

They stood for a moment or two eyeing one another. Drummond and Blenkinsop were dressed like identical twins, Drummond being looked upon as the office fashion-setter. They wore shapeless check trousers, braided jackets and curled-brim bowler hats. Celluloid cuffs overshot their wrists to cover the ends of frayed cotton gloves, while raised collars with cheap stick-pin ties hoisted their necks to a becoming angle of supercilious hauteur.

'Off home, old man?' continued Drummond, solicitously. 'Very sage. Married men have responsibilities, eh, Blenkinsop?'

Blenkinsop dangled his head, uttered a tragic laugh and, standing stork-like upon one leg, began to wipe the toe of his other boot against his calf.

'Blenkinsop is shortly about to dabble his feet in the waters of matrimony,' explained Drummond.

'Congratulations,' said Tupman.

'We're celebrating,' said Blenkinsop.

'You must join us in a tiddly,' said Drummond.

'Very kind of you, but no,' replied Tupman. 'Very kind,' he added hastily as Blenkinsop clutched him by the arm.

'Shan't take "no" for an answer,' said Blenkinsop, firmly. 'Eh, Drummond?'

'Certainly not,' said Drummond, seizing the other arm. 'Tupman couldn't be such a cad as to refuse to drink a health to the future Mrs Blenkinsop. Could you, Tupman?' he demanded fiercely.

Tupman had no wish to appear unsociable and even less to be involved in a public dispute.

'Well—as it is a rather special occasion—just one,

perhaps,' he agreed weakly. He could handle one drink, surely?

'Good man!' said Drummond.

'This way,' said Blenkinsop and they hustled him toward the 'Lazarette'.

The tavern was warm and cosy with an atmosphere redolent of tobacco, rum and the rich flavour of the meat and potato pies for which the 'Lazarette' was justly famous. The bar was curved and of polished mahogany. Behind it large mirrors reflected regiments of bottles and gave an extra dimension to the room so that a man leaning on the counter would sometimes have the illusion of looking through to yet another area of bright conviviality.

It was well-patronised but not uncomfortably so. Tupman recognised one or two old acquaintances, fellow-clerks from nearby shipping offices, seated against the wall and casting hopeful eyes at those ladies of the night permitted entrance by Ma Gammon—a mountainous woman who prided herself upon running a decent place, although not above a little trafficking in the crimping game. The rest were made up of a few woollen-shirted seamen brown as berries and with money to burn, a couple of second mates, a handful of apprentices and an assortment of stewards. In one corner Thammy-the-note-cracker sat at his usual table, open for business.

As they pushed their way to the bar the old longing returned to Tupman. He could almost taste the liquor burning down his throat and a dormant memory pricked at his conscience. He would have one, he promised himself. Just one and no more. He deserved it; he had earned it; Blenkinsop was a good fellow and it would be unreasonable to refuse to drink a health to the man's future wife.

'What is the lady's name?' he asked, propping his elbows upon the bar as Drummond snapped imperious fingers for attention.

Blenkinsop seemed taken aback at the question.

'Who?' he asked dimly.

'Gladys,' interposed Drummond quickly. 'Gladys Mitchell.' He winked knowingly at Tupman. 'Taken too much aboard. He'll forget his own name next.'

'Ah.'

It was true that Blenkinsop did seem a little under the weather. He had a tendency to sway and lurch and laugh suddenly and immoderately.

'Hollands is your tope, I believe, Tupman?' Drummond pushed a glass into Tupman's hand. 'Rum for you, Blenkinsop, old man. Brandy for me.' He threw a shilling carelessly upon the counter and raised his glass. 'To Gladys. And may the Lord make her grateful for what she is about to receive, eh, Blenkinsop?'

'To Gladys,' responded Tupman, raising his glass in turn. He had an innate dislike of coarseness, of the pointed innuendo, and although Blenkinsop leered in reply he thought he caught a hint of embarrassment in his expression, so he added, 'And may I add my congratulations and wish every happiness to you both.'

'Thank you,' said Blenkinsop and swallowed his rum at a gulp.

The gin had a cloying sweetness, a peppery warmth that slid down his throat to greet him like an old friend. In his pocket his fingers sought and met the comforting jingle of his week's wages. He selected a shilling promising himself that he would forgo his cocoa money for the following week. Doris would not suffer, he would see to that. But it was only fair and just that a man in the company of friends should stand his corner. One drink, of course, quite clearly meant one each. He rapped smartly upon the counter and ordered another round.

Time passed in a haze of pleasant conviviality. Drummond insisted upon cigars, paying with a pound note and waving away objections.

'Callon's crinkle,' he told them, laying a knowing finger

alongside his nose. 'What the eye don't see, the heart don't grieve over, hey?'

Tupman puffed contentedly at his cigar, laughed uproariously at a number of risqué jokes, met a host of new acquaintances including a couple of seamen and the second mate of a Callon ship, and came to the conclusion that Drummond and Blenkinsop were two of the finest fellows alive.

Drummond seemed to know everybody and, once or twice staring into that other room beyond the mirror, Tupman noticed him making the rounds and exchanging civilities with Thammy-the-note-cracker and Ma Gammon and a beetlebrowed man in a brown suit and nut-cracker whiskers. They seemed to be conducting business of sorts for he thought he saw money change hands, but before he could concentrate an increasingly defective vision upon the scene his latest friend the second mate insisted upon his taking a glass of hot spiced rum. He obliged the gentleman by toasting his health, then the fumes seemed to rise to his brain, the second mate's face ran like wax and he had a confused memory of falling backwards down a deep dark well over the brink of which peered the solicitous features of Drummond, Ma Gammon and the owner of the nut-cracker whiskers. Then darkness closed in and he floated gently and peaceably on the waters of oblivion.

He came to with the impression that his skull was bursting. His head ached abominably, his heart was racing madly and his skin felt cold and clammy. Bile rose into his throat and suddenly he was seized in a grip of mortal terror as the world tilted upon its axis and he found himself slithering down a steep slope while demons roared and howled in his ears. Then his back met a solid object with a crash that jarred the breath from his body.

He sobbed and forced open his eyelids and met the aching blue of the sky. He closed his eyes again quickly and a torrent of ice-cold water sluiced over him to bring him retching and coughing to his knees. He made weak swimming motions with his arms and opened his eyes again to see the unmistakable face of nut-cracker whiskers looming above.

Tupman tried to speak but his tongue seemed glued to the roof of his mouth, then a boot hooked him in the ribs and a voice bawled:

'On yer feet!'

He obeyed dazedly, still trying to collect his scattered wits, struggling out of nightmare to face a reality worse than any horror he could have imagined.

He was aboard a ship! Of that there was no doubt; the demon voices he had heard were the sailors hurrying and scurrying about their work. Ropes were straining and sails booming in the wind. He staggered weakly as the deck lifted once again beneath his feet and he became aware of a tumble of other bodies lying sprawled in ungainly heaps. Even as his senses slowly absorbed the scene a familiar ungainly shape began to crawl painfully from beneath the pile of drugged humanity. Blenkinsop!

He watched his fellow clerk creeping across the deck like a broken insect until he reached a pair of straddle-legs encased in heavy boots. He looked up pitifully into the unrelenting face of Tupman's erstwhile friend the second mate.

Blenkinsop whimpered and tears of self-pity ran down his face.

'No, please,' he begged. 'No. Not me.'

A pail of water drowned the plea in his throat and a hand reached down dragging him to his feet and flung him toward Tupman.

The remaining bodies were stirring. One burly veteran, who must have had the constitution of a horse, dragged himself to his feet, shook a head like a bull, assessed the situation, tottered to the rail and vomited over the side.

Nut-cracker whiskers planted massive fists upon his hips and addressed himself to the rest.

'My name is Quail. *Mister* Quail. Mate of the *Gladys Mitchell,* bound for Valparaiso round the Horn.'

It was unbelievable! Unthinkable! He'd been crimped! Shanghaied aboard an outwardbounder! The *Gladys Mitchell*—a Callon ship surely? Where had he heard that name before? And he became aware of Blenkinsop snivelling beside him. 'Oh, the devil!' he was sobbing. 'The rotten lying, cheating devil! Not me—I shouldn't be here! He sold us both! Both!' He foolishly took a step toward Quail and raised his voice in a squeak of protest. 'It's a mistake! I shouldn't be here!' He pointed to Tupman. 'It's him you were to take. Not me! You must put me ashore at once!'

Quail's hand snaked out, Blenkinsop's head jerked and he fell to his knees. A long livid weal showed at the side of his jaw and his ear seemed to flower into bright scarlet. Quail's hand returned to his side holding a short length of tarred hemp with a heavy knot at one end. He breathed deeply and stared down at Blenkinsop.

'You'll speak when spoke to, and not before, and then in a respectful manner.'

He turned his head and continued with his address as though nothing untoward had taken place.

'This is Mister McConnell. Second mate. His task is to make seamen of you.' The beetle brows clamped down in a minatory frown. 'Carry on, Mr McConnell. Move 'em along,' and turning on his heel he stomped away, the rope-end twitching in his hand.

McConnell reached out and gripped Blenkinsop by the throat, yanking him to his feet and dragging off the high stiff collar in the process. He pushed Tupman toward the foremast rigging.

'Up aloft,' he yelled. 'And look sharp about it. Move, damn your eyes, move!'

Tupman stared dazedly at the web of rigging stretching

far above his head. Something stung him across the shoulders and he yelped in anguish.

'Up aloft, I said. And jump to it when you hear a command!'

McConnell, grinning evilly, swished a length of teaser in the air—a knotted piece of signal halyard that cut like a whip. 'Up with you, and out along the lower tops'l yard. You—,' he called to the bow-legged veteran who was now placidly washing his face in a bucket of salt water. 'Go with 'em. Show 'em the ropes.'

The veteran knuckled his forehead, grinned, 'Aye, aye, sir,' and shoved Tupman and pulled Blenkinsop toward the rigging.

'Up with you, lads,' he said. 'T'ain't nothing to be afeared of. Fust time's the worst, as the feller said to his missus.'

Tupman hesitated and received another lash from the teaser for his trouble. He clambered awkwardly on to the bulwarks and caught a sickening glimpse of the sea rushing past like a mill-race. He closed his eyes, gripped the ratlines and commenced to climb.

The old seaman was up after him like a monkey, coaxing, wheedling, swearing, instructing: 'Hang on to the shrouds, never the ratlines. Don't look at your feet. Don't look up, don't look down. Keep moving, keep moving, keep moving.'

He stumbled and slipped and found the rigging to be tarred and sticky. The monstrous rotundity of the mast seemed to approach closer and closer until, as he climbed higher, the rigging tapered to a point below a wide wooden platform. He could go no further. He could hear Blenkinsop gasping and sobbing behind him and far below the hateful voice of the second mate bawling:

'Up you go. Up and over. Up and over.'

Tupman, looking up, saw in total disbelief, an inverted triangle of rigging stretching out toward the edge of the overhanging platform. It wasn't possible. It simply was not possible. No human being could be required to clamber, virtually upside down, out into space like a fly without wings. He gripped the stays, pressed his face against the ratlines and shuddered, refusing to move another inch.

The old salt, clambering up and down and chattering encouragement like a Barbary ape, hung beside him as much at home as a monkey up a tree.

'Over the futtocks, lad,' he exhorted. 'Up you go. Up and over.'

He gripped Tupman's hand and guided it to one of the stays. 'Now the other hand,' he hissed.

'Move! Move, you pox-faced soldier!' roared the voice of Mr McConnell. 'Liven him up, there, matey! Liven him up,' he called to the seaman.

Tupman's other hand reached over his head and gripped like a vice. His body was now bent like a bow. He made the mistake of looking down. The ship seemed to have shrunk to a slender ellipse and the second mate's upturned face was little more than a pale blur mouthing oaths and obscenities. The ship rolled slightly in the swell. At this height the pendulum motion of the mast was exaggerated and to Tupman's horror his feet left the security of the rigging of their own accord and he found himself swinging free at the full stretch of his arms.

He kicked wildly, then a firm hand grasped his ankle and pushed his foot to the temporary security of a lateral rung. His other foot followed suit as though it had a will of its own and for a moment or two he clung thankfully to this precarious ladderwork of tarred hemp, his body swaying with the movement of the ship and almost parallel with the deck below. Then the seaman's voice urged again.

'Up. Up. Up. Up and over.'

His arms felt as though they were being wrenched from their sockets. He could neither return nor hang for ever. Somehow he succeeded in scrambling up, stomach churning as each roll of the ship threatened to cast him off and plunge him to the deck below. The saliva of terror dribbled from his mouth, then suddenly his head was level with the platform. From here the topmast rigging reached high toward the sky. He gripped the shrouds and hauled himself sobbing to comparative safety.

He lay face down for an eternity, gasping relief; then Blenkinsop's terror-stricken face appeared over the edge.

His fellow-clerk's eyes had the blank, empty look of the demented and his mouth gaped wide in a round O of fear, and as he dragged his trunk into view it was evident that he had vomited up his distress. His face was white as parchment and his breath rasped the pitiful prayer of the helpless. 'Ah, God, ah, God, ah, God, ah, God . . .' He saw Tupman and screamed, 'Help me! Help me! Help me, damn you, help me!'

Tupman stood up, and the platform swayed gently. Stepping back his hand sought and found a downhaul running from a block beside the massive solidity of the mast.

The sailor was muttering and cursing somewhere below, then Blenkinsop's body heaved up and he sprawled in a shuddering heap upon the platform.

Tupman surprisingly discovered that the simple action of standing up had a steadying effect. He even found a momentary sense of exaltation. A temporary triumph of the spirit over flesh. In fact, now the worst was over, it was quite pleasant up here. A little world of his own, safe and secure. He looked around and took stock of his surroundings, readjusting his vision to a panoramic view of the Mersey.

On one side the docks stretched for miles; thickets of ships and forests of masts. On the other, the sands of Egremont and New Brighton shores were peopled with pleasure-seekers dotted about the beaches, splashing and skylarking in the froth of waves. Bathing machines looked like tiny wheeled caravans, and the ribbon of the promenade and the long stretch of the piers gave an overall appearance of an animated child's toytown. Steam ferries puffed and hooted, curdling the water in their criss-cross passages.

He had been concentrating so much upon sheer survival that he had not imagined for a moment they were so close inshore. His impression had been that they were far out to sea and lost forever. The thought sobered him and he looked back over the great sprawl of Liverpool. Somewhere, beneath that pall of smoke and behind the distant clank of railway yards, were wife and family. He knew with absolute certainty that he would never see them again. Valparaiso round the Horn, Mr Quail had said, and he knew enough of shipping to understand what that meant. Nitrates from the west coast ports. Valparaiso, Coquimbo, Antofagasta and Iquique on the hell coast. A two-year voyage, at least. Tears stung his eyes and he looked again, bitterly, at the sporting crowds on the beaches, so near and yet so impossibly far away.

The sailor came quickly into view. He climbed the topmast rigging for a few rungs then swung himself lightly to stand beside them. He grinned at Tupman through broken teeth.

'You'll do,' he said. 'We'll make a tarpaulin of yer, yet.' He stirred the whimpering Blenkinsop with his foot and shook his head. 'I dunno about this one. I reckon he'll finish his time as a hunk. A galley swab,' he explained. He stuck out a hand. 'I'm Amos. Amos Twobody.'

Tupman shook the proffered hand. 'Tupman,' he told him. 'Oliver Tupman.'

There was an exasperated hail from the deck below.

'Right, lads,' said Amos. 'Next stage. Up you go.'

Blenkinsop was sitting on his haunches. They looked up to follow the seaman's pointing finger.

'What we do is we go out along the yard. After coming over the futtocks, it's child's play,' he said. 'Child's play.'

Far above their heads hung an enormous pole of timber,

thick in the middle and tapering towards the ends. It creaked and groaned as it swung in the wind. The canvas sail was furled tightly but just above it the upper topsail roared and boomed in the wind's pressure.

'You first,' said Amos, and pushed Tupman toward the topmast rigging.

He climbed slowly and carefully. At this height the wind was no longer a playful, buffeting breeze. Now it whistled and shrieked in fury and plucked with a thousand fingers. Moreover the rigging was narrower and steeper, alternately tautening and slackening at the movement of the more slender topmast.

Quite suddenly and unexpectedly he found himself level with the topmast yard. It was far more massive than he had imagined. No pole, but a varnished trunk planed smooth. He waited, wondering what was next expected of him, then Amos scampered up beside him, reached out, took hold of a rope leading from far aloft to the deck below for some strange purpose beyond Tupman's ken, stepped with the agility of a cat on to the swaying yard, and held out a helping hand.

Tupman stared in renewed terror. Below the yard hung a footrope, a long line of tarred hemp loosely looped in stirrups. He foolishly looked down and his head swam. The deck now seemed no more than a sliver of wood floating in an aquamarine sea. He looked along the yard-arm and swore that nothing would persuade him to release his precious hold upon the rigging and trust himself to that swaying, groaning length of greasy timber suspended eighty feet above the deck. Then Amos seized him by the hand, plucked him from his perch and he found himself sprawling across the boom, lying on his stomach while his legs vainly flailed the empty air and his fingers desperately clawed for a hold upon the unyielding bulk of canvas. Only the uncertain balance of his body saved him from tumbling headlong from the yard, then his hands found the robands holding the sail and his feet the footrope which immediately sagged beneath his weight to add a new dimension to his terror.

The yard was slippery, encrusted with dried salt and bird droppings, but a long slender rail ran along the top. It gave a firm handhold and he began to gingerly ease his way along, reaching out one foot for the safety of the next stirrup, then drawing the other foot after it.

He must have been halfway along the yard when without warning the footrope tautened, lifting him high until for one paralysing moment he believed he was going to be pitched headlong over the yardarm. Lying belly down he turned his head to see Amos moving along crab-wise, comfortably balanced and one arm towing the gibbering figure of Blenkinsop after him.

Amos grinned. 'Move along, lad, move along. Out to the clew o' the sail. Shift yerself, lad.' Then to Blenkinsop: 'Come along, you great babba, I'll hold yer hand.'

Tupman wriggled and squirmed his way along until his shoulder met the wire supporting stay running aloft. He looked out and down and discovered that he had, at long last, reached the end.

The extremity of the yard extended far beyond the deck of the ship. The sea rushed far beneath in foaming arrows thrown aside by the sharp cleaving bows. He watched fascinated as the encroaching waves seemed to fold back upon themselves. His legs ached and his fingers were numb, the nails broken and bleeding. Unconsciously he wriggled into a more comfortable position, standing almost upright and supporting himself by gripping the wire stay. It thrummed and trembled in his grasp and the yard swung slowly, creaking and groaning to itself as though engaged in a private labour of its own. A block banged noisily and above his head the taut canvas of the upper topsail snapped and snarled in the torment of the wind.

Ahead, a line of bell-buoys marked the channel and now, almost abeam, he could clearly see a ferryboat disembarking passengers at New Brighton pier. There was a balloon-seller waiting by his stall and, even as he watched, a yellow balloon suddenly leapt into the air to climb rapidly, bobbing and weaving an invisible pattern on its way to freedom.

He thought again of wife and children, and then—without thought, knowing exactly what he must do—he deliberately released his hold and allowed himself to fall . . .

He seemed to float through the air for an immeasurable time. He heard a shout from Amos, even saw the hand reaching out to save him. Almost disdainfully he ignored it, saw sails and sky wheel above his head, then he hit the water and for a moment was convinced his back was broken.

But the sea had welcomed him with open arms to draw him down and down into lung-bursting depths. He opened his eyes and glimpsed a shadow, a great black shape that rushed past to spin him round and round like a top. Then it was gone and he was caught in the turbulence of the wake, a tumult of water that rolled him over and over then spewed him to the surface.

He rose, coughing and spluttering, half-drowned but alive, and already about fifteen yards astern of the ship. A row of white faces appeared at the rails, mouths open in shouts of wind-torn advice. Someone waved an arm and a line snaked through the air but fell far short and the ship towed it further and further from reach.

He hoped they wouldn't lower a boat for him. He had no intention of returning. To make doubly sure he raised his arms despairingly above his head and allowed himself to sink.

He stayed under as long as possible then floated to the surface again. Now the ship was at least forty yards away and still on course. He raised one weak arm, rolled over and slipped down into the green and lasting peace of the cold depths.

When he drifted to the surface again he saw the ship billowing away, throwing out even more canvas. Obviously he was no more than a piece of flotsam, jettisoned over the side, no longer of use and easily replaced.

He felt abysmally tired and the sea was weighting his clothes, tugging and dragging him down. He trod water and heard his death knell, a deep-toned dirge that clanged mournfully across the wide chasm of the river.

The clanging grew louder and suddenly the black shape of a bell-buoy loomed before him. The tide was running, ebbing fast, and he could see the surge of water against the buoy's heaving barnacle-encrusted sides. He struck out for it and with his last reserves of strength reached the dolorous iron haven. There was a small gallery running around the buoy. He waited until it dipped toward him then scrambled up, rasping arms and legs in the process. He stood up unsteadily and grasped the struts of the bell housing.

From close quarters the clamour of the bell was deafening and he wondered how long it would be before he was rescued. Then he saw the boat pulling toward him and he knew he was saved. He had time to puzzle over which day it was and would he be in time for work on Monday morning? before willing hands reached out to drag him into the sternsheets of a dory stinking of fish, and row him toward the beach of pleasure-seekers and the waiting ferry.

Chapter Fourteen

The sky lay across the horizon like a sheet of crumpled paper crisped and burnt at the edges.

'Mackerel sky,' commented Jeremy, seated on the hatch, contentedly polishing his boots.

The sun which for days had been a constant companion,

cheerfully dodging in and out of stray tufts of cloud, now had a pale, watery, anxious look.

'Set storm canvas,' said James. 'We're in for a blow.'

Baines put aside his abacus—a counting frame of wire and beads, constructed by the carpenter under Anne's directions—and stared out at the sea. The long Atlantic rollers had flattened like a sullen animal cowering before its master. The air was still and sultry and the *Pampero* ghosted along with the sails barely drawing.

The bos'n received his orders quietly and soon the hands were hurrying aloft to take in sail. The yards rattled down and new heavy canvas was hoisted to be bent on to double gaskets. Chains were attached to the ends of the lower yards and secured to the braces.

'Batten her down, Mr Armstrong. Tight as a cork.' James looked at the sky. The light was changing to a murky sulphurous yellow. 'We haven't much time,' he added. He sent Anne below and gave Jão his instructions.

Kate, taking her turn at the cooking range, felt once again the onset of a dizziness that had been overtaking her with increasing frequency these past few days. It was accompanied by a tightness in her chest and an ache in her limbs and joints. At times she was seized with chills as though her veins were filled with ice-cold channels of water. Her teeth would chatter and she would find herself shaking as though with the ague. It was not seasickness because she had long recovered from the first bout and had not been afflicted since. No doubt it was some other mysterious malady of the sea and she would recover once they again set foot on dry land. It might even be caused by their diet for they had to survive on heavily salted meat as tough as old boots and tainted by the smell of brine casks. She longed for fresh vegetables instead of the monotonous sequence of dried peas, lentils, rice and oats. Oats, many of the passengers complained, were for horses, not men. But they had finished the store of potatoes a couple of days ago and there would be no more until they reached America. She sighed, stirring a stew of peas, lentils and bruised meat. America seemed a long way off. Sometimes looking at the empty horizon she had a conviction that there was no such place, that they were doomed to wander this waste of water forever.

The tantalising smell of bacon sizzling and smoking arose from her neighbour's frying pan to remind her that all emigrants were not poverty-stricken. Some had disposed of small-holdings at favourable prices and were obviously well-to-do; certainly they seemed to consider themselves a cut above the others and put on enough airs and graces to satisfy a convocation of bishops.

There were six women busy at the range when a couple of seamen arrived and, to their great indignation, set about dousing the fires. Shrieking like fishwives the women grabbed ladles and knives, prepared to defend their half-cooked provisions to the death, until a well-aimed bucket of water extinguished both fires and ardour. Choking clouds of steam and ash drove them away clutching precious cooking pots and pans, swearing—reported one of the sailors—worse than packet-rats.

Jeremy carried the cauldron of stew and helped Kate below. They sat on the edge of their bunk while Jeremy pounded up hard ship's biscuit and sprinkled it into the stew for body.

'A morsel of thickening clamps the stomach wonderful,' he said. 'Us'll need all the packing we can get. I reckon we're in for one of them storms the captain spoke about.'

On the quarterdeck James marshalled his forces and prepared the ship for battle.

The emigrants were driven below, the hatches secured and tarpaulins battened down. All ventilators were removed, the shafts plugged and covered tightly with oiled canvas. The cabin skylights were similarly protected. Every possible ingress through which the sea might force a way was firmly stopped and caulked. The two clinker-built ship's boats were upended and double-lashed to the skids. The wire lifts of the heavier yards were replaced with chains while royals and topgallants were fished and sent down. The standing rigging was checked and tautened. The bow anchors lashed even more firmly to the cat heads.

He watched the hands aloft swinging about like acrobats but without their usual laughter and ribaldry. They worked with a contained urgency, only occasionally sparing a glance toward the ominous streaks of cloud spreading fanwise across the sky, or down at a sea slowly heaving like molten lead.

James was satisfied. Baines had picked his crew well. There were a few black faces among them, reminders of the earlier voyage; most had paid off and disappeared into the stews of Liverpool, but one or two had evidently developed a taste for seafaring and signed on for another voyage. The rest were Western Ocean men, reputed to be the toughest seamen in the world. The weather now blowing up would soon prove their worth. He could hear the cook clattering and banging in the galley, hastily preparing the last hot food they would receive until the storm had passed. Or taken them under.

Baines stood at his side, methodically buttoning himself into oilskins. Mr Armstrong was superintending a couple of the job watch stretching lifelines along the deck. James noticed approvingly that the young man did not stand by wasting his breath in exhortations to endeavour, but lent a hand himself, straining with the others to bowse the lines tight until they sang like bowstrings. In the strange unnatural stillness he could even hear the chink of crockery as Jão and Anne busied themselves packing away the breakables.

He studied the ship carefully. Under her bald-head rig, and with storm sails hung out, she had a stubby fighting look about her. She was close-reefed under lower courses, foresail, lower topsails and staysails. From the mizzen mast the boom of the spanker reached out to creak above his head, the fore-and-aft sail which would help keep steerage way flapping and filling as the wind veered and shifted fitfully.

The *Pampero* crouched in the sea, pricking her ears as the sails filled; her head rose high as though scenting danger; she snarled at the sea foaming about her bows; then she lay still and quiet again; waiting.

He spared a thought for the emigrants enclosed in a suffocating prison of near darkness, helpless and ignorant of the ways of the sea. Then shrugging aside the thought he watched the crew swarming down to the deck to congregate about the hatch, lighting pipes and looking anxiously toward the galley.

James surveyed the disposition of his forces with satisfaction. The ship was battened down tight as a cask, the crew were hard-bitten professionals, survivors of a hundred such battles. He nodded to Baines.

'Hands to dinner. And an issue of rum, if you please.'

Baines had been waiting patiently for the order.

'Aye, aye, sir,' he said and, smacking his lips in anticipation, rolled away on his mission of good cheer.

The light was fading rapidly and there was a leprous look about the sky. The waves slopped and slobbered and the surface of the sea was etched with strange eddies and cross-currents. To the south and west a dense bank of cloud stretched motionless across the horizon, its underbelly clothed with a sinister olive tint. It looked like the lair of some obscene beast out of nightmare. A low rumble emerged from its depths, coppery light flickered above. To the north the horizon was jagged against the dome of night.

James closed his eyes and tried to concentrate upon a mental sketch of the size and direction of the storm. Its track should be north and east with hurricane force winds revolving about the centre. He remembered Buys Ballot's Law: Face the wind and the area of low pressure will be to your left. He wondered if Mr Buys Ballot—whoever he might be—had ever been faced with an Atlantic hurricane? With fitful winds that at first veered right around the compass? With a wind capable of trowelling a city flat, of churning the ocean like clay on a potter's wheel until the rim stood ninety feet high, a spinning wall of water engulfing everything in its path.

Meteorology was not so much a science as a black art. He understood the principles but, as was frequently the case, theory bore little relationship to practice.

The track should be plotted and the area divided into four quadrants, said the books,

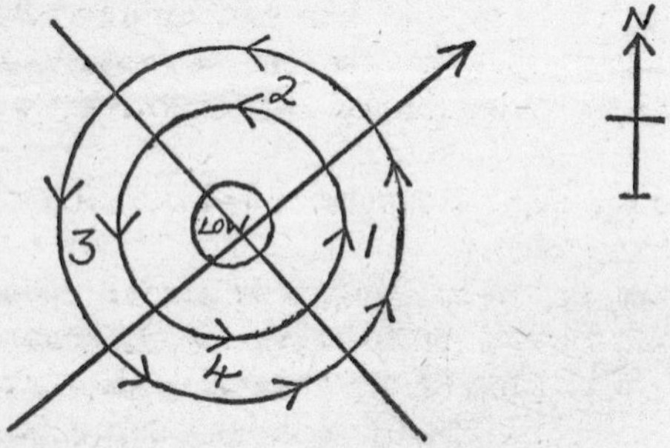

the most dangerous areas being the first and fourth. From the fourth quadrant a ship would be blown into the track of the storm which then would pass over it only to draw it back again into the fourth segment until wind and sea had chewed the ship to driftwood. Sectors two and three were safer; if any measure of safety could be found in a hurricane. On the outer rim of the second quadrant it was possible to be thrown off like mud from a cartwheel. The third was undoubtedly the safest, with the storm moving away.

But he would not know until the first big wind drove

down upon them. At that moment everyone's lives would depend upon his instant response. In the meantime there was nothing left to do but wait.

Anne came to stand beside him.

'Will it be bad?' she asked.

'Very bad,' he answered, simply. Anything short of the truth would be an offence to this remarkable woman.

'What of our passengers?'

'They must endure.'

She nodded gravely. 'Poor creatures.'

'And you must go below, Anne, and stay there. Imagination is the worst enemy. No matter what you divine to be happening on deck, you stay below. Is that clear?' He spelled it out firmly.

'I understand,' she said. Her hand sought his and their fingers locked together. 'But not yet, James. Not yet.'

'There is a little time left,' he admitted, glad of her company.

They stood side by side, not speaking, content in each other's strength.

They watched Baines making his rounds. A last minute inspection, checking and testing. Saw him stoop, pick up a small piece of timber and throw it over the side. It made a faint splash as it hit the water, then bobbed away, rising and falling, dipping into the troughs until it disappeared from sight and it seemed as though it had never been.

The carpenter's mallet made sharp rapping sounds as he methodically hammered home the wedges into their cleats, tucked in an errant corner of tarpaulin, secured the hatches drum-tight.

Mr Armstrong tossed the remains of his meal over the side, tightened his belt and sauntered across to take up his position at the lee braces. His shark's mouth grinned toward James, then he manfully bit into a chaw of tobacco, settled his back comfortably against the lines coiled about the belaying pins and settled down to wait.

He would do, James thought. He would do very well. As second mate Mr Armstrong had perhaps the most dangerous job on the ship. His function was to remain in the waist ready to cast off and slacken away the braces when the order was given to tack or wear.

The storm had also been marshalling its forces. It began with a patter of hail, rattling against the sails and making the decks slippery and treacherous underfoot, hissing across the sea, blinding their vision.

'Go below, Anne,' said James.

She squeezed his hand and hurried away, head bowed against the stinging hail.

Baines and two of the hands trooped on to the quarter-deck. The seamen joined the lone quartermaster at the wheel. Baines stood beside James.

'Stand by, if you please, Mr Baines,' said James quietly. He turned his face directly into the driving hail, seeking the wind pressure.

The wind had shifted quickly, coming in off the beam.

'Port tack, Mr Baines.'

'Port tack,' roared Baines to Armstrong. 'Stand by to come about.'

Armstrong slackened off the lee braces.

'Mainsail haul!' bawled the bos'n.

The yards swung round as the storm leaped out of the south, a wild shrieking fury that laid the ship almost flat. The helmsmen struggled with the kicking wheel, holding the rudder against the pressure of the sea.

The *Pampero* shoved her starboard bow deep under water and her port quarter lifted high. Then, relieved of the top hamper of royals and topgallants, she raised her head and angrily threw a mane of green water high in the air. The wind caught the wave and contemptuously threw it away. But now the gale was roaring at them from the port quarter, driving the ship before it.

They were in the first quadrant, James thought, and calculated that the next shift of wind would come from south and east. They would run before the storm as far as possible and then attempt to claw their way to the north.

The hail had stopped. Foam was blowing in dense white streaks from the crests of long steep waves. The *Pampero* rocked and shuddered to the pounding shock of the sea. She lifted and heaved and flung herself forward to worry at the waves like a terrier at a bone. The rigging was producing a wild skirling of its own, while the chain lifts clashed like cymbals. The deck lifted and canted beneath their feet, then fell away again.

Baines wiped his face. 'I've known worse,' he said.

'It'll get worse,' James told him. He must remember: the eye of the storm always bore eight points off the wind.

The storm must have been playing with them for it suddenly fell upon them with the impetus of an avalanche. It roared down upon the ship, driving before it a wall of water mountain-high.

The sea burst upon them, dragged the *Pampero*'s portside bulwarks under, swept across the deck like a ravaging monster.

Armstrong and his sailors disappeared, buried in an ocean of green water. James saw a seaman picked up, turned over and over before being smashed into a bloody mess against the base of the mainmast. The sea swirled around him, foaming and eddying red, then it carried the broken body away, out into the depths of the ocean until the sea lapped around it and drew it under.

The mass of water chewed and chomped its way along the deck, foaming and frothing, roaring like a wild beast. The port lifeboat burst its bonds to explode into a thousand flying fragments. A shattered, jagged-edged length of planking whirled through the air like a flail. James and Baines ducked their heads and at the same instant heard the whirr of the wheel spinning freely. One helmsman was jammed against the rail, his cheek laid open to the bone. He clutched his face moaning while the sea surged about his legs. The other two dazedly picked themselves up from the scuppers where the flying piece of timber had knocked them.

Already the ship was paying off, turning beam on to the sea, sails stretching and banging, the spanker boom lurching from side to side. The mizzen topsail blew out with a sound like cannon fire and was promptly torn to shreds.

Baines and James reached the wheel at the same time. James jammed his foot on the brake, slowing down the spin until Baines could grab the whirling spokes, then he added his own weight and heaved and pulled until the veins seemed about to burst in his head.

The ship was awash, buried in the sea, heeling over until her lower yards were dipping into the water and the waves licked hungrily at the corners of her sails. The masts creaked and groaned under the stress. The wind howled triumph from a black sky. White spume tore from the tops of waves as steep as green cliffs. The stern slid into the trough and a wall of water smashed into the deck housing, wrecking the cabin skylight before thundering along the deck to meet a group of mizzentopmen desperately clawing their way aft along one of the lifelines. It swept them from their feet until they hung out like washing on a line. One lost his grip to be pounded into the scuppers.

On the fo'c'sle head the carpenter and a couple of hands were struggling to control the fore topmast staysail in an effort to drag the ship's head round.

The two helmsmen now added their combined weight to the wheel and together they brought the helm down. The mizzentopmen struggled on to the poop and fought to haul the spanker to windward. Mr Armstrong surfaced, spewing out water like a whale, took in the situation at a glance and eased off the sheets to take the driving force out of the foresail. The ship began to swing sluggishly, creaking and groaning as the centre of gravity reasserted itself. Then the *Pampero* straightened herself spilling torrents of water from the scuppers. The wind was now its own worst enemy. It ballooned the staysail until the sheets hummed and tautened, and lent its insane strength to pushing the head round.

The *Pampero* raised her head high in the air and the sea cascaded the full length of the deck to break into foaming rivers, thundering against deck houses and hatch coamings, roaring against the base of the masts, smashing furiously against the break of the poop. Then the ship shook herself free, rolling the water from her back. She sliced through a giant wave like a knife and the wave parted to run away, purling beneath her counter.

Baines plucked a couple of the mizzentopmen toward him and thrust them at the helm. The injured helmsman was stumbling in circles, his hands over his eyes, crooning to himself that he was blinded.

James pulled away the man's hands and examined him quickly. A splinter had sliced open a flap of skin at his hair line and the blood had evidently run into his eyes. He pushed the man into the charge of a tall, gangling seaman calmly coiling the spanker sheet neatly upon its belaying pin.

'Take him to the cabin below,' he told him. 'Tell Mrs Onedin to stitch him up.'

Then he turned away to concentrate his full attention upon a world gone completely mad.

Above deck it was possible to meet the devil face to face but in the pandemonium of the emigrants' quarters chaos reigned supreme.

Battened down in near darkness, the oil lamps swinging crazily from their hooks, hearing the keen of the wind above and the surging rush of water at the other side of the hull they had been afraid. But when the storm struck and the ship lay over they went mad with terror.

A tier of bunks tore loose from their supporting stanchions and crashed to the deck carrying with it those occupants who had thus far succeeded in clinging to their shelves. Bodies tumbled higgledy-piggledy and a man was roaring: 'Me leg is broke, me leg is broke.' Women screeched and children howled, and even Jeremy's faith in the staunchness of the ship was sorely tested. He kept his head, braced his back against one tier of bunks and his feet against the other. The moment the ship righted itself the survivors picked themselves up and began to run about like sheep in a pen.

Kate was moaning, but he had taken care to wedge her in firmly using boxes and the hamper and an old piece of timber. Jenny clung to his legs weeping and crying out, 'I want to go home. I want to go home.' He stroked her hair and thin shoulders and tried to comfort her.

They could hear the flow of the sea as it broke over the deck above them. Enormous masses of water, rushing tumultuously, crashing and roaring only inches above their heads. Their dark box reverberated to the sound of the maelstrom above. Whenever the ship rolled, which was often, sea-chests and baggage flew about. When the ship dipped they thought they were going to the bottom. The lamps swung and jumped and one suddenly leaped through the air to crash to the deck in a pool of spreading yellow flame. Being colza oil it burned slowly and was quickly stamped out. Had it been paraffin the entire ship would have been ablaze.

Many of the Irishers, Jeremy noticed, had fallen to their knees in attitudes of prayer, crossing themselves, and imploring with wailing supplications the mercy of a multitude of saints, while others of different persuasion called upon the Redeemer, begging for mercy for past sins.

It hardly matters, Jeremy thought wryly, we are all in the same boat. Then he turned his attention to Kate. She had been poorly, very poorly, ever since they had been shut below. He conjectured that it was probably due to the absence of ventilation, the result of breathing in much-used air. Such a thing could not be healthy. Kate would be as right as rain, he reasoned, once the storm had passed and she could breathe God's good clean air instead of this vile choking miasma. Her skin was clammy to the touch and cold, cold as ice. She had slept almost constantly from the time she had laid down, only waking fitfully to retch thin black bile. But he was glad she could sleep. Sleep was known to be a great healer. Awake she would not be able to endure the knocking about and tumbling every time the ship heaved and rolled

He sent Jenny to fetch a piece or two of timber from the smashed bunks. She returned with a couple of broken lengths with nails still sticking out. He tapped them into place with the heel of his boot, makeshift fence rails that would prevent Kate rolling out on to the floor. He laid Jenny gently beside her and finished his work. It looked like a coffin.

They seemed to be enclosed in the sea. It was all around them, above and below, rushing and thudding against the hull, crashing overhead. But down here the ship, in spite of its torment, was dry, dry as a bone. It renewed his faith in the strength of the timbers. A ship must be wondrous built indeed to withstand such a battering and not leak so much as a cup of water.

The man with the broken leg was being attended to by his friends. His first wild roars had fallen to an anguished sobbing. Another man was bent double clutching bruised, or perhaps broken ribs. By common consent the women and children had been consigned to the bottom shelves, their menfolk standing beside them, braced against the bunks, the only method by which balance could be maintained against the unpredictable lurchings of the ship.

Jeremy lodged himself firmly and concentrated his mind upon the wonders of America. Land for the taking, they'd said. As much land as a man could cover in a day's walk. Free. He'd have some of that land, he promised himself. More land than his master had farmed in his entire life. In America a man was his own master, so they said. Rich, unbroken land, ready for the plough. He gloated at the thought. A few years' hard work and he'd be—he'd not tempt providence by saying rich—but comfortable. Yes, they'd be comfortable. He'd build a cottage for Kate and Jenny. Grow their own vegetables. Potatoes, greens. And a cow or two for milk. He'd heard that American cattle were great shaggy hairy beasts, herds of them roaming vast pastures. No matter. A cow was a cow no matter where you found it. But at first, of course, he must earn enough cash money to make a start. He'd need seeds, plough, plough horse, mattock and spade. America may be generous with its land but no doubt implements cost hard money there just as elsewhere. He had listened to his fellow-emigrants discussing the same problem and the consensus of opinion had been that the best source of income came from building railway roads. For building these railway roads, it was claimed, a man could earn as much as ten shillings a day and all found. It seemed an incredible sum and bore out the general impression that America was a country where the streets ran with gold. Jeremy made a rapid calculation: why, in six months at building railway roads he would have earned enough to buy everything a man needed to start a farm.

He was lost in his private dream world when the first avalanche of water hit the ship, laying the *Pampero* yardarm-under and almost driving her below forever.

One moment he was wedged quite firmly between the tiers, the next he found himself lying horizontal. No one could sustain that position. His knees buckled and he fell to the floor with a jarring crash that knocked the breath from his body. Then the floor became a wall and he found himself slithering to the bottom. He grazed his head against the shelf of a lower bunk, cracked his ribs against a stanchion to finish with a tangle of other bodies with waving arms and legs, against the shipside. He knew it was the side of the ship only because of the rougher planking, the massive ribs and a slimy cold due to the constant run of the sea outside. But the world had turned topsy-turvy. He saw the flame of a lamp apparently turning on its side; then the glass blew out with the heat.

Another tier of bunks tore free. He saw a stanchion snap like a twig; then the entire system of shelves fell upon them.

Those beneath fought tooth and nail to extricate themselves from the press of bodies above. Those above yelled and kicked at those below. Men, women and children were screaming in pain and fear. Jeremy put out a hand, touched a leg, found a shattered bone and his hand came away sticky with blood. He struggled to his feet, all sense of direction lost. A man clinging desperately to a stanchion, his feet waving frantically in the air, looked around, mouth agape with terror. Then he let go and his body plummeted through the air to land with a thud upon a group of his countrymen pulling themselves dazedly to their feet. Boxes and hampers leaped high to make strange parabolas of flight, scything all before them.

Some fought to reach the ladders leading to the deck above. But the great square of the hatch was no longer a ceiling but a leaning wall and the ladders, bolted firmly to the floor, lay at an impossible angle.

Jeremy discovered that his back was bent and pressed between shipside and deck like a fly. He became aware of the appalling vomiting of the sea inches above his head.

Then the ship righted herself and Jeremy screamed as the axis turned, gravity reasserted itself and he dropped like a stone to land bruisingly on all fours. Then once again he was caught up in the inevitable swarm of bodies, somersaulting, twisting and turning, rolling over and over, clawing, kicking, scratching, screeching and yowling, plunging amid the wreckage of bunks and trunks and chests and baskets. The spilled contents of burst baggage littered the hold like a rubbish dump.

He stood up shakily and his ankle gave way beneath him. He tested it gingerly, decided thankfully it was a sprain and not a break, and limped across to Kate.

She and Jenny lay where he had left them, the nailed planks having held against the pressure of their bodies. Jenny was crying hysterically, but Kate seemed to have slept through it all. She was breathing shallowly, a soft sibilant whisper more like the gasp of a runner at the end of a race than the natural breath of a sleeper.

He kneeled down and covered her with the blanket then turned his attention to Jenny.

'T'is all right, my poppet,' he told her. 'There's naught to fear. T'is only a great beast of a storm. T'will soon pass. Just rest easy. Easy, my poppet, easy, now,' he comforted, only to hear, above the cries of the injured, the roar and race of the sea and an insane shrieking from a wind so monstrous wild it passed all belief.

He touched the deck with exploratory fingers. It was dry. Dry as a nut kernel. Then he remembered. Beneath this floor was yet another cellar, filled with a thousand tons of cargo. He derived comfort from the thought. A ship fashioned to carry a thousand tons would take a power of sinking.

Night fell like a black curtain. The moon tore loose from a ragged mass of low-lying cloud. For a moment it trailed a comet-tail of bright stars; then vanished to leave nothing of its presence but a pale ghost-light touching the edges of the cloud. The sea was a floor of white foam. The wind an overpowering concussion, a concentrated weight of air that forced the breath back into their lungs and squeezed like a giant hand, one moment flattening them against the rails the next lifting their feet so they seemed to dance a mad fandango. James and Baines clung to the rails while the entire ocean's atmosphere streamed furiously past carrying with it flat sheets of water sliced from the tops of waves. The labouring ship had the appearance of a submerged half-tide rock. Water spilled from the scuppers only to be flung back again. The sea frothed and cascaded over the hatches, broke in fountains of spray about the masts.

There were now four helmsmen at the wheel, lifelines about their waists, struggling and fighting to keep the ship on course. The *Pampero* slewed and plunged and kicked like a maddened horse trying to shake free of its traces. The wind hurled her forward striving to drive her under. The sea followed astern, seeking to gulp her down. The crew had taken cover, for no man could hope to survive in that seething maelstrom.

The air was filled with flying water and the universal roaring deafened them as though their ears were stopped with wax.

The storm plucked at the sea and tore it to shreds. It piled wave upon wave into immense columns of water then threw the entire mass at the sky. Its mad fingers churned the ocean into a vast whirlpool, a boiling cauldron that lifted the ship high in the air to crash down again in a series of jarring shocks that threatened to shake her to pieces.

Then suddenly, as though it had exhausted its strength, the wind stopped. There was a lull, an uncanny silence broken only by the sea slopping about the decks, gurgling through the scuppers, gushing through the wash ports.

'By God,' said Baines. 'It's stopped!' He pushed himself away from the rail and spoke in utter disbelief.

James also released his hold upon the rail. His fingers felt as though they had been clamped permanently into position. He shook his head in an attempt to clear a constant singing in his ears.

Then the pale disc of the moon peered down through

a funnel of cloud. Around the ship the sea rose and fell confusedly as though sapped of its strength.

'We are in the eye of the storm,' said James.

He had to think, and think quickly. But his brain seemed numbed with shock. He took a stiff-legged pace or two along the breadth of the quarterdeck, shaking his head savagely in an effort to rid it of this infernal singing. The singing changed to a humming, then a deeper thrumming. He suddenly realised that the noise came not from inside, but outside, his head. Then he saw Baines, mouth agape, slowly turning in wonder.

It was the cry of the storm. The booming of a great wind endlessly circling the centre.

They seemed to be at the bottom of an immense well surrounded with walls of swirling clouds. Dense vaporous masses towered to the sky in ever-changing patterns. Lightning flared and scorched. Thunder raised a distant clamour.

The helmsmen drooped exhaustedly over the wheel. James's brain cleared. They hadn't much time. They must work quickly. They had been caught in the first quadrant. To survive they must head for the second. He walked across to the compass binnacle and squinted at the compass card. The binnacle light had long been extinguished but by the sickly light of the moon he could just make out the north-seeking pointer.

'Mr Baines.' He gave his orders sharply and clearly. 'Relief to the wheel. Damage report from Mr Armstrong. Call all hands. Bring her round and steer due north. Then I want every man you can spare aloft. The moment the wind hits us take in every stitch of canvas and heave to.'

'Aye, aye,' said Baines, and his foghorn voice bellowed: 'All hands! All hands!'

'The ship is yours, Mr Baines,' said James formally. 'I am going below for a few minutes.'

He made his way to their quarters afraid of what he might find.

A single oil lamp spluttered fitfully overhead and he stepped off the companion ladder into eighteen inches of water. The saloon was deserted but for a chair floating on its back and odds and ends of debris bobbing about as though the storm had prised its way in and ransacked the accommodation like a burglar in the night. There was a beribboned hat, a potato masher, a high-button shoe, and a drawer half-filled with a soggy mess of books, papers and items of clothing, stained from the contents of a jar of ink.

'Anne!' he called. 'Anne!'

He sloshed toward a door and peered into a short-cross alley. There seemed to be less water here.

'Anne!' he called again.

The door of their stateroom opened and Anne's head emerged.

'James!'

He waded toward her only to stop at arm's length and stare incredulously at her bruised and swollen face. Her right eye was almost closed and the swelling on her cheek reached down to a puffed-out upper lip.

She gave him a lopsided grin. 'It's nothing, James. The storm cracked our heads together.' She stepped aside and he saw Jão grinning up at him. The steward was engaged in mopping up the floor and wore a massive bump above his left eye like a trophy.

Their stateroom was not quite such a scene of disaster as the saloon. But it would do, he thought ruefully, it would do. The carpet had been rolled up and rested oozing water from both ends against a bulkhead. The injured seaman lay strapped to the settee, his head raised upon a cushion and swathed in bandages. He was sound asleep and snoring stertorously.

'I gave him a mixture of rum and laudanum and then stitched up his poor face as best I could.' She sighed. 'I am no surgeon, James. I am afraid the unfortunate will bear the scars to his grave.'

Rum and laudanum, thought James. A mixture powerful enough to stun a horse.

'He does snore rather dreadfully,' she added.

He looked again at her battered features. 'You must lie down,' he advised, gently. 'Really, my dear. A bunk is the safest place.'

'Nonsense,' she answered, briskly. 'There is a deal of clearing up yet to be done. Carpets ruined. Bedding soaked.' She brushed a teasing strand of hair away from her face. 'I am afraid the saloon has quite defeated us. The sea poured in faster than we could bale.'

He looked at her in amazement. She never ceased to surprise him. Here she was after living through the fury of an Atlantic hurricane, going about her housewifely duties as though she had been subjected to nothing worse than the inconvenience of a few slates blown from a roof.

'I'll attend to it right away,' he said, wonderingly.

'Is the storm now over?' she asked.

'By no means,' he assured her. 'This is but a lull. I intend to turn the ship to face wind and sea and heave to. We haven't much time,' he added.

She nodded gravely. 'Then I must not detain you.'

He gave her an affectionate peck upon the cheek and hurried away as lighthearted as a schoolboy. She really was a most remarkable woman, he thought. Most remarkable.

He heard the clank of pumping as he climbed the stairway back on to deck, and saw that Baines had not been idle during his absence. The carpenter and his helpers were already busily repairing and shoring up the shattered skylight. Four of the crew were swinging rhythmically on the handles of the Downtown pump.

'She's taken no more than a couple of feet of water,' said Baines. 'But we might as well dry her out.' He jerked his head. 'There's plenty more where that came from.'

It was an eerie sight. The moon poured down a sickly greenish light that painted the funnel of clouds a ghastly hue. The confused mass of turbulent water showed bone-white teeth as the *Pampero* crept stealthily on her new course, heading slowly across the eye of the storm. The ship moved fitfully, jerkily, as though limping toward her goal. The yards creaked and the sails slatted. What little wind there was in the storm centre seemed to be as confused as the sea. It would send out a licking tongue, pushing the ship forward, then, as though regretting its temerity, would withdraw once again into the cavern of its throat.

James looked up to the gently swaying masts and saw that the mizzen and main topsails had blown to shreds. A couple of the crew, stretched across each yard, were slicing through the gaskets. The remnants of the mizzen topsail blew free to hang for a moment in the air before fluttering away to fall in the sea like a great wounded bird.

The foremast seemed to be alive with figures. A group on the topmast yard were busily furling the lower topsail while two dozen men strung out along the heavy lower yard waited to haul in the lower course. Beneath them some of the younger men were congregated about the fife rail, ready to pull upon the spilling lines. Even so the men on the yard would have their work cut out. Storm canvas weighed two pounds to the square yard, dry, and when the ship nosed into the wind they would have little time to spare.

'Any damage, Mr Baines?' he asked.

Baines shrugged. 'She's come out of it well. We lost one boat and three of the wash ports has carried away. Fo'c'sle head rails bent and twisted. The jib-boom's hanging on like a broken tooth. I got some of the hands chopping it clear now.'

James nodded. He could hear the intermittent chop of axes, muffled curses, and could just make out a few shadowy figures clambering about at the bows.

'And we are four hands short,' added Baines, matter-of-factly. He ticked them off on his fingers. 'One below being 'tended by Mrs Onedin. One I saw go over the side, and two more just disappeared.'

James nodded again. It was only to be expected. More men were lost washed over the side than ever fell from the mast.

'Mr Armstrong?' he asked.

'He's doing fine,' said Baines. 'Just fine. A very promising officer, sir. Very promising,' he added with a proprietorial air.

James searched the deck and was relieved to see Armstrong's close-cropped shark-head among the group at the fife rail.

He called him by name and the young man broke into a loping trot toward the quarterdeck.

James remembered something else. 'Send a bucket party aft,' he told Baines. 'To bale out the saloon and remain on call until this business is over.'

Armstrong arrived as Baines bawled his orders.

'You know what we are about to attempt, Mr Armstrong?'

Armstrong had learned his lesson. 'Aye, sir.'

'Good,' said James. 'When we have completed the manoeuvre, you are to go below and get some sleep. You will relieve Mr Baines at . . .' He fished out his watch and was surprised to discover how much time had passed. It was a few minutes after two. In another four hours it would be daylight. 'At four bells.' He grinned crookedly. 'I doubt you will hear them. You must make your own arrangements.'

Armstrong grinned back. 'Aye, aye, sir.'

'And—Mr Armstrong.'

'Sir?'

'You have done very well, Mr Armstrong. Very well, indeed.'

'Thank you, sir,' said the young man and swaggered back to his post, his shark's head held high.

The bucket gang trotted up, made their way aft, and below to the saloon. At least Anne would no longer be left alone with a useless steward and a drugged sailor. He turned and slowly surveyed the ship and the calm centre of the storm. If there was anything left undone he must think of it now. Shortly it would be too late. He tried to plot the track in his mind's eye. The entire body of the storm would be moving across the sea at a speed of about twenty knots, carrying them with it. But because of the inertia of the water the centre would pass over them if they remained here much longer.

As the *Pampero* laboured toward the tempestuous sanctuary of the second quadrant James cast an anxious eye toward the great wall of cloud inexorably bearing down upon them from the west. It was appreciably closer. If it caught them the ship would be sucked into the demoniacal regions of the fourth quadrant and methodically battered to pieces. One of Albert's aphorisms drifted into his mind: 'The sailing ship master relies on God; the steamship master on his engines.' He wished with all his heart that he had one of Albert's steam contraptions under his command at this moment; he'd steam across this damned cess-pit and straight out the other side! The *Pampero*, damn her, seemed to be moving at a snail's pace!

He strolled across and looked at the compass card.

'Nothing to the west'ard,' he reminded the helmsman sharply.

'Nothing to the west'ard, aye, aye, sir,' the man responded in his monotonous chant. The others, idling by the wheel, shuffled their feet and grinned sheepishly.

'Mr Baines,' snapped James. 'Once we are under bare poles I shall require the helm lashed amidships. All hands to go below—and they are to batten themselves in.'

'Aye, aye,' answered Baines, placidly, having already quietly passed the same order to the bos'n. There was little sense in risking men's lives unnecessarily. With the ship hove to, head to wind and sea, there was nothing anyone could do but wait.

There was a ragged cheer from aloft as a sudden gust caught and bellied the remaining sails. The *Pampero* lurched forward, gathered speed and pushed her head into the whirling mass of cloud. The wind, James was thankful to note, had plenty of easting in it.

He had no time for further reflection before the storm was upon them again. The *Pampero* bucked like a horse and a cold sea smashed over the foredeck.

'Bring her round and heave to!' The wind tore the order from his lips whirling the words beyond human hearing.

Baines understood. Every man aboard understood. The ship had to be coaxed around to lay about six points off the wind. Then the wheel would be lashed down. If her gear held out she would ride out even the fiercest of weather. The hope was that aided by the windage of masts, spars and freeboard, she would spin out to the rim of the second quadrant.

Practice, as always, differed from precept.

The wind hit them on the starboard quarter driving the lee bulwarks under. The first and hardest task was in making fast the foresail. It was clewed up and then the watch, precariously strung out along the yard, fought five hundred square feet of maddened canvas. They started to pass the gaskets on the weather yard while the sea raged beneath and the yard cock-billed, pointing at the sky. The gaskets burst and the ballooning sail roared defiance. The hard cases at the tip of the yard swore and cursed as the footropes jerked taut and the spar swung and swayed. They scrabbled at the unyielding canvas and tore out their fingernails while the *Pampero* scudded before the wind and the troughs of the hungry sea grew steeper.

James and Baines watched anxiously from the quarter-deck. It was the age-old problem of the sailing ship. Being wind-borne it derived its power from the very element which was now in danger of destroying it. At the hub of the wheel the sheer fury of the wind would drive the *Pampero* round into the fourth quadrant. The force decreased toward the rim so they needed to exploit the combination of centrifugal force and the surface track of the storm to push them out through the whirling spokes. But lower courses were driving sails and this driving sail was hurtling them into the danger sector.

It was in James's mind to order it cut free. Lose the sail and save the ship; but moving out towards the rim they would once again require the push of the wind. He was about to give the order when he saw that the weather side was at last under control. The lee side was much less formidable—like squeezing the air out of a balloon, it would kick and jump and finally die with an expiring gasp.

The next problem was to haul the ship around to head to sea

The helm was eased, the *Pampero* rolled abominably. The storm spanker and mizzen staysail drummed and lashed from side to side. The fore topmast staysail flapped and billowed then strained to bursting as the bows came round. The hands aloft gathered in the last of the big square foresail, the *Pampero* turned reluctantly to face the wind, the seas ran diagonally under her counter and she snugged herself down, breasting the waves and ignoring the shrill manic shriek of the wind.

Deck canted at an acute angle, helm lashed amidships, the *Pampero* drifted bodily down wind with the seas storming over the weather rail. She rolled abominably, but deep in her holds a thousand tons of cargo counterbalanced the pendulum swing of the masts.

Baines crossed his fingers in propitiation to the gods of

the sea. James clasped his hands behind his back, straightened his shoulders and expelled a long-held breath. He grinned at the wind: although it still snarled and cuffed at the ship it seemed to be slowly retreating into the vastness of its lair like a cowed and beaten animal.

The *Pampero* drifted sideways through the night. Then, as the eastern sky showed an almost indiscernible lightness, a pale opalescence that changed the sea from a white-streaked darkness to a ragged metallic grey, the tempest struck one final blow. Out of the boiling ocean rose a huge wet paw. It reached as high as the topmast before swatting the ship in a passion of thwarted fury.

It buried the entire foredeck beneath a black mountain of water. The *Pampero* reared, the stern lifted high in the air, the ship started to slide under. There was a deep rumble from below as the heavier cargo began to shift. For a fleeting moment James had a vision of the iron rails destined for the Union Pacific Railroad breaking loose and thundering toward the bows. There was a reverberating clang, a screech of torn metal as though a giant had burst its bonds. Then miraculously the *Pampero* raised a shoulder while the sea tore and clawed its way along the deck carrying everything before it. They saw the second lifeboat disappear forever in a welter of foam. The capstan was wrenched from its mountings. The ship's galley collapsed into a mass of twisted timber and metal. The emigrants' cooking range shattered into fragments. The sea roared up against the quarterdeck to explode into a towering breaker that engulfed the wheel and deck housing and carried away spanker boom, sail and standing gear.

James had locked an arm about the rail. The deluge of water smashed the breath from his body and threatened to drag him over the side. He felt the rail buckle; something snapped; his arm went dead, numb of all feeling; he was slithering across the deck, floating away. Then a hand grasped him by the collar, his head surfaced and he saw Baines clinging to the bent and twisted rail with one arm, the other stretched out to pluck him from the boiling surf.

The stern heaved and the water cascaded away. James stood up unsteadily and tried to reach for the security of the rail, but his left arm refused to obey his command. He put out his right hand to lift this strange dead weight, and felt the shattered bone. The arm swung uselessly from its shoulder socket. He frowned in perplexity. His brain seemed to work slowly, unwilling to accept the evidence of his senses.

Then they both saw the fore topmast spinning through the air. It hung high for an interminable time then plunged like a dagger into the very vitals of the ship.

The *Pampero* screamed. The great wooden blade thrust itself deep into the hatch covering the emigrants. It ripped through the protective tarpaulins, splintered the three-inch thick hatchboards as though they were so much matchboarding, and tore a ragged gaping hole as wide as a sluice gate.

James shook his head. His vision was muddied and there was an aching pain somewhere in the region of his right ear. He put up his hand and it came away with a sticky mixture of salt water and blood. He opened his mouth to call for all hands, but only a croaking sound emerged. There was a tumultuous ringing from somewhere and he realised that Baines was clanging the ship's bell. Voices shouting in the wind. Feet tramping on deck. His legs turned to rubber and he sat down heavily. He felt maudlin drunk, although he had never been intoxicated in his life. He grinned up at a circle of faces and began to sing softly to himself. Then many hands hauled him to his feet and with rough gentleness carried him aft. The wind seemed to be no more than a soughing captured in a seashell. Then the night closed in and he fell into a pit of darkness.

Jeremy was scrabbling on all fours when the hatchway burst open. A gale of wind filled the hold and blew out the remaining lamps to plunge them into a terrifying darkness. Then the sea poured in; a vast Niagara of water that bowled over those in its immediate path, flushed out the occupants of the lower bunks then surged along the floor carrying on its crest a tidal wave of possessions and desperately flailing bodies.

The water closed over Jeremy's head then subsided as it gathered speed and rushed to the fore end of the ship. The undertow almost dragged him from his knees.

We're done for, he thought, and tore at the boards penning Kate and Jenny in their bunk. He dragged Kate to her feet, found one of Jenny's imploring arms and hauled the child out into the passageway.

He stood up panting with fear. Kate hung in his arms like a rag doll, head lolling, limbs hanging slackly. Jenny clawed at him, shrieking in terror.

The hold was a bedlam of sound. The pounding roar of water, the scream of the wind and the animal howling of the emigrants trampling one another underfoot in the panic to escape.

Jeremy propped his back against the mast rising like a tree, roots planted in the keel, its head reaching for the clouds. He hoisted Jenny on to one arm and realised that the water was no more than ankle deep. Then the deck canted and the wave rushed back.

Men were fighting to climb out through the hole above their heads only to be smashed down again by the inrush of the sea. Jeremy blinked, accustoming his eyes to the new darkness and saw a faint grey light filtering through a gaping gargoyle mouth spouting black water into the hold. They would come for them, he reasoned. Robert's brother would not leave them to drown like rats in a trap. The water was not very high, it had not yet reached his knees. There would be far more danger in being knocked down and trampled by the mob than of being drowned by the rising waters. Kate was a dead weight in his arms and Jenny clung to his neck, sobbing and whimpering. He locked his big ploughman's hands together and lodged his back more firmly against the strength of the mast. Help would come. They would wait.

On deck they worked with the fury of the possessed. They had hauled a hatchboard from the forepeak and half-carried, half-swum it as far as the hatch. They shoved it into place across the hole. The sea threw it back. They retrieved it and the sea laughed and washed it overboard. Twenty men struggled to drag a bolt of canvas aft. The sea rolled them into the scuppers. It picked up the canvas and playfully pitched it to the other side of the ship. They rigged block and tackle and hauled it along the deck. They had the faces of madmen and laughed like madmen at the wind and the sea. A dozen tailed on to the haul, a dozen struggled to guide the snake-body along. The snake lashed its tail and smashed them into the bulwarks. They rose again, pounced and tied the tail with ropes and payed out slowly as the sea lifted them from their feet and poured into their mouths and lungs. They surfaced again and spat at the sea.

Baines ploughed among them. He stood like a rock while the sea tried to pluck him away. He swore and he cursed and he sang, and once, when the sea raged waist high, he cuffed it back again.

The *Pampero* kicked and bucked and fought the sea, savaging the waves like a mad dog. She bit and chewed while the sea gnawed at her exposed flank and the wind shrilled through her rigging. She lifted her head and white torrents boiled over the decks and the seamen marched the bolt of canvas toward her open wound like ant-surgeons with a tamp of wadding.

Armstrong, called from a sleep as deep and profound as any philosopher, fought with an exhultation he had never before known. The sea buried him time and time again, but his hands remained clamped to the lifelines and he rose as though from the dead to spew out mouthfuls of water. He survived and learned that he hated the sea. The sea was the enemy. So as his head rose from the welter of foam he, too, snarled his challenge at the sea and the wind.

The block creaked and groaned and the rope moaned under the strain as the canvas came inexorably to the site of the torn hole.

The carpenter waited dour and unemotional as though he were awaiting a meeting of the elders of some isolated Scottish kirk. He had a mouthful of nails and his belt was hung with the tools of his trade; axe, hammer, maul, knife, saw and chisel. He stood upon the hatch, one hand holding to a downhaul, the other hooked calmly in his belt. He swayed with the pull of the sea, but with Scottish obstinacy kept his feet and waited patiently for his work to be brought to him.

They dragged the canvas into position and threw it across the gap. The wind tried to tear it out of their hands. The seamen laughed and shouted insults. They had spent a lifetime fighting the fury of the Atlantic, hanging by toes and nails to yardarms, buffeted by tempests of wind. The sea was always with them. So they lay their bodies to the bucking canvas while the carpenter hammered in nails and Mr Armstrong and his gang lashed it down with rope. The canvas strained and bulged under the weight of the sea, so they ripped off a door from the after accommodation and laid it across and covered it with an old tarpaulin. Then they rose, gasping and sobbing with their efforts while the sea slobbered and gurgled about their feet and the dawn broke into a hideous puce light as though the earth had vomited its bile into the sky.

When the wind soughed and sheets of driving rain beat the sea flat, they knew they had won. The *Pampero* was coming back on an even keel. The ship was rising like a cork, the sea running off her decks, back to the swell of the ocean and the wilder reaches of the storm. They stood and looked at one another and grinned like demons. They had survived.

Baines put Mr Armstrong in charge of the ship, sent two men to the wheel, packed the rest off below and then he and the carpenter set off on their tour of inspection.

James swam back out of unconsciousness like a drowning man breaking the surface. His arm ached abominably and seemed to be clamped in a vice. He made a supreme effort and raised his head an inch above the pillow then sank back again into a wave of darkness. The lids of his eyes were like shutters of lead. He prised them open and a double moon rocketed across the sky. He closed one eye and focused the other. The moon creaked and spluttered, burned with a yellow flame and the oil lamp swung into his vision.

'James,' called a voice from the depths of a cavern. 'James,' it echoed. 'James.'

A second moon loomed into view and he reopened his spare eye to resolve the pattern of light into Anne's face peering down at him.

'Drink this,' she said, and he greedily swallowed a glass of clear fresh water.

Her voice seemed to boom at him. 'Lie back,' she commanded. 'Mr Baines has everything in order. The storm is passing.'

'Ah,' he said in a long, long sigh. 'Ah.' He had meant to say a great deal more, ask a thousand questions, but all he could manage was this foolish, 'ah.'

'You have a broken arm,' she told him, slowly and clearly, that there might be no misunderstanding. 'But it has been set and splinted. You have also had a knock on the head which has doubtless affected your sensibilities.'

A hand as cool as her voice touched his forehead and he sighed with satisfaction.

'Remarkable,' he said, looking at her idiotically. 'Most remarkable.'

An enormous wet seal rose from the bed of the sea and shook a spray of water over him. The seal snorted good-naturedly and transformed itself into Baines's beaming face.

'What, what, what, what?' he muttered querulously.

The elephant seal seemed to understand and trumpeted its news. The storm had struck its last blow and run away defeated. It had inflicted a fair amount of superficial damage—the seal barked with laughter—James wheezed in concert with the humour of the situation—the sea had torn away the starboard anchor, laughed the seal, and James tried to nod his head in vigorous appreciation of the joke. Ripped it out and bore it away, roared the seal raising a flipper to wipe moisture from its eyes. Thereby—overcome with the hilarity of the situation—restoring buoyancy to the *Pampero*'s head. One of the hand-forged links of the anchor cable, added the seal, sepulchrally, had pulled out like drawn toffee.

James giggled, imagining Cousin Wilberforce at his toffee-boiling. Then he thought of Robert's kin. 'Passengers,' he demanded. 'Passengers?'

The seal changed places with Baines. 'They've taken a battering,' he said. 'We reckon on three or four feet of water in the 'tween decks, but if they've kept their heads they'll be as right as rain. We're pumping out now,' he added as the seal took his place once again and James floated away into a limbo of drowning seas and pounding engines and churning paddles and a cold-faced Albert saying: 'I told you so.'

Once he sat up to grip Anne by the shoulder and mouth at her: 'Iron ships! Iron ships! I'll take the world with iron ships!'

She stroked his face and laid him back and smiled, 'There, there,' as though to a babe. 'Sleep, James, sleep,' and waited by his side while the storm moved away trailing its coat of rain and the sky turned blue and the sun burned away the cloud.

The *Pampero*'s sails stretched to the new wind like a butterfly spreading its wings and her decks dried white with the salt of the sea.

The seamen opened the hatch and dragged out the emigrants. They emerged into the light of day stunned with disaster. Six had broken bones, one a shattered jaw. Four children and two women were dead.

One of the women was Kate. They had had to prise the stiffened corpse from Jeremy's arms. He was the last to leave. His back planted firmly against the mast, the child curled asleep on his shoulder in the sleep of total exhaustion, the water swirling about his knees, he seemed obdurately determined to remain in this noisome dungeon forever as though unable to face the promise of reality beneath a clear sky and the inexorable movement of their little world through time and space.

The emigrants had gathered about the hatch, collecting and sorting the remnants of their possessions and endlessly telling each other tales of their adventures, while the sailmaker sewed the pitiful lonely bundles into canvas shrouds ready for burial.

Anne found Jeremy sitting alone, numb with misery. She took his hand. 'I'm sorry,' she said. 'It is God's Will.'

He shook his head. 'That's what they allus tell us. Crop failure. Empty bellies. But it's the poor He takes, never the rich.'

A group of Irish women were keening over their children, the men standing around, awkward and solemn. Jeremy raised his eyes and saw Jenny talking excitedly to another little girl about her own age. He heard a rhythmic clanking as the crew set about pumping out the 'tween deck; the chop of an adze and the whisper of a plane as the carpenter busied himself fashioning a new topmast. Seamen were swarming aloft renewing lines and tattered sails. Voices called to one another. One group was actually singing.

The ship was coming to life again.

The women's lamentation rose on the air, spread out, and was lost in the wide grey emptiness of the sea.

The *Pampero* disembarked her human cargo at Castle Garden, a round fortification of yellow stone at the southern tip of Manhattan which served as a sorting office for the emigrants.

James and Anne watched them troop ashore. James's arm was in a sling but the bone had mended and felt quite comfortable. He wiggled his fingers luxuriously. It had been a clean break and in a day or two he should regain the full use of the limb. In the meantime he was anxious to be off again to their discharging berth at South Street in East River. Mr Purdy's New York agent had already advised that the freight on rails had risen from fifty-five to seventy dollars a ton and was still climbing. Moreover he had fifteen thousand bales of English cloth and five thousand bales of blankets to dispose of, with New York manufacturers clamouring for the stuff. From the latest newspaper reports the civil war looked as though it might be a long-drawn-out and bloody affair. Apparently there had been an indecisive engagement at a place called Bull Run. An army needed uniforms and blankets. War, James concluded, could be a profitable business for those not actually engaged in the affair.

Anne tugged at his sleeve and he came out of his reverie to see Jeremy and Jenny standing on the shore and looking back at the ship.

'Did you give him anything?' he asked.

Anne avoided his gaze, knowing James's dislike of giving. Money, in his view, was something to be earned.

'Five pounds,' she said, adding quickly, 'My own money, James.'

He looked at her face. The contusion had almost disappeared; almost but not quite; it gave her face a slightly twisted, puckish look.

'Nonsense,' he said, brusquely. 'A man needs a start in life. The company can well afford it.' He coughed his dry, half-embarrassed cough, then remembered to add, in case his generosity should be misunderstood, 'Let us hope he doesn't waste it.'

She smiled at him. Really, she thought, he is a quite remarkable man.

The ship was already casting off, the tug pulling and snorting impatiently.

Jeremy stood watching for a long time until the *Pampero* disappeared from view behind the stubby round fortress tower that enclosed the Garden. Then he hoisted Jenny upon his shoulder and made his way toward the medical office. He would put in for some of that free land, he decided and never, ever again, set foot aboard another ship. There was security in land. He stamped his foot upon the unyielding ground. He would stand firmly upon his legs in this new land of America. That much he knew.

Chapter Fifteen

Callon looked for all the world like a little gnome in a nightshirt. Propped by pillows he lay in an enormous half-tester bed with curtained sides rising to the ceiling like domed minarets. The bobble of his nightcap hung rakishly over one ear as he growled farewell to lawyer Grogan.

Grogan gathered his papers and nodded a non-communicative face as Daniel was ushered into the sick room. Then he was gone slipping through the doorway like a dark wraith and leaving no record of his presence beyond the latent smell of burning wax.

'The man's a fool,' grunted Callon. 'All lawyers are fools. Pettifogging word-splitters to a man.' He patted the quilted eiderdown. 'Sit down, Daniel, sit you down.'

Daniel eased himself carefully on to the edge of the bed and looked sympathetically at his benefactor. Callon seemed to have suddenly acquired the shrunken look of old age. There was a greyness to his face and every inhalation of his breath seemed unwilling to remain in his lungs, so that when he spoke it was in a series of puffs and gasps.

'Are you feeling better, sir?' he asked, solicitously.

Callon grinned sourly. 'Just putting my affairs in order. But I'm not done for yet. Not by a long chalk.'

The effort of speaking gave rise to a paroxysm of coughing. He thumped his chest. 'Pass me a spoonful of that jalop, my boy. The tall bottle. It's recommended as a physic for the bronchals.'

He supped from the spoon held out by Daniel and pulled a wry face. 'The feller that concocted this potion should be made to swallow his own medicine.'

But the syrup did seem to have a soothing effect; the harsh rasp died away to a soft gurgle.

'I have been making a new Will.' His features twisted once again into the semblance of a derisory grin. 'Don't be embarrassed, my boy, you are not mentioned. But I have taken thought for your future.' He pushed himself upright and his eyebrows came down in the old familiar scowl. 'It's time you and Emma named the day. Have you spoke to her?'

It was the moment Daniel had been dreading.

'Not yet, sir,' he replied, uncomfortably.

Callon grunted peevishly. 'Take my advice and do so without delay, otherwise she'll keep you dangling forever.' He took a few long shallow breaths. 'I've no son, you see, Daniel? No son. You understand the problem?'

Daniel blinked and shook his head.

'You are unusually obtuse,' snapped Callon, testily. 'Emma has no knowledge of the world, no knowledge at all. When I'm gone she'll like as not up and marry some good-for-nothing, fortune-hunting wastrel who'll squander a lifetime's work at the gaming tables. I've seen it happen, my boy. Too often, too often. An heiress is considered fair game by society tuft-hunters.'

'Perhaps,' Daniel suggested delicately, 'Miss Emma has no predilection for matrimony?'

Callon snorted. 'Female fancies! I've made it plain to Emma where her duty lies. She accepts your proposal or she doesn't get a pennypiece! I've wrote to tell her so.' He was overcome with a further explosion of coughing. Daniel poured out another spoonful of Doctor Bronson's Soothing Syrup and settled Callon into his pillows.

He was aghast. He and Emma had fallen into a trap of their own baiting. He wondered what her reaction would be. One of fury, he imagined.

Rackerty-rack, chickerty-chack. A clattering train drumming past fields; a flash of cows; a flight of poles; a wayside station passed in a roar; thunder of darkness; burst of light; blur of smoke; a scatter of houses; wail of whistle.

Emma sat unseeingly in a first class compartment of the down train from London, her father's letter crumpled in her hand. She could not understand how any father could be so cruel. The threat was clear and couched in terms of brutal simplicity that left no room for equivocation. She either accepted Daniel Fogarty or she would be married off to that odious creature Captain Bredin, the business sold lock, stock and barrel and the money held in trust for her first child. He had given her a choice which was no choice. Daniel—dear honourable Daniel—had not yet proposed; and when he did he would fully expect her refusal. In all conscience she could not do other; had she not given her word? She could not accept—but the alternative was too dreadful to contemplate. She wondered if perhaps she *could* persuade him? A marriage of convenience? Daniel was ambitious. He would have control of the company. And the purse strings. Would he be generous? She rather thought so. If they could enter into another agreement? A marriage in name only, thus avoiding that other, rather sordid side of wedlock. He might be persuaded. Naturally there would be no romance; not a vestige, there never could be. He did not love her, if love was what she thought it meant. But that in itself could be an advantage, releasing both from the unpleasanter obligations of the marital bed. If she put it to him tactfully as a solution to both their problems? . . . After all it wasn't as though they actually disliked one another; on the contrary they took considerable pleasure in each other's company. He had made a quite admirable escort; courteous, attentive, obliging; never once by word or deed overstepping the thin line they had drawn between them. He was *trustworthy.* That was the word: *trustworthy.* But how could she possibly face him with what amounted to a betrayal of that very trust?

In a fret of frustration she drummed her fingers in time with the movement of the train and her mind repeated in rhythm: *Should I, or shouldn't I? Should I, or shouldn't I? Should I, or shouldn't I?*

Shortly after the *Pampero* berthed in Liverpool James announced he thought it high time they gave a small dinner party.

Anne received the pronouncement with a mixture of surprise and protestation. Surprise because it seemed such an odd request coming from a man with such a pronounced dislike of what he usually described as 'witless socialising' and protestation because of the lack of suitable accommodation.

She looked around the tiny cottage parlour helplessly.

'How many guests do you have in mind?' she asked.

James had clearly given the matter considerable thought for he promptly ticked them off on his fingers: 'The Frazers. Albert and Elizabeth. Robert and Sarah. John Elder and the Holts, if they can be persuaded. My lawyer, Tapscott. Young Ellerman—he seems to have his head screwed on the right way. About a dozen I should say.'

She blanched at the thought. James apparently picked his guests as though forming a board of directors. Furthermore she had never given even the smallest dinner party in her life before. If but one of this list of notables accepted she would require rather more than a shoulder of broiled mutton with caper sauce.

'But, James!' she wailed. 'We simply do not have the room!'

He grunted as though that were a small matter and whisked her around to visit Elizabeth.

Elizabeth seemed to be in one of her moods. She greeted their arrival with a wan smile, conducted them to the drawing room and rang for tea. Anne noticed that there were blue circles about her eyes and her face had a pinched and haunted look. She fidgeted restlessly and kept up an inconsequent chatter as though building a defensive thicket of words against the terrors of silence.

But she had little to fear on that score, thought Anne, for James seemed bent on monopolising the conversation, constantly interrupting to ask impertinent questions as to the cost and upkeep of the household, how many servants were in employment, how many rooms? He fingered the curtain material, examined the carpets and plumped himself into the chairs.

'You always were of extravagant tastes, Elizabeth,' he told his sister, accusingly, swallowed his tea, gulped down the cucumber sandwiches, remembered to bid Elizabeth a formal good-day and regards to Albert, and hustled Anne from the house.

'Where are we going?' she asked breathlessly trying to keep up with his long strides.

'To look at some property,' he said. 'And add your father to that list. He's an entertainment in himself.' Having made one of his rare jokes he gave a short barking laugh and quickened his pace. She tugged his arm and stopped him in mid-stride.

'James!' Her face was flushed as much from excitement as exertion. 'You are thinking of buying a house?'

'Why not? The cottage is too small. You said so yourself.'

'I only meant . . .' she began.

'Exactly,' he replied as though her earlier plaint had decided the issue beyond all argument. 'We are going up in the world. Come along.' He took her arm and wheeled her around the corner into Huskisson Street.

They stopped outside a quite smart residence in the middle of a terraced row. A short flight of whitestone steps led to a pillared doorway. Number 21 had a black-lacquered door with a highly polished brass knob. Although by no means as imposing as Elizabeth's establishment it did have a look of quality with an array of spear-headed iron railings protecting the basement quarters, and a sandstone mullioned bay window overlooking the street.

James tugged the door bell and they heard the bells jangle into silence in the interior.

She waited with her heart fluttering frantically like an excited bird in a cage until there was a shuffle of feet and the door leaned open to reveal a bowed beldame with a hooked nose and a mob cap pulled down over untidy grey hair. She eyed them suspiciously until James produced a card with a flourish.

'You will be the caretaker,' he said. 'We have come to inspect the property. I have an introduction from Tapscott, Wainwright and Co.'

The ancient backed away sniffling up its beaked nose and looking for all the world like an aproned Mrs Punch.

The house was single-fronted and therefore only half the size of Elizabeth's and certainly the rooms were not so grand, but Anne fell in love with it at first sight. She obediently followed James's whirlwind progress, marvelling at the spaciousness after the cramped quarters of the cottage and already planning colour of curtains, shades of carpet, patterns of wallpaper and *furnishings* . . . ! Her heart almost stopped at the thought. Did James realise how much furniture would be required to fill so many rooms? She determined not to mention the fact while this inexplicable madness was upon him.

The front room overlooking the street was evidently the drawing room and opened by means of an elaborate system of folding doors upon the dining-room. It was enchanting, she thought, altogether too enchanting.

James then subjected the house to a second, more thorough, inspection. He took a seaman's jack-knife from his pocket and poked and probed and jabbed his way from room to room, from top to bottom, as though surveying a ship; and all under the disapproving eyes of Mrs Punch.

His final inspection was of the basement kitchen where he seemed to expect some sort of criticism from her, so she dutifully examined the massive cast-iron kitchen range taking up the space of one entire wall. It contained a fire in the centre, with at one side a lidded copper boiler for drawing off hot water, and at the other a two-tiered baking oven. Above the fire was an iron top with detachable lids. It was the grandest cooking range she had ever seen. Then her heart plummeted at the thought of cleansing and feeding this monster; it would surely require hoppers of coal and a mountain of blacklead. She wondered if, after all this expense, she dare ask James for help in the kitchen?

James was probing at the cracks in the flagged floor. 'Well?' he asked as she finished her inspection.

'It is a quite enormous range. Much larger than anything I have ever used before.' She ran a finger over the surface. 'And it is quite filthy. In dire need of a thorough cleaning.'

'Is it efficient?' he demanded.

'Oh, yes,' she responded eagerly. 'I am sure it would be most efficient.'

He sniffed and put away his pocket knife. 'Then the rest will be the cook's problem, not yours.'

She stared in disbelief. A cook? James really must have taken leave of his senses. She thought she should make some form of protest, however weak, simply to remind him of the obligations of running an establishment of this size.

'That would be a scullery maid's work. No cook of any consequence would soil her hands . . .' she began.

'Very well. Cook and scullery maid. How much would they cost?'

'To live in?' she asked.

'Naturally. I have no intention of cooking my own breakfast.'

She looked at him, but he was smiling.

'I daresay I could find a quite decent cook for about twenty pounds a year. A scullery maid—around five or six pounds.'

He grunted. 'And I expect you will require a housemaid?'

She looked again quickly, expecting sarcasm, but intercepted nothing beyond a look of earnest inquiry.

'A housemaid would certainly be of great assistance.'

'And a parlourmaid,' he added. 'And there, I think, we must draw the line. If you think you can manage, that is?' he questioned anxiously.

If she could manage! 'Oh, James!' she cried. 'Oh, James!' She would hug him if it were not for the presence of Mrs Punch. 'Of course I can manage! Of course!'

'Good,' he said. 'I knew for a fact that Elizabeth employed far too many servants. Needless extravagance. Quite needless. You can hardly move in that house without tripping over some half-witted domestic. Elizabeth has no sense of values. Never had.' He stamped a marauding cockroach into extinction. 'Well? What do you say, Anne? Are you satisfied with the place?'

'More than satisfied, James. It's beautiful! Beautiful!'

'Right,' he said. 'We'll take it. If the price is right,' he added with his habitual caution.

She could not believe her ears. It was too good to be true. As they made their way back to the hall a tiny alarm bell rang. James was never motivated by the inspiration of the moment; he invariably planned carefully beforehand.

'Can we really afford all this?' she asked timidly.

He grinned at her. 'The company can. It will come out of profits.' He grinned even more hugely. 'Some of Robert's fifteen per cent will go toward paying the servant's wages.' He put his hand on her shoulders and to her intense surprise kissed her lightly on the cheek. 'Don't worry, little Anne, we struck a bargain once, remember? When I move up in the world, you move with me. And now,' he demanded briskly, 'how soon can you give that dinner party?'

Seated at the dinner table she remembered she had estimated six or eight weeks, a month at least, a notion which he had promptly pooh-poohed and given her a fortnight, not a day longer. She had not believed it possible; and no doubt without James's driving energy and genius for organisation it would not have been. He packed her and Elizabeth and Sarah off on vast shopping expeditions while he haunted the house, bullying and harrying the workmen—painters and plumbers and paperhangers and carpenters and joiners until every room sang with curses. But he had been as good as his word. In eight days the house had been redecorated from top to bottom, inside and out. Cartloads of furniture had been installed and an army of seamstresses kept busy sewing curtains and valances and flounces and bedspreads. She had interviewed troops of would-be housemaids and a succession of cooks all richly endowed with impeccable references. From this company of paragons she had eventually chosen a Mrs Raven, a lizard-like woman with a no-nonsense air and a light hand with pastry.

She had had one fierce quarrel with James over the matter of tableplacings. James had wanted to marshal his forces like a general going into battle with all the big guns at his end of the table and the lesser lights below the salt. She had remained adamant and eventually appealed to higher authority in the shape of Elizabeth and Sarah and Sarah's much-thumbed *Lady's Guide to Etiquette*. Under this combined onslaught James had given way, only insisting that her father be placed out of harm's way and guarded by members of the family.

Anne ran a satisfied eye around the table. Elizabeth, strategically placed between Mr Alfred Holt and Robert, was keeping the table entertained with an account of her visit to the Royal Amphitheatre where she had witnessed a dramatic entertainment entitled *Hawkshaw, the Detective*, in which the great detective had uncovered a dastardly plot to malign the good name of a lady of quality. The audience had screamed with terror and many ladies had fainted when, in the last act, Hawkshaw had revealed a real skeleton in a real closet. Elizabeth's histrionics as she acted out the convoluted plot brought a smile even to the saturnine features of John Ellerman, a quiet young man who ate in brooding silence. Elizabeth reached a triumphant denouement, whipping off imaginary wig and whiskers. 'I am—Hawkshaw, the detective!' she declaimed.

Only Albert, Anne noticed, forebore to applaud. He contented himself with dabbing his lips with his napkin and murmuring: 'Perhaps we should consider ourselves fortunate that detective Hawkshaw confines his talents to the stage.' There was a decided inflection upon 'we' and the remark seemed to be aimed like an arrow directly at Elizabeth.

A slow flush spread from Elizabeth's shoulders to her face. From the tilt of her chin and the sudden snap of anger in her blue eyes it was evident that she was about to indulge herself in a tart rejoinder.

Anne rose to her feet. 'I think, ladies,' she announced, 'we shall leave the gentlemen to their cigars.'

Amid a general hemming and hawing and shuffling of chairs the ladies glided through to the drawing room, hissing and gobbling like a flock of bright-coloured swans.

Frazer grinned as James circulated port and brandy and pushed forward a box of cigars.

'Well, Onedin, I hear you made an eventful voyage?'

'The sort of event I could well do without.' James rubbed his chin and smiled ruefully, but his eyes were bland. 'In fact there was a time when I wished I'd had the *Pampero* fitted with one of Albert's auxiliary engines.'

He helped himself to a cigar and saw his guests rising to the bait. Albert opened his mouth and leaned forward to speak but then gave precedence to Holt's seniority.

Alfred Holt had a sensitive face, a high intellectual forehead and the calm eyes of the thinker. He stroked his side-whiskers with a finger and shook his head.

'I think you have the boot upon the wrong foot, Mr Onedin. Sail should be auxiliary to engines, not vice versa.'

'Mr Ellerman, do you have an opinion?'

Ellerman habitually used words sparingly as though afraid their currency might suddenly be devalued. He held up one hand and itemised on his fingers. 'Capital cost. Freight. Capacity. Resolve that equation and ship operation becomes no more than a matter of book-keeping.'

James looked across at Elder. 'You are an engineer, Mr Elder. Can you solve the computation?'

'I venture to suggest that Mr Ellerman is over-simplifying the problem.' Elder examined his fingers as though he had never seen them before. 'There are too many variables.' He looked across at Albert. 'I think Mr Frazer would agree?'

Webster helped himself liberally to the brandy decanter while lawyer Tapscott inhaled a mound of snuff. Albert's normally reposed features were now illuminated by the light of fanaticism. Words tumbled out in a headlong rush as though a pent-up volume of ideas had burst through a dam of ignorance. Confident in the support of three of the most powerful visionaries in the world of steam-driven vessels he rose in revolt against his father.

'The days of sail are numbered—only there are some who are too blind and too obstinate to recognise a fact when it is thrust before them. Sailing ships have reached the limit of design and capacity but the upper limit of a steam-driven ship is not yet in sight. Its size will be defined only by the strength of iron and the power of steam.'

Frazer interposed: 'The wind blows free for every man's use. Coal costs twelve shillings a ton.'

Robert thought it time to add a leaven of reason to the bread of argument. James was up to something, there was no doubt about it. A new residence and influential guests smacked of log-rolling. The man seemed to be spending money like water. He wondered when he would see the colour of his share. There would be a reckoning shortly, he promised himself. In the meantime he decided to give cautious support to Frazer.

'Fires burn money,' he said sententiously. 'The greater the fire, the greater the expenditure.'

'Well put,' assented Frazer, pleased to find an unexpected ally. 'The greater the power, the greater the consumption.'

Elder shook his head. 'A fallacy, Mr Frazer. My compound engine gives a higher efficiency per ton of coal than any other yet devised.'

'But it does burn coal,' Frazer stressed drily.

'Of course it burns coal, ye loon!' snapped Elder, his Glaswegian accent crashing across the table like the grate of broken crockery. 'Ye canna get something for nothing!'

'The wind—' began Robert, tentatively, trailing behind Frazer's argument.

Elder rounded on him. 'The wind blows a ship where God wills. Steam drives a ship where man wills.'

James had sunk low in his chair. He watched the smoke from his cigar spiralling toward the ceiling and listened to the growing heat of argument with satisfaction. He had chosen his guests with care. Holt would soon be a force to be reckoned with. Elder's reputation was already made. Ellerman was up-and-coming, a born organiser with an acute financial brain. He would pick their wits and then make his decision. He sank even lower and drew evenly upon his cigar.

'I believe,' Holt was saying, 'that I have developed an engine of even greater thermal efficiency than Mr Elder's.' He smiled half-apologetically at Elder. 'But the proof of the pudding will be in the eating. We shall see when the *Cleator* is launched next year.'

'What,' prompted James gently, 'is a compound engine?'

The three engineers began to talk at once but it was Albert's voice which finally dominated.

'A revolution in the economics of shipping,' he declared. His voice, losing its accustomed mannered drawl, rose in a high pitch of excitement. His long thin hands modelled a boiler out of the air.

'Power is contained within a boiler. Its source, the conversion of water into steam. The steam drives a piston and the piston drives the engine. This was the fore-runner —the slow-running single-expansion engine. Power output low, coal consumption high. The secret of Mr Elder's invention is to first admit the steam to a small cylinder, where it achieves but a proportion of its expansion, then pass it to a second, larger, cylinder, where the expansion is completed. Each stage operates a piston in the process thereby achieving a far higher output of horsepower and therefore greater economy per pound of coal.' His hands made cycling motions. 'A double-expansion engine. Two pistons giving twice the power at half the cost.'

'A saving of thirty to forty per cent, in fact,' conceded Elder.

'Fifty per cent for the *Cleator*,' said Holt.

'I visualise a ship of iron in which is installed a set of compound engines with two high-pressure and four low-pressure cylinders, a coal consumption of under two pounds per horsepower per hour, and a boiler pressure of only forty pounds per square inch.' Albert glared round the table defying disagreement.

Frazer grinned at his son. 'If she doesn't shake herself to pieces first, she'll blow up.'

'Not so,' Elder contradicted quietly. 'My company have, at his moment, plans on the drawing board for a ship to be engined double-expansion at sixty pounds steam pressure.' He smiled thinly at Frazer. 'It seems even my Lords of the Admiralty have developed a nose for the winds of progress.'

Frazer snorted his contempt. 'The Navy! They can afford to back their folly with taxpayer's money.'

Webster sat up and rumbled to life. 'Her Majesty's Navy does not indulge in folly, sir!'

Frazer smiled disarmingly. 'You will allow, Captain Webster, that the Board of Admiralty has a somewhat longer purse than the rest of us.'

'Poppycock!' snarled the old man. 'Poppycock, sir! A navy that has the wit and imagination to build an ironclad such as the *Warrior* stands in little need of reprimand from a tuppenny woodship builder!'

'The *Warrior*,' said Albert scathingly, 'is nothing but a converted full-rigged ship, hopelessly out-of-date. There is a common misconception—that to fit a sailing ship with an engine produces a steamship. It does nothing of the sort! It produces a hybrid, a monstrosity of the seas that is neither fish nor fowl!'

'It sounds like a good red herring,' said his father derisively. 'Which shape takes your fancy, Albert? A box?'

Albert regained his composure. His voice dropped into its habitual easy drawl.

'Why not a box, pointed at one end? Although I prefer to think of it as a steam-driven floating warehouse.'

Ellerman nodded thoughtful approval.

Frazer was tiring of the game. He wondered again at Onedin's object in bringing them together. Surely not for the sake of rancorous argument? He decided to put an end to the matter once and for all.

'How much space,' he asked, 'will be taken up by machinery and coal?'

'About one third,' said Albert.

'Then such a ship would never compete for profit. A sailing ship would carry fifteen hundred tons of cargo against your Puffing Billy's five hundred.'

'My ships,' said Holt, 'will be designed to carry three thousand tons at ten knots with a range of eight thousand miles.'

James came out of his reverie. A tingle of excitement ran through his veins. He had now all the information he required. He looked around the table. Holt's calm pronouncement had produced a pool of silence while each man assimilated the implications. Only Frazer continued obstinately to shake his head.

'Even so powerful a ship as that envisaged by Mr Holt could not compete against the sailer. A sailing ship makes no stops for coaling, pays no costly fuel bills, suffers no machinery repairs or long overhauls. The capital cost is enormous—my yards can build four clippers for the price of one steamer. Furthermore just one of those clippers will sail circles around Mr Holt's ten knot plodder.' Having stated his case Frazer stubbed out his cigar, pushed back his chair, clamped his features into the obstinate lines of a man beyond the reach of argument and scowled defiance around the table.

Holt smiled: 'Let me remind you, Mr Frazer, of Aesop's tortoise and hare. While your hares are streaking to Foochow in ninety days, my tortoise is plodding to the same destination in sixty-five. A sailing ship makes best headway along the arc of an ellipse. A steamship uses the vector.'

Albert caught James's eye: 'It travels in a straight line,' he said.

James spoke directly to him: 'You claim that size is limited only by the strength of iron and the power of steam?'

Albert nodded.

'Could you build a ship to these specifications: Four and a half thousand tons; a speed of thirteen knots; a range of six thousand miles?'

Albert hesitated. 'Well—yes—'

'At what cost?'

Albert again hesitated: 'There are so many factors—no one could possibly give a figure without careful computation.'

'Approximate.'

Albert licked his lips and looked toward Holt and Elder for encouragement.

'Around seventy-five, eighty thousand pounds . . . ?'

Eyes alight with interest the engineers nodded agreement.

'Very well,' said James. 'Build it.'

Robert blanched. His mouth ran dry. He knew it! The man was raving mad! Seventy-five thousand pounds! The horrors of bankruptcy stared him in the face. He would have none of it! Withdraw from the confounded company immediately! He tried to speak, to protest, but his tongue seemed to have stuck to the roof of his mouth.

Albert was first to find his voice: 'You are quite serous?' He sounded as though he could not believe his ars.

James gave a passable imitation of Albert's drawl. Shouldn't have broached the subject otherwise,' he said anteringly. 'You may recall once telling me that should ever be of the mind to invest in a steamship I should onsider your yards at my disposal. It was the occasion, s I recollect, of your introduction to Elizabeth.'

If James imagined that the memory might revive a ense of obligation he was rapidly disillusioned. Albert's ace suffused with anger. Frazer chose that moment to ntervene.

'Eighty thousand pounds is a tidy sum of money. How lo you propose to raise it, Onedin?'

James looked toward the lawyer.

'Mr Tapscott?'

Tapscot blew into his handkerchief. 'It is Mr Onedin's ntention to raise the sum of one hundred thousand ounds by public subscription.'

'Eighty thousand for the ship. Twenty thousand perating capital,' said James.

Frazer looked at him sharply. 'You had already arrived t a costing. And alerted your lawyer. You would appear o have given the matter considerable prior thought?'

'Why not?' asked James, mildly. 'A man does not pend one hundred thousand pounds on impulse. For no nore than the expense of a dinner I have had confirnatory advice from the best brains in the country.'

Holt chuckled: 'I think we must digest your effronary with the same pleasure we have applied to your ospitality.'

Elder grinned. 'Someone must engine the ship. Perhaps his would be an opportune moment to put in a bid for Randolph and Elder?'

'That,' returned James gravely, 'is something you must ake up with Frazer and Son.'

'Just a moment, if you please,' interposed Frazer. 'I'm

too old a dog to learn new tricks, but I'll not stand in my son's way. I'll back Albert if he's a mind to accept the order; but you must realise that to build such a ship will mean a heavy investment for Frazers. Enlarged yards. New slipway. Machine shops. Our profit margin's going to be tight. Very tight. I reckon Frazers should have an interest. Say, fifteen per cent?'

'Five per cent. Directors shares. To Albert alone. Not to Frazers.' James glanced toward Tapscott and received an affirmative nod.

'Ten,' countered Frazer. 'To Albert.' He grinned evilly. 'So if you go down you take only one of the Frazers with you.'

'Done,' said James. 'Tapscott will draw up the contracts.' He pushed back his chair and stood, stretching his arms. 'Now that is settled, gentlemen, I think we'd better join the ladies.'

Elizabeth looked up as the door opened and the gentlemen returned. The ladies had been discussing *ad nauseam* the subject of the engagement of Captain Fogarty to Miss Emma Callon. She felt angered and betrayed. She caught Albert's eye. He seemed flushed and excited. To her surprise he walked over and kissed her affectionately. Actually on the mouth and before the entire company! She returned his kiss and found herself blushing like a bride.

Anne greeted James. 'Did the dinner party go well, dear?' she asked smiling.

'Very well,' he replied, elaborately casual. 'It has just cost me a hundred thousand pounds.'

The story of the Onedin Line will be continued in another volume.